CW01624538

# Doris & Dave's 'Greek Adventure'

Written by David Chorley

Woodbridge Publishers
1200 Century Way, Thorpe Park,
Leeds, LS158ZA



First Edition

ISBN (Paperback): 978-1-916849-04-4



*If applicable*
Cover Design by Woodbridge Publishers.

WOODBRIDGE
PUBLISHERS

# Acknowledgements

I would like to thank Woodbridge Publishers, who have been incredible throughout this process.

*I dedicate this book to all my family and friends, who have supported me through this process but have been completely oblivious for the most part.*

*However, I would also like to dedicate this book to two supportive individuals. Firstly, my one-eyed cat, Gerrard and my girlfriend, fiancé, best friend and future wife, Lorna. –Please note that this is in no particular order; the latter is one person, not four individuals.*

# Chapter 1

I was in my back garden on a sunny Saturday afternoon, watering my fruit trees, when my peace and tranquillity were rudely interrupted. I could feel the presence of a quietly observing Doris from over the garden wall.

Not one to encourage small talk, I pretended I hadn't noticed.

However, there was a slight problem. Although the wall was tall and Doris was short, she would overcome this obstacle by standing on a stool so she could peer over.

Sometimes, she would say nothing and would just observe. Other times, she would speak.

I was hopeful on this occasion, as it wasn't going to be the latter.

"Morning *Dave*, lovely day for it, isn't it?"

*Bollocks, she wants a conversation.*

"Hi Doris, how are you?"

"I've got a proposition for *you,* and I think you might *like* what I'm about to say," she said with a glint in her eye.

I put the empty watering can on the cast iron table and waited.

"Doris, I do like *older* women, but don't you think you're a little *old* for me?"

"Not that kind of *proposition,* Dave, just listen," she added, resting her arm on the wall.

"Well, that depends on one major factor - firstly, does it have anything to do with AVON?" I asked.

"Why AVON?" she asked.

"Because every time we speak, it's about AVON and your *many* alleged bargains."

"Well, yes, it is about AVON," she said.

Her face creased with another smile, all very thin-lipped and gummy. It wasn't a pretty sight.

"Doris, have you forgotten to put something in this morning?"

She looked confused.

"What do you mean?" she asked.

"Your false teeth? They really help, especially when you smile," I added.

"Oh *shit,* sorry, back in a *mo*," she said, disappearing and reappearing in a matter of seconds.

"Bloody hell, that was quick," I said.

"Yeah, I keep them on the table by the back door."

"Right, where was I?" she asked.

"You were about to mention AVON," I said.

"Oh yeah," she said.

"How can *anything* to do with AVON benefit me, Doris?"

"You haven't heard what I'm about to say yet," she shouted.

"I don't wear perfume," I added.

"Listen!" she shouted.

"How long will this take?" I asked, but she wasn't beaten.

"Listen, one word, Greece!" she shouted, like she'd just won big at bingo.

I looked up, and she had my focus, though I wasn't expecting it to last.

"Have I got your attention?" she looked smug and cheery.

"I heard you the first time. I'm all ears, Doris."

"I have won a competition through AVON for 14 nights on a Greek island for *two* people."

She looked elated, and rightly so.

"Ok, so you want me to drop you and one of your bingo friends off at the Airport?"

She looked puzzled, “No, I mean, me and you.”

“Eh?” I said, confused.

“Listen, none of my friends are available. They’ve made other plans, and we have to take this holiday within a month.”

“Oh right, I see,” I said.

“Dave, you are my *only* hope.”

“So you’re Princess Lea, and I’m Luke Skywalker then?”

I asked

“Who?” she asked, her face puzzled.

“Doesn’t matter.”

“Dave, this is real, a *free holiday.*”

“Doris, what can I say, I’m speechless.”

“It’s not like you to be stuck for words, Dave,” she laughed.

She leaned on the wall and smiled.

“Don’t be - just say *yes,* and you’ll be one step closer to a *free* holiday,” she laughed and grinned and did a little dance on the stool.

“Careful, Doris, you’ll be going nowhere if you fall off that thing.”

I pondered for a moment.

“Which part of Greece is it?” I asked.

She handed me the details.

"Right then, let's have a look."

She waited patiently while I read the contents, specifically the small print.

"I've never been to Greece, Dave, so this is something very special," she was bursting with enthusiasm.

Flicking through the pages, I looked up at her.

"It's on the island of Naxos - I've been to a lot of Greek islands, Doris, but this one is still on my to-do list."

"Well, you can tick this one off your list then," she said.

"At least it's not somewhere obvious, like Crete or Corfu. This looks a bit special, somewhere a bit different."

"Well, if you say so, Dave."

"It says it has the perfect blend of lively and traditional, so no kiss-me-quick hats here."

"That's a shame, Dave. I was going to take my hat."

"I'll let you off, Doris."

"It says here that it's a perfect blend of lush green mountain back drops, tranquil fishing villages, small towns with a nice vibe, and great seafood; we've hit the jackpot here."

"Which part of Greece is it, then?" she asked.

"The Aegean Sea."

"Ageing sea, aren't all seas old?" she asked.

"Yes, it's a *very* old sea."

"What do you think then?" she asked.

"What do I think? I think I might become a member of AVON myself at this rate."

She looked confused.

"They only sell perfume, Dave, sorry."

I looked up at Doris and began to nod my head slowly and smile.

Her face lit up as she knew what the answer would be.

"Don't just stand there nodding like a donkey. Are you coming or not?"

"Count me in," I said.

I had to admit, I'd rather be going with a lady at least the right side of 40, as opposed to 70, but beggars can't be choosers.

I stood there with what amounted to a golden goose ticket in my hand.

Doris smiled.

"Oh, Dave, that's amazing. I'm so pleased you'll come, and since you know so much about Greece, you'll not only be my companion, but you'll be my guide too."

My smile became a frown, like polish that had been stripped off an old oak table. My mouth felt dry, and I needed a glass of water with some time to reflect.

Doris was still buzzing.

"Knowing you Doris, I'll be your *minder* too, so - *no* scrapes on this one, please, no wandering off, and no vanishing."

She interrupted me mid-flow.

"Yes, Yes, Yes, I *promise*."

"So, next Saturday it is. I will quickly email my boss and let him know that I need a short notice holiday, but he'll understand; he's good like that," I said hopefully.

"Oh, Dave, I can't wait. Right then, I'm off to the shops to buy some bits, so I'll see you next Saturday."

She climbed off her stool and disappeared into her house.

*14 nights in Naxos with Doris; I'm not sure I'll be posting this on Facebook anytime soon.*

The following Saturday arrived, we boarded the plane without any dramas and landed on time at Mykonos Airport at 1:15 p.m.

To get to Naxos, we needed to get a connection by means of a boat transfer. It wasn't any hardship; a mere 45 mins, and we'd be there.

As we entered the airport terminal and joined the queue at passport control, we could already feel the warm heat of the Greek sun.

The distinct lack of air-conditioning in the terminal made it a stuffy encounter.

Doris wiped the sweat from her brow.

“Oh, the heat in here, Dave. Why doesn’t someone switch on a fan?”

“They have Doris, but unfortunately, it just blows warm air around the room, which is quite normal for Greece. They don’t do plush airport experiences.”

“Should I ask that nice man if he can put the air-con on?” she asked, pointing at a steward.

“It is what it is, Doris. This shouldn’t take long, so stop flapping,” I said.

“Have your *passport* ready; we are getting closer now.”

She fiddled with bits in her handbag, pulled out a plastic wallet, and readied it in her hand with a firm grip.

“Go on then, let’s have a look at your mug-shot,” I asked.

“I will not,” she said.

“Give it here.”

She passed her plastic wallet to me.

“Doris, this is your bus pass; where’s your *passport*?”

*Please tell me she hasn’t lost it on the plane.*

She began to ruffle through the contents of her bag again while I quietly hyperventilated.

“Found it, here it is,” she looked at me, her face etched with relief.

“Right, give it here. I will look after it for you from now on.”

“I keep hearing staff talking in a foreign language Dave. Is that normal?”

“Oddly Doris, *yes***.** We are in Greece, so that qualifies as another country, and they speak their own native language.”

She smiled, with her gums and teeth protruding through her skinny lips.

“Oh, I see, yes, of course, that’ll explain it then,” she said as she continued to people-watch.

“I must say, some of these Greek men look rather dashing, Dave.”

“Easy tiger, we’ve only just arrived, and you’re already on the pull,” I said.

“I’m wasting no time. I’m too old for wasting time, Dave.”

“Just calm yourself and keep walking.”

I placed my hand on her left shoulder and gently nudged her forward.

“Right, we’re next in the queue. Have your passport ready, Doris.”

“Why do they need to see it?”

“To keep an eye on you, that’s why.”

She handed the passport to the clerk and waited.

He flicked through it, looked at her photo and looked back at her.

“Not aged a bit, have I darling?” she said.

He smiled awkwardly and handed it back to her.

"Thank you, next, please."

I handed him mine and waited. Again, he looked at my photo, then looked at me and smiled.

"You like the older ladies?" he asked.

I was gobsmacked.

"No, it's not like that, just holiday companions."

He laughed, handed me my passport, and I made a quick exit.

"What did he say to you?" Doris asked.

"He said I looked good for my age and the Greek women will love me."

"He did not."

"Go and ask him."

"Ok, I will,"

"Doris, come here. We are through the gate now, and you can't go back."

"I need a gin & tonic, Dave."

"Right, well, the faster we get out of here, the faster we get a drink."

# Chapter 2

We collected our cases without any drama.

"This is worryingly easy, Doris, hassle-free. Let's just keep it that way for the next 14 nights, eh."

My thoughts of joy were never far from thoughts of dread.

"Agreed, Dave, it's all very easy, this travelling lark. I should have done it years ago."

"I just hope getting to our villa won't be much of a drama. I could murder a drink." I said.

"Here, have some of my water, Dave."

"I meant a *real* drink."

She wheeled her case behind her, leaving me to struggle with two carry-on cases and my own large case.

Cases are always filled with contents that we will never need, let alone use. I looked around at all the other holidaymakers pushing cases of various sizes.

It all looked excessive, and we were no different. We, too, were a part of the Brits abroad system, 'take as much crap as possible but use very little'.

"What have you got in these cases, Doris, bricks?"

"No, just shoes and stuff."

"Stuff, like what?"

"Well - I like to bring towels; you can never have enough towels, Dave."

"They will have towels there. No bloody wonder your cases are like dragging slabs of concrete."

Moments later, we met with our Olympic Holiday rep outside the terminal entrance.

She was tall and elegant, 20-something, with a typical animated smile and a sense of jolliness about her; all standard issue with holiday reps naturally, but *she* was special, and definitely a 10/10 in the looks department.

The holiday rep smiled, her face beamed, and it actually looked like she liked her job.

"Welcome to Mykonos. My name is Sally, and I will be your tour guide today."

*She can be my guide any day*, I thought with my eyes transfixed, although I was doing my best not to stare.

"Dave, put your tongue away."

"I don't know what you mean?"

“We’ve been here a matter of seconds and you’re already like a dog on heat.”

“What do you want me to do, Doris? Look at my feet when I’m talking to a pretty girl?”

She had teeth that glowed; she had definitely spent her wages at the dentist.

“‘Dave and Doris,’ for Villa Stavros on Naxos, I believe,” I asked.

The rep smiled. She glanced up and down her clipboard and flicked the pages that flapped about in the wind.

“Oh *yes*, found you - Stavros will take your luggage, so just make your way over to bus number 37, and I will be with you shortly,” she confirmed.

“Thank you,” I said.

Doris looked at me, “So, we’re staying at Villa Stavros, and the bus driver’s called Stavros. Do you think the villa is *his* by any chance then, Dave?”

She chuckled.

“I don’t care if it’s Stavros, Bill, Bob, Barry, or Ben who owns the villa, as long as it’s nice,” I said.

We made our way onto the bus, grabbed a seat somewhere in the middle, and made ourselves comfortable.

I’m a bit funny about where I sit on a bus. The front is too noisy, the back is, well, too far back, and the middle is just about right.

Sometime later, the last few people climbed aboard, closely followed by the holiday rep.

She closed the door behind her with a push of a button. It squeaked and creaked before closing, like it hadn't seen oil on its dusty hinges in years.

The driver sat in his seat, spoke a few words in Greek on his radio, and started the engine.

The bus rattled into life with the unmistakable smell of diesel.

"Does this thing have an air-con, Dave?"

"I think we're lucky it has wheels, Doris."

The holiday rep switched her microphone on and rose to her feet.

I was waiting for the customary words we all expect to hear at this point

"Hello, everyone, and welcome to the beautiful island of Mykonos. We will shortly be boarding the ferry to take us to the Island of Naxos. Can everyone *hear* me at the back?" she asked.

"*Yesssss,"* several passengers mumbled and grunted.

"Wonderful, so our driver today is Stavros, and he will be doing seven drops, which will be for nine hotels in total. It won't take too long, so allow between 20 and 40 mins or so."

"For those of you who haven't been to Naxos before, you are in for a *real* treat," she said.

The coach quickly made its way to the port and drove onto the waiting ferry.

"Okay, so once we have parked on the ferry, you can leave the bus and make your way upstairs. Can we all please reassemble back on the bus when we arrive at Naxos?" she asked.

"What if we can't find the bus?" came a voice from the back. There's always the one.

"There is only one vehicle deck in the basement, so just head for the lowest deck. You can't get lost."

Her instructions were greeted with nodding heads and the sounds of chatter.

"Right, come on then, Doris, let's go explore the boat for a bit."

"Why don't we just stay on the bus, Dave? The girl said it will only take about 40 mins."

"Because up on deck, we can get some fresh air and grab a drink."

"We have bottled water in our bag," she added.

"Doris, it's not up for debate. Come on, move your arse."

The crossing was shorter than she'd suggested. The captain must have had a heavy right foot, but I wasn't complaining.

We soon arrived at the port of Naxos. It was unlike most Greek Island ports; it looked stunning. White-washed houses with blue wooden shutters were scattered across the landscape.

It was busy and noisy as expected, with the sound of mopeds whizzing along and port staff in blue and grey uniforms blowing their whistles and directing traffic as it disembarked the boat.

We all quickly returned to our seats on the bus and awaited further instructions.

The holiday rep resumed her position at the front of the bus and switched on her microphone.

"So - has anybody been to Naxos before?" she asked.

There was a brief pause, and then a voice shouted from the back of the bus, "Yes, several times, we love it here."

It was some random woman in her 60s I'd have said. She already had a chocolate tan, like she'd never left the island, and her face was weathered by someone who had clearly spent most of her life sitting in the sun, cooking, from 9 a.m. till 9 p.m. We know the sort, face like a leather handbag, never seen a beach in her life, the type that sits by the pool, smoking, eating crisps, getting fat, and reading trashy magazines.

Doris peered over the top of her seat in the direction of the woman.

"You look like you've had enough sun already, luv," Doris shouted.

"Doris, is that your way of *making* friends?" I asked.

"I was just *saying*," she replied.

"Well, just say it in your head."

I glanced at the woman. She had a face like a slapped bottom.

The rep continued to talk.

"Very good, well, that's a good advert, ladies and gents, one happy customer returning year after year," she said.

She was doing her best to hold onto the seats on either side of her as the coach began to move forward down the ramp.

"Ok, before I tell you a little more about the island, we will be dropping you off at the following hotels."

She looked at her clipboard like an actor who had forgotten their lines. Flipping over the pages, she made a few notes. Her pen had clearly run out of ink, so she leaned forwards toward the driver and gestured to him. He passed her a pen that he had wedged behind his ear, and she composed herself.

"She looks like it's her first day on the job," said Doris, shaking her head.

"Give the girl a chance," I said.

"Just because you fancy her, Dave."

I didn't respond.

"Ok, so first *drop,* Villa Stavros."

I put my hand up and then put it back down again, but I wasn't sure why I just did that. It was the kind of thing you'd do at school when the teacher read your name out first.

I looked at Doris and gave her the thumbs-up as the rep continued to talk.

Doris looked at the rep.

“She drinks more water than my tomato plants,” she said, laughing to herself.

“Yeah, well, look at how good your plants look; it’s doing the same for her, lovely thing she is.”

“Bloody hell, you’re smitten.”

“She’s a bit young for me, but it’s not a crime to look.”

“Yeah, well, she’s not that special, Dave.”

I looked at Doris and smiled, “She’s like a Formula 1 car, a lovely piece of handcrafted engineering.”

“Then why don’t you ask her if you can climb in?”

“Because I’m too old, Doris, I wouldn’t fit in the seat.”

Doris laughed.

The rep continued to read out hotel names.

“And the last hotel is Hotel Zantos,” she added.

Some moans came from the back; someone had booked the short straw hotel. We have all done it. It’ll be situated on top of a hill somewhere, surrounded by goats, and it’ll be a half an hour's walk to the beach.

“So that concludes our drop-off locations, ladies and gents,” the rep paused, took another sip of water, and continued, “So, who would like to hear a bit more about the island?”

Cheers and moans could be heard in equal measures around the bus. Some tired-looking faces clearly just wanted to get to their accommodation.

"Naxos - is part of the Cyclades island group in the Aegean Sea. It is one of the most popular and glamorous Greek islands, known for its 35 beaches, 12 fishing villages, lush green hills and mountains, great restaurants, and amazing bars."

"Sounds amazing!" shouted Doris.

"For those of you who like a more party atmosphere, the main town is very lively, with lots of bars," she added.

Doris leaned over to me, "She likes the sound of her own voice this one."

"She can talk to me anytime, preferably one-on-one," I replied.

The rep continued.

"Oh, Dave, there's more to life than just sex, you know."

I looked at her.

"Really, when you've been single as long as I have Doris, I beg to differ."

"You can catch a ferry to neighbouring islands; the details can be found in your booklet. Paradise and Super Paradise Beach welcome a diverse crowd - so anything goes, all of which you can read about in more detail in your welcome packs," she said.

"She's reading from her booklet."

"Bloody hell, give the girl a break Doris. She has a lot to remember."

She paused for breath and gulped what was left in her bottle. I looked at the booklet in our welcome pack and read out some particulars to Doris.

"Area: 105.2 km², Max length: 15 km, Max width: 10 km, Population: 10,134, Island group: Cyclades,"

Doris nodded, but I could tell by her blank expression that she hadn't listened to a word of the detail.

"Well, what do you think so far, like what you hear?" I asked.

Doris smiled.

"Oh yes, Dave, I can't wait to get started," she said with a cheeky grin.

Moments later, the coach came to a stop.

"Ok, who is getting off at Villa Stavros?" the rep asked.

I stood up, arm aloft again.

"Yep, that's us," I shouted as we gathered our hand luggage.

We got off the bus and waited by the roadside.

The driver opened the luggage compartment and grabbed our cases whilst the rep approached us with her clipboard pressed to her chest like it was part of her outfit.

"Welcome to Kolo Beach. Villa Stavros is just up that short path. It's wonderful, the views are amazing, so I am sure you'll have a lovely time staying here."

"We can't wait," I said.

"I will be in the bar area at 8:30 a.m. tomorrow for a 1/2hr welcome meeting for all new residents," she added.

Doris looked confused.

"But there's only us staying here," she added.

"That's ok. There will probably be others who arrived here earlier, so you won't be alone."

She might be easy on the eye, but she won't be easy on the wallet. From past experience, meeting with a holiday rep on the first day of your holiday is more about them trying to up-sell some trips for double the cost, but I smiled and nodded anyway.

"Great, absolutely, we'll see you then," I said.

The bus pulled away, leaving a plume of dust behind it.

"So what time are we meeting her in the morning then? Doris asked.

"We're not," I replied.

"I thought you fancied her?"

"Doris, she's not about to ask me to marry her; unfortunately, she's just trying to sell us some holiday trips."

"But she'll tell us about all the *trips* we can go on, Dave."

I looked at her and smiled.

"We can grab all the information we need from the tourist information office in town."

Her face suddenly registered.

"Agh, I see, very clever Dave, we cut out the middle man, I get you."

I was pleased the coin had finally dropped, and my apprentice was learning.

"Alright, you *know* best, Dave."

I looked at the villa in the distance.

"We've made it, Doris."

"Not yet we haven't; we've not seen the inside," she said as we made our first steps across the road.

"AVON - would they let us stay in a shabby accommodation?" I asked.

"They won't be getting another order from me if they do, Dave."

Approaching the gate to the villa grounds, we could see a man walking towards the entrance. He opened the gate with a beckoning wave.

"Welcome to Villa Stavros. My name is *Stavros*," he said, reaching to grab our bags.

"Hiya luv, I'm Doris, and this is Dave."

"Welcome," he said with a bemused smile.

"Come, follow me," he said.

Stavros looked like how we imagine all Greek men to look like in their 50s; thick curly black hair, short and stocky, sporting an unruly black tash that sat under a big nose; it was a bit like a dead rat.

The hotel was typically Greek, with whitewashed walls, blue wooden windows, and blue wooden shutters. There were plants and flowers of every colour imaginable scattered as far as the eye could see. Some were in pots of all shapes and sizes, others grew wild, and some hung from baskets on the wall.

"Lovely flowers, Stavros," I said.

He looked at me and smiled.

"You liked gardening?" he asked.

"He's more of a dustpan and brush kind of guy," said Doris.

"I like my shrubs, yes," I said, ignoring Doris.

"Lovely garden, Stavros," I added.

Doris laughed.

"Bloody hell, Dave. Are you on the charm offensive or what?" she said.

"Stavros, you have a lovely garden, mate."

He laughed, "more luck than judgement," he said.

This was seriously nice.

*Well done, Doris,* I thought.

Stavros escorted us to the bar/reception, dropped the bags, and went behind the counter, where several keys hung from hooks on the wall.

"Ok, so - one double room then, huh," he looked at me, puzzled.

*Oh, bollocks, it's a double, it's one room, well of course it would be, it's for two people, why would I think it would be two rooms?*

"Let me explain - Doris, my *friend,* has won this holiday as part of a competition she had entered back in the UK. It was for two people, and I guess that means one room, it's no problem," I explained.

Stavros smiled.

"Oh, I see, this isn't a problem. You can book yourselves in as 'Mr and Mrs Smith' if you prefer?"

*This guy is a comedian.*

"I am only teasing you, my friend. For a moment, I was thinking, this guy likes the *older* ladies. Don't panic, my friend, you have twin beds."

Doris didn't see the funny side. She looked pensive and unamused.

"Well, sharing a double wouldn't have been so terrible, Dave," she stood with her hands on her hips.

"I like older women, but that's a little extreme," I said.

I did my best not to laugh.

"Ok, right, let me show you to your room," he waved the keys in his hand and led the way.

The studio was a good size. It had just enough essential furniture and, more importantly, two beds, which were a comfortable distance apart. It also had a nice little kitchen area situated next to an open-plan living area. This was tidy, and this will see us right.

The walls were whitewashed, with tasteful pictures scattered about. Looking up, there were oak beam features in the high-pitched roof. You could smell the wood, and it felt cosy; it felt Greek.

"The beds are a bit far apart, Dave," Doris said, looking at me to suggest they needed to be closer.

"Don't panic. They aren't nailed to the floor, so if you two *love birds* want to get closer, you can just push them together."

*This bloke should be on stage.*

I wanted to slap him; I imagined his reaction if I slapped him across the face.

"Good, there will be no risk of me waking up in the middle of the night to find you spooning me then," I said.

Placing the bags to one side, Stavros walked towards the patio doors, drew back the curtains, and opened the doors to reveal a wonderful view of the sea and surrounding area.

The balcony was as impressive as the main room; AVON had done good.

We all leaned on the balcony railings side by side and admired the view.

"Look at the views of Myko and Kolo beach, the fishing village of Pinta is to the left, and the main town of Naxos is to the right. It's not far, so it's a 10 min walk to the fishing village of Pinta, the beach is just across the road, and the main town is just a 15 min walk," he said.

"What if we get too *hot* at night," Doris asked.

"The air conditioning, that's also included," he said.

He looked around as though something was missing.

"Oh, there it is," he held aloft the control for the air-con and smiled.

"Is there a *remote* for the TV?" Doris asked.

"Of course, it sits in a slot at the side of the TV," he said, pointing to the flat-screen TV on the wall.

"So – enjoy my friends, I will let you settle in," he said.

He walked towards the front door, opened it, and then looked back to face us, "If you need *anything,* just ask."

He stepped forward, then stepped back again as if he'd just remembered something.

"Oh, before I go – breakfast is from 7:30-9:30 a.m."

"Great, thanks, Stavros," I said.

"Oh, also – the maid will change your bed linen every day, but if you don't wish to be *disturbed*, then you have a sign that you can hang from your door handle," he smiled. He was enjoying this, but I wasn't.

"He's a funny guy, Dave."

"He's alright."

We both leaned on the balcony and continued to admire the view.

"Doris, welcome to the start of our Greek *adventure*."

"Well, before we do anything else, I think it's time for a Gin & Tonic, wouldn't you agree, Dave?"

I nodded.

"I like your thinking, Doris."

# Chapter 3

She appeared with our G&Ts.

“Doris, let’s raise a toast.”

“Why not!” she said, her face lit up with a creased smile.

“To our Greek adventure,” I said.

Our glasses were raised aloft and clattered as they met. Doris, not one to let her cold drink get warm, gulped half the contents immediately.

“Calm yourself, Doris; it’s a marathon, not a bloody sprint.”

“I just get giddy sometimes. I love gin, and it makes me feel young again.”

“Yeah, it’s the giddy bit that worries me,” I said.

I gently sipped mine in a more civilised fashion.

I leaned on the balcony railing and looked out over the top of the olive trees below and observed the wonderful view across the sea.

The breeze was warm and gentle, and the smell of the flowers from the garden below added to the zest from the fresh lemon in my drink. I can't speak for Doris, but my senses were further simulated by the smell from a nearby BBQ. It felt good, being right here, in this moment.

"Right, well, I don't know about you, Doris, but the smell of that grub is making me hungry."

She slurped her drink like someone who had no teeth. It sounded wet and horrible.

"Agreed, Dave. What are you thinking?"

"I'm thinking a few more of these, and then a walk into town?"

"Sounds like a plan, Dave."

She took another big gulp, and then suddenly, without warning, her teeth fell out of her mouth and landed on the floor by her feet.

"Party trick, Doris?" I asked, creasing with laugher.

I turned to face the other way to help save her blushes.

She quickly bent down and put her teeth back in, like I hadn't noticed. Credit where it was due; she didn't drop her drink. Her fingers flapped about as she tried to re-fit her teeth in her baggy mouth.

"Have you ever considered implants?" I asked.

"Oh Dave, don't be so perverse. I think I'm a bit old for breast enhancement, don't you?"

"I meant *your teeth, not your breasts."*

"You've used that word again. Stop it," she shouted, all flustered.

"What?" I asked.

"Breasts," she replied.

I put my empty glass down.

"Right, let me nip to the local shop for some *provisions,*" I said.

"What for?" she asked.

"Well, let me think - because we'll need bottled water, some bread, butter, milk, etc for the morning."

"We get breakfast," she said, all confused.

"It's just good to have bits in," I added.

"Oh, I see. You need some cigars."

"Good thinking, Doris. Yeah, I'll see what they have."

"I'll get us another drink then," she said whilst sucking on her lemon.

"Do you always suck on your lemon?" I asked.

She looked at me as if sucking on a lemon was completely normal.

"Yeah, been doing it for years."

"It's probably why you have no teeth then."

"Are you going to the shop or what?" she shouted.

On my return, Doris appeared with a glass in her hand.

She was wearing one of her summer dresses. It looked like something from the 1980s series – "The Love Boat".

"What do you think, Dave? Will I pull tonight?"

I paused for thought.

She also wore gold sandals and had a matching handbag.

"Do all ladies north of seventy wear gold sandals?" I asked.

"Gold all the way, Dave."

"You look delightful."

"Thank you."

"You're all glammed up, but I was planning to stick my flip-flops on, maybe a pair of shorts and a tee. I'm not doing formal."

She looked disappointed

"Oh - did you not bring your *dinner jacket* then, Dave?"

"Oddly enough - *no,* and that's because we're on a Greek Island and *not* on a Saga Holiday for the over 70s," I said.

"Excuse me – I'm over 70," she said, shaking her head.

"How old are you exactly?"

"A lady never tells," she said.

"Oh yeah, of course," I said.

"Ok, I'd better get ready then. Wouldn't want to look too shabby hanging out with a *lady."*

Laughing to myself, I opened the crisps and crunched on some local cheese & onion alternatives to Walkers.

I walked into my bedroom, put the packet of crisps on the bed, and opened my wardrobe. Time was of the essence, and I had to make a quick decision on what I was wearing.

*Flip-Flops, tick, shorts, tick, tee, tick, wallet, tick, cigars... where's my cigars?*

Half an hour later, I was ready. I grabbed my cigars from the side table and stuffed them in my top pocket.

I walked out onto the balcony, where Doris sat waiting.

"Doris, may I escort you to dinner, madam?"

She smiled. She was enjoying this, and she looked happy.

"Why thank you, kind sir," she said, linking my arm as we left the villa.

"Should we call a taxi, Dave?"

"It's a short walk, we'll be fine."

"It's *dark,* Dave," she moaned as I closed the door behind us.

"Just link my arm, and I will see you right," I reassured her as we made our way down the path.

We soon got closer to town, and the shops and tavernas became more plentiful, as did people, but not to the point of excess; they were just enough. According to Tripadvisor, this was a hidden gem of an island, and so far, it was living up to my expectations.

"Doris, what about that little restaurant over *there*? It'll have a view of the harbour, *and,* it's a fish restaurant judging by the smell. I'm craving some calamari."

She nodded. "I love fish and chips," she said in her broad Wigan accent.

"Not sure if it'll be like the fish n chips you're accustomed to in Wigan, but you can ask!"

We walked into the restaurant and made our way across the timber deck floor towards one of the sea-view tables. As we grabbed a prime spot with a good view, we were soon greeted by a keen waiter.

"Hello, welcome, how are you? Can I get you some drinks? Are you ready to order?" he asked, all nervous and all fingers and thumbs.

He was no older than 18 but looked about 8, and he had a nervousness about him like it was his first day on the job. Fiddling with his note pad, he began to fluster.

"Hello, very well, thank you. I would like a beer and a …"

"A large G&T for me, please, ice and a slice," said Doris, interrupting me mid-flow.

Nervously writing on his pad, the waiter dropped his pen on the floor. It rolled under the table, so he bent down and fumbled about with his hands, trying to find it.

“I hope you’re not touching me up under there, young man?” Doris said, all serious.

“Sorry, madam. Found it.”

The waiter quickly rose to his feet, holding the pen aloft like a prized possession. He then started to write our order on his pad. His pen was clearly out of ink as he kept doing a swirl on his paper in a frantic attempt to find some ink. It failed, so he decided to make a quick escape towards the bar to avoid any more embarrassment.

“He’s a nervous chap,” Doris said.

“I’d be amazed if we get the drinks we’ve ordered,” I added.

“Well, if he gets it wrong, I’ll be having words with his boss,” she said.

“Behave yourself, Doris, or he’ll be spitting in your soup,” I said.

“I’m not ordering *soup*,” she added, all matter of fact.

“He’ll stick your fish down his underpants then,” I laughed because I knew what reaction was coming.

“Oh, Dave – don’t be vulgar.”

Moments later, we had our drinks, complimentary bread in a basket, and some olives. He’d made a good recovery. I ordered calamari, and Doris, not one to disappoint, ordered cheese on toast.

“I thought you wanted to ask if they could do fish and chips?” I asked.

"I've just seen someone being served fish, Dave, and it still had its head on."

She looked horrified.

"At least you know it's fresh," I said, taking a sip of my beer.

"I don't want to see its eyes looking back at me, Dave."

"The fish might look the other way," I said.

She looked puzzled.

"Doris, *seriously*, cheese on toast?"

She took a big bite and crunched so loudly that bits of cheese and crumbs stuck to her face and chin.

"I know, I know, but I like what I like, and I need to get used to all this foreign food first before I'm brave enough to try new things," she said.

I stuck my fork into my fried calamari, forced a load in my mouth, and chomped away on squid rings infused with garlic and lemon. It was bliss.

"How can you eat those things with all those legs?" she asked, shaking her head.

"Seriously, the French eat *frogs*, so this is nothing," I added.

She looked confused.

"They eat *frogs*?" She asked.

"They eat the head and everything," I added, taking another mouthful of squid.

“The French are perverts,” she said.

“Why are they perverts?” I asked, laughing.

“They’re perverts, Dave - end of.”

“*Fuck* - You really do hate the French then?”

“Dave, don’t use the F word,” she corrected me again.

“What’s wrong with using the *F word* in the right context?” I asked, shrugging my shoulders.

“I mean the word *French,”* she stated.

“Bloody hell, what you like,” I said.

“Would you eat *French* cheese?” I asked.

“No, I *bloody* wouldn’t.”

“What have *they* ever done to you?” I asked.

She stopped chewing, took a swig of her drink, and paused for thought.

“I *once* went on a coach trip to France. I remember having some garlic bread. It was all wet and horrible. I’m sure the French waiter urinated on it,” she said, all very serious.

I laughed rather loudly, drawing the attention of a few fellow diners who sat at other tables.

“Dave – I’m *serious*,” she said.

“I’d better not order any garlic bread then, eh!” I added.

“No, it’s fine. This is Greece, not France,” she said.

“So, you wouldn’t be offended if I order French cheese?”

“Don’t you dare, I’ll scream!”

“But you’re not offended by me eating squid legs?”

“No, it’s gross, but I can live with it.”

“Good to know because I’ ll be eating a ton of it.”

“What, tonight?” she asked.

*“No,* I mean while we are here.”

The bar got increasingly busy with a mixed crowd, a healthy blend of locals and tourists, and there was a nice holiday vibe about the place. The smells of great food continued to waft about the place as more food was served to the neighbouring tables.

We finished our food and moved-on to our dessert with more alcohol. Doris slurped on her G&T and proceeded with the annoying habit of crunching on her ice.

“Do you have to do that?” I asked

“Do what?”

“*Crunch* on the ice,” I said.

She smiled and crunched on another piece of ice like a defiant school child.

Suddenly - her false teeth dropped into her glass. I looked at her in horror. She looked back at me, flustered and flappy. Sticking her skinny fingers into the glass, she wildly tried to grab her teeth.

It seemed to take an age. She finally grabbed them, poured some fizzy water over them, and proceeded to put them back in her mouth.

"Doris, they're not in properly, they're wonky."

She fumbled with her fingers in her mouth and eventually secured them in place.

"You alright?" I asked

"Not sure."

"How do you mean?"

She looked uneasy and uncomfortable, but this wasn't about her teeth falling out; something else was wrong, something else was bothering her. She kept adjusting her dress at the waist, and her face contorted with discomfort.

"Doris, what's up? You look a bit restless?"

She paused for thought as the cogs in her mind processed an answer.

"Hmmm - my stomach feels a bit iffy, to be honest, Dave."

She then belched out loud - how nice. I looked around to see if she had caught anyone's attention.

"Well, it can't be the food; you've only had cheese on toast; not exactly a recipe for botulism, is it?"

She had another expression of discomfort etched on her already creased face. I had seen fewer creases on a well-used road map.

"Well, yeah, I only had some crisps earlier when you were out, but they were a bit salty for me, so I washed them down with some tap water, but it tasted a bit gritty, so I didn't drink much of it."

*"Wait* a minute. You had tap water? The tap water here isn't suitable for drinking. There's a notice on the wall in our kitchen, *hence*, I purchased bottled water."

"Ohhh, Dave, I don't feel too good."

Her face creased again as she did another belch. The belch was quickly followed by a rather wet-sounding fart. It was loud and raspy, and the plastic-coated chair cover did nothing to muffle the sound. Such anti-social noises hadn't gone unnoticed, as a couple on a nearby table looked over and began to discreetly chuckle.

Moments later, Doris rose to her feet.

"I think I need the ladies, Dave."

"I think *you do,* Doris, don't hang about, will you."

Before she could walk away from the table, she let out another almighty fart, so loud that people on the surrounding tables stopped their conversations and looked over. It was an observation of mass. Some chuckled, while others looked less amused, shocked, and even horrified.

"Doris, don't hang about," I said, pointing towards the ladies.

I looked at some of the people sitting at other tables, made eye contact, and smiled at them apologetically.

Doris began to walk slowly towards the toilets. Again, she let out another roar of thunder from her pants. She took another few steps forward, but her progress was in slow motion, like she was wearing concrete wellies. Maybe walking slowly was her attempt to slow down the inevitable. Maybe the turtle's head was about to touch the cloth?

"Doris, just get to the bloody toilet fast. This is beyond embarrassing."

Moments later, the worst possible episode occurred. Much to my horror, and the horror of the people now watching this box office hit, Doris farted again. This time, it was even louder than before, and to make matters worse, the offensive sound was accompanied by what appeared to be the sounds of her following-through.

What could only be described as another loud wet fart was quickly accompanied by a lumpy brown substance that had deposited on the floor.

Oh fuck - this was now a social crisis of a biblical scale. I was trying hard not to imagine the brown slop running down her leg.

I just sat there, speechless, unable to move or make any kind of decision that might help her.

She then scampered off to the toilets whilst a waiter quickly grabbed some napkins and placed them over the offending substance.

He was retching in the process. I felt his pain as I watched him scooping it up. Others watched in disbelief, talking quietly amongst themselves. I was simply gobsmacked.

Suddenly, one lady caught my eye. She left her table and began to walk away, placing a cigarette in her mouth as she left the restaurant. I could see her a short distance away. She lit her cigarette, took a big drag, and exhaled. The smoke bellowed above and away from her on the breeze. It wasn't a bad idea; smoke the smell away. I glanced at the packet of cigars in my shirt pocket, and I was tempted, very tempted.

I couldn't just sit there, either. I've got a granny who's just shit herself, and I'd better do the gentlemanly thing and check if she's ok.

But – I needed a cigar first,

*fuck it; it might help me compose myself before I go in there.*

I leaned back in my chair, lit a cigar, took a drag, and slowly allowed the smoke to waft in my mouth. I pretended I was somewhere else, with someone else, but after several puffs of my cigar, I couldn't erase the thoughts of a distressed Doris. I had to go and help.

Stubbing my cigar out, I left the table.

The waiter approached me, only this time, his standard issue smile had been replaced with a frown.

"The ladies are just over there if you want to see if she is ok," he kindly suggested.

"Thank you," I replied.

I knocked gently on the WC door.

“Doris, it’s me - how are you feeling?”

“I’ve bloody soiled myself. How well do you think I’m feeling, Dave.”

She was clearly still in the final throws of substance depositing, as I could hear the unmistakable sound of diarrhoea splashing against porcelain.

“Just take your time. I will go and ask the waiter if I can borrow a towel.”

“A towel, what am I going to do with that, make a nappy?” she shouted.

“Well, here’s a thought, Doris, should I nip to the chemist?” I suggested.

“What for?” she shouted.

“Some nappies?” I asked.

“Dave, now is not the time for humour,” she said.

I did my best to reassure her, but it was a bit like asking a shitting dog to stop shaking.

I walked back to the bar area and grabbed the waiter's attention. At the same time, I observed a calm being restored to the restaurant, and people went about their business as normal.

Old news, people had forgotten already.

The waiter looked concerned.

"She's ok, but clearly not over the worst, so she might be in there for some time," I said.

I did my best to reassure the visibly stressed waiter.

"Ok, no problem. Was it something she had eaten earlier today?" he asked.

I liked his style, deflecting from the prospect that it might be the restaurant that was liable.

"Yeah, don't worry, she'll be ok. I will check on her again."

Moments later, I returned to the WC and knocked, but there was no reply. I pushed the door, and it opened, but she wasn't there.

*Oh fuck what now?*

I then heard some laughter and clapping from the bar area.

I walked back into the restaurant area to find her talking to the waiter in just her underwear, with her knickers stained brown.

"Doris, you need to ask for a towel to hide your blushes, and I need to get you back to the villa before you get arrested," I said.

Another waiter arrived at the crime scene, and placed a man's jacket over her shoulders.

"Thank you, darling, that's very kind of you," she said with a slight smile.

"You're very welcome, madam," he said.

He was desperate to remove her from the premises, and I struggled not to laugh in that moment.

"Thank you, I will get her home and return your jacket tomorrow if that's ok?" I asked, and the waiter nodded with approval.

"Of course, sir, please take your time, and I'm very sorry your *partner* isn't feeling very well," the waiter said with a sympathetic smile.

"She's my *friend*, not my partner."

"Oh, I see, sir."

Doris looked at the waiter and laughed.

"Don't believe a word of it, we're lovers, alright. He's quite a catch, don't you think?" she shouted.

"Doris, pipe down," I added.

I looked at the waiter and shook my head.

At this rate, the whole bloody island will believe I'm shacked up with her.

What do I need to do to convince people otherwise, get posters printed and do a mail-shot?

We made our way up the road, leaving the drama for one night behind us.

"Talk about making a bloody grand entrance on our first night," I said.

"Oh, Dave, I feel so deflated."

"Oh, you're definitely deflated."

She looked sad, “Don’t mention *shit* again, please, Dave. It makes me feel sick, and never mind about me soiling myself. What about my lovely dress? It’ll be *bloody* ruined.”

“Ruined, it’s my street cred that’s bloody ruined.”

She looked at me and laughed.

“You don’t have any street cred, Dave.”

“Yeah, I know. I have even *less* now. Thanks, Doris.”

“Don’t mention. You’re very welcome, Dave.”

# Chapter 4

I woke early. I'm not the best in the morning, but in "holiday mode", I have no problem wrestling the mattress from my back.

I put the pan of hot water on for a brew. The Greeks don't provide kettles as a rule because, unlike the British, they don't drink tea.

Doris was nowhere to be seen, conspicuous by her absence. I wasn't complaining; it was peaceful, and I was enjoying the moment.

I leaned on the balcony and looked out over the gardens.

*Where is she?*

I glanced at my watch. Even at 7:22 a.m., the sky was blue and cloudless, bees were already busy flirting with the hanging baskets, and I could smell the irresistible aroma of fresh bread that lingered from the bakers nearby.

My thoughts reverted back to Doris.

*Maybe she had a moment of resourcefulness and went for some fresh bread?*

Then suddenly, there was a bang on the door. I nearly dropped my cup.

*Maybe she had forgotten her key?*

I opened the door to be greeted by a short, squat, bearded Greek man sporting a string vest and a hairy chest that would have given Tom Jones a complex.

"Hello - are you with an *elderly* lady?" he asked.

"Hmmm, yes, of sorts. She's staying here, why?"

I was thinking the worst.

"She is ***crazy***. She came to my farm and asked if she could hire a sheep. She is ***crazy***; she scared my sheep," he was ranting.

"A sheep?" I asked, bewildered.

"Yes, a sheep!," he shouted.

"So, where is she now? I'm really sorry. I'm sure there's been a misunderstanding?" I said.

"She is here," he said.

Doris could be seen walking up the path.

"You tell her she is ***crazy***."

"She already knows, mate. I don't need to tell her."

"If I see her on my land again, I will shoot her."

"Bloody hell, mate, that's a bit harsh."

"Listen, she is a crazy lady. I already have one at home and don't need another."

I shook my head in disbelief. Was this shit really happening?

He then walked off all dramatic, waving his arms in the air.

Doris arrived at the doorway with a sheepish grin.

"Please explain to me why you are scaring animals and upsetting the farmer?"

"Dave - I'm sorry, I got chatting to a man in the bakers."

"Sounds harmless enough," I said.

"No, listen, he was a bit deaf. I asked him where I could hire a *jeep*, so he pointed to a farm house just across the road. When I knocked on the farm door, I asked if I could hire a *Jeep*, but he must have been hard of hearing too because I think he thought I meant 'hire a *sheep,'* and he wasn't best pleased."

"Why would you think you could hire a Jeep at a farm, Doris? Did you not query that with the man in the bakers?"

She shrugged her shoulders.

"Let's re-cap Doris, just to add some clarity to this madness."

"Do we have to?" she groaned.

"So you got talking to a deaf man in the bakers, who led you to a deaf man at a farm?"

"Yes," she said.

"Have you been smoking *weed,* Doris?"

"Weed?" she asked, confused.

"Never mind," I said.

"So then, what happened?" I asked

"Well, he asked me to leave."

"And did you just leave?" I asked.

"It wasn't my fault I went through the wrong gate and scared a flock of sheep."

"How did you manage to scare the sheep?" I asked.

"Well, one got too close, so I panicked and swung my hand bag at it," she added.

"So then what?"

"The crazy farmer started hurling abuses at me."

I was lost for words.

"Doris, let's introduce a golden rule that under no circumstances are you to leave the villa without me, understood?"

"Sorry, I meant no harm. Anyway, on a *positive* note," she said.

"Positive? No such word exists in your world!"

"No, listen."

"Go on," I said.

"I've got us some *fresh* bread from the bakers," her face lit-up as she revealed her bounty.

"Oh, so it wasn't an entirely wasted journey then, eh Doris? Nice, come on, let's get inside," I said, "And listen to me, please. No more scrapes with the locals."

"I'm sorry."

"No more talking to deaf people in the Bakers."

"I won't, I promise."

"Stay away from the *sheep*."

"I will."

"Can we just keep a low profile from now on, *please*, or we'll be kicked off the island at this rate."

"Agreed," she said.

"Right, let's go into town later and hire a Jeep from a man who isn't deaf. Do you think we can manage that? Or will we come home on the back of a woolly four-legged animal?" I asked.

She laughed.

"Ok, Dave, point taken."

"Right, it's ten past eight. Fancy grabbing some breakfast?" I asked.

"Don't think I could risk food just yet, not after last night," she said.

"Good call. Let's have a coffee inside, and then we'll go," I added.

We eventually made our way into town. I loved this place already; the buzz, the vibe, the sun on my face.

"Right, you sit on this bench while I just pop into that car rental place and sort us out with a set of wheels."

"Can't I just come in with you, Dave?"

"No, I will be faster alone."

"Why don't you tie me to that tree over there like a dog?" she groaned.

"Doris, take a chill pill. It doesn't take two of us to hire a jeep. I won't be long."

It *actually* took longer than anticipated. The paperwork was excessive compared to normal. The last time I was on a Greek Island, I walked into a rental shop, pointed to a vehicle, paid some money, and walked out with some keys.

"Ok, we're all sorted," I said, waving the car key in the air.

She looked elated.

"Which one is it?" she asked.

"That one there," I pointed to it parked in the bay.

"Oh nice, Dave, so that's what a *jeep* looks like?"

"That's right. Notice how it has wheels and not legs, Doris."

She laughed.

"So what make is it?" she asked.

"It's a little Suzuki Jimney with a rag-top roof, perfect for island life."

"Any air-con?"

"It's a convertible, Doris. We don't need both."

"Agh, yeah, ok, I get it," she said, nodding her head.

"I'm sorry I didn't bring my driving licence, Dave."

*Bloody hell, I'm not.*

"Yeah, a real shame that, Doris."

"Before we get excited and go sightseeing, let's grab some extra provisions."

"Like what?" she asked.

"We'll need some bottled water for starters."

"Good thinking, Dave. I've just drank the last drop."

"Exactly, and remember the bottled water concept, Doris. It is the alternative to tap water that won't give you a soggy bottom."

"You're not funny, Dave. My bottom is my business."

"Oh really? I think half the town has seen your bottom already."

"They *have* not," she insisted.

"Have you not seen the local newspaper this morning?" I asked.

"What do you mean?" she asked.

“There was a picture of your bottom on the front page,” I said.

“No there wasn’t.”

“Well, I think they had edited that bit out of the picture, but you could still see some of your flesh,” I said.

She looked horrified, “*How?”*

“They had cameras in the toilets.”

“That’s illegal, Dave.”

“Where’s the paper? Show me.”

“I’m winding you up, Doris.”

“You’re an *arsehole,* Dave.”

“Takes one to know one, eh.”

“Right, come on, jump in, let's go.”

After a short drive up the road, I pulled over at the first shop.

“Right, this will do, Doris.”

“Any special requests?” I asked.

“A tall, dark, handsome man, please, Dave.”

“It’s not that kind of shop tiger.”

“I like those smoky bacon crisps, oh, and some chocolate.”

“It’ll melt!”

“Yeah, it will - in my *gob.*”

“Is that it?” I asked.

"A spade."

"A what?"

"A spade."

"Oh, I see, so I can dig you out of the next mess you get us in?"

"No, I saw it once on tele, where a man got his jeep stuck in the sand and used a shovel to dig his way out."

"Bloody hell, this is a Greek Island, not the sand dunes of the Sahara. Calm yourself, woman." I said.

"You can't be too *careful,* Dave."

"With you, yeah, I couldn't agree more!"

"Right, don't play with any of the switches, please; I will be back in a minute."

"I won't."

I had no sooner grabbed a few bits when a local man came running into the shop, his face contorted with fear. He began shouting at the girl on the till, who then translated his shouts to me.

*"Excuse me*, is the jeep outside - *yours*?" she asked while the man frantically waited for my answer.

"Yeah, why?"

"I think you need to hurry," she pleaded.

I ran outside the shop - to my horror, I watched the jeep slowly roll down the hill.

You couldn't write this shit.

I began to run after it, followed by the Greek man. His face contorted with fear.

Doris was screaming at the top of her voice and waving her arms about frantically.

“Help me, help me, help me.”

It was no use. Just as I thought we were catching the vehicle, it gathered more speed and began to pull away from our breathless efforts.

I stopped for a moment, gasping for breath, the local man doing much the same. We both looked on with horror as the jeep reversed across the road at the bottom of the hill.

We gasped as we watched it pass several sunbathers on the beach as they lay on their sun beds, oblivious. It remarkably missed them all by inches and then plunged into the sea.

# Chapter 5

I stopped momentarily, got my breath back, and continued running down the hill.

"Ouch, fuck! that hurt," I shouted as I hit another stone hard on my left foot.

My progress was more camel and race horse.

The Greek man was already at the bottom of the hill, but that was less about his fitness and more about his choice of footwear, I'm sure.

"Come on, what's taking you so long?" he shouted.

"Usain Bolt has no chance against you, pal, does he?" I asked.

"Who?" he replied.

We ran onto the beach and made our way towards the carnage. Sunbathers just watched in astonishment, or awkwardness, in a very British way; the types who 'stand and stare' as opposed to 'run and help'.

To our relief, we could see that the jeep had come to a halt on a rock, so only the rear of the vehicle was submerged in the sea.

We both ran toward the vehicle.

Doris was sitting and physically shaking.

I tried to open the passenger door, but it was jammed. Another local had also arrived on the scene. He tried to open the door, but it didn't budge, so he tried the driver's door instead, but it was all in vain.

"Someone bloody help me, please," shouted Doris, her face creased with fear.

The Greek man pointed to the rear of the vehicle.

"Hurry, it's filling up with water. She has to climb over the top," he shouted.

"*Dave,* I'm trapped."

"Remove your seatbelt, Doris. That's no good for you now."

*"What if I float away?"*

"Listen, you're not trapped. You actually need to unclick your seat belt," I shouted, but she was frozen in fear.

The Greek man pressed his face against the glass on the passenger side.

“We need you to listen carefully. We have no time,” said the man.

I climbed over the door, dropped into the passenger seat, unclipped her seat belt, and grabbed hold of her, gently shaking her to get her to focus.

“You’re going to have to jump over the top,” I shouted.

“I can’t. I’ll get wet, Dave,” she shouted.

“You’re already bloody wet,” I shouted.

“Where’s my handbag,” she shouted, looking around for it.

“You’ll be in a body bag if you don’t do what I tell you, Doris.”

“I’ll catch you; just do it. You don’t have time. The vehicle is filling with water,” I shouted.

“I’m not moving,” she said in defiance.

“Doris, there’s a *shark* in the back seat,” I shouted, pointing to the seat behind her.

She suddenly grabbed hold of the door frame and cocked a leg over the top.

I helped her with her other leg, and within an instant, super gran had left the vehicle.

The Greek man carried her in his arms onto the sand and carefully seated her.

“You ok? It wasn’t too hard, was it?” I asked, and she nodded her head.

"I thought the shark trick might do the job," I laughed.

"You shouldn't lie. I thought you were serious."

"I was."

"I didn't want to get my knickers wet. That's what made me jump out, Dave, not the bloody shark," she said.

The man looked at her and smiled.

"She's one brave lady," he said.

She moved her fingers and toes, and started to bend her limbs back and forth like a rag doll coming to life.

"Nothing broken, it would seem – just my pride, eh," she said as she brushed the excess sand off her clothes.

I reached inside my top pocket and pulled out a pack of tissues; the first few were wet, but the rest had survived. I pulled one out and handed it to her.

"Here, use that to wipe your face," I said.

"Thanks, Dave."

She began to wipe her face and arms, handing the wet tissue back to me and grabbing a fresh one.

"She okay?" he asked, looking at me.

"She's fine, mate, and hey, listen, thank you. I'd still be in the shop without you," I said.

He looked at Doris and smiled.

"You are a very brave lady," he said, patting her on her head like she was a pet dog.

She looked up at him and frowned.

“Do you mind? You’re spoiling my hair with your fat Greek fingers,” she said.

“Doris, he helped to rescue you from certain death.”

He looked at me and laughed.

“Thanks again for your help,” I said, putting my hand on his shoulder.

“Ok, no problem, I must go now,” he said.

“Would you like a lift?” I asked, looking back at the stricken jeep.

He made no comment.

“Where’s he going?” she asked.

“Home, probably.”

“Here, take a drink of water,” I insisted.

She gulped away at the bottle.

“Have you lost your hearing aid by any chance?” I asked.

“She gulped on the bottle like a new-born lamb whilst wiping away more sand particles from her wet face.

“Dave - I’d rather hire a s*heep* next time,” she smiled.

“You might want to remove the seaweed hanging off your head, Doris. I know there are health benefits from using Kelp and suchlike, but I think I’d try Holland & Barrett instead of using the raw material.”

She poured the rest of the bottle of water onto her palms and splashed it on her face, removing any remnants of the sea.

We both looked at the jeep and looked at each other.

"Hand-break cable must have snapped," I said.

"Good job. I didn't leave a damage deposit, or I'd be royally buggered right now," I added.

She shook her head in disbelief.

"What are we going to do?"

"Well, there's a good chance they won't believe it's a failed hand break, so I will…"

She stopped me mid-flow.

"Dave - I have a *bit* of a confession."

*"Go on, I'm all ears."*

"I thought the hand break was an umbrella," she said.

*Like you need one in this climate.*

"Eh?" I said.

"So I grabbed hold of it, but it was stuck, so I pressed something, and then it started rolling down the hill. *Sorry,* Dave, it's all my fault. I didn't realise, I'm so sorry."

"Bloody hell, Doris, you're hurting my head."

"Are you mad at me?" she asked.

"Mad, no, why would I be mad? It could have been worse. You at least haven't shit yourself."

She looked at me, all guilty.

"Oh please, Doris, tell me you haven't?"

"No, I bloody haven't."

"Do you know Bear Grylls, Doris?" I asked.

"Grylls, are they a bit like burgers?" she asked.

"No, he's a bloke you see on tele, demonstrating what it takes to survive in extreme environments and under extreme circumstances. That's who I am when I'm with you."

"There's not much difference between you two then, is there?"

"Oh, there is Doris. He gets paid for it, I don't!"

"Well, you did get a *free* holiday, Dave, so that kind of counts as payment," she justified with a half-smile.

"What are we going to do?" she asked.

"Let me think - I have an idea, but we have to move fast."

"Dave, we need to move fast?" she shouted.

"That farmer you were harassing over the sheep, he'll have a tractor, and that will help us drag this jeep out of the water," I said.

She nodded.

"Great idea, Dave, but I'm not sure he will want to help us."

"I'll sort it out. That will at least put the vehicle back on dry land, and we can then look at the damage to the rear and what water damage there is to the interior. We'll need to take the carpets out, dry them, stick several air fresheners in them, and hope for the best. We might just blag it."

"What are our chances?" she asked.

"Slim to none."

"I'm impressed, Dave."

"What with such great odds?" I asked

"I like a flutter," she added.

"Don't get too giddy - the farmer has to agree to help us first."

"Right, well, what are we waiting for?" she asked.

She stood up and placed her hands on her hips like she was ready for the next challenge.

We walked a short distance back to the farm, arm in arm. I feared she'd roll back down the hill if I let go.

"You ok, feeling alright, no pain?" I asked.

"I'm fine, Dave, nothing a Gin & Tonic wouldn't cure."

She looked at me, "What about you? any pain?"

"Only in my neck, Doris."

"Well, here we are, Dave. The last time I saw that gate, the horrible farmer was chasing me out of it."

"Listen, we need a plan, Doris."

"What are you thinking?" she asked.

"I *think* if he sees you, he might grab his gun."

She had one of those creased faces again, like she'd just sucked on a lemon.

"Listen, he won't help us out of kindness. I might need to *bung* him a few quid for his troubles," I suggested.

"I'm with you all the way, Dave."

"No, you're bloody not. Wait here, I won't be long. We need to crack on, so *I'll* go talk to him."

I walked up the path and arrived at the door to the farm house. I could hear the distant bark of a dog with large lungs. Let's just hope it stays where it is. I could see several chickens strutting about the yard, doing what chickens do best, scratching at the dust and pecking the ground for grubs.

There were several old buildings and plenty of farm-type machinery scattered about, including a tractor that looked pretty useful.

*Right, deep breath, Dave, compose yourself.*

I knocked on the door and waited. Moments later, the door opened, and the farmer stood before me.

"Oh – it's *you* again. What do *you* want?"

"Hi, I have come to apologise on behalf of my friend."

He looked bemused.

"Ok, no problem, just tell her that I will shoot her next time," he began to close the door.

*"No, wait,"* I shouted

"What do you want?" he moaned with his hands on his hips, all snobby.

"I *really* need your help."

"Keep talking. I'm listening!"

"Our jeep has got stuck in the sand, and we need to move quickly, so I was wondering, could you *please* help us?"

"Hmmmm," he continued to scratch his chin.

"I'm *very* busy," he said.

"I wouldn't ask, but we are kind of desperate."

"I'm busy, *sorry*. I can't help you."

He wasn't playing ball, so I needed to use plan B.

"Ok, how much?" I asked.

His pondered.

"Ok - I will give you 25 euros."

He laughed.

"25 euros, you think I'm that cheap, huh?"

"Ok, 40 euros?" I asked.

He laughed again; he was enjoying my pain.

"50 euros, and we have a deal, yes?" he suggested.

"Bloody hell, ok, we have a deal."

He glanced over his shoulder at what appeared to be his wife sitting at the kitchen table. He then mumbled something to her in Greek and closed the door behind him.

He opened up the palm of his right hand, waiting for me to stuff 50 euros in it. I opened my wallet, took out the cash, and placed it in his hand.

“*Ok, let’s go,*” he shouted.

We made our way toward the tractor. He then stopped and looked at me.

“I will meet you at the beach. There is no room for you in the tractor. It’s not safe,” he said.

“Ok, no problem, I will go and grab Doris.”

I ran down the path toward her. She was standing by the gate with an expressionless face, as though she was expecting a negative outcome.

“Well, what did he say?” she asked, all concerned.

I turned around and pointed towards the tractor that could be seen a short distance away.

“Dave, you’re a hero,” she shouted with glee.

“How much did it cost you?”

“Cost?” I asked.

“Nothing, just my charm, Doris, nothing more.”

“You’re full of shit. How much?”

“Enough!”

“Come, we need to get back down the hill, Doris; no time to be dicking about.”

When we arrived at the scene, the farmer had already grabbed his winch and hooked it up to the front bumper of our stricken vehicle.

“Bloody hell, Dave, he doesn’t hang about.”

“Dam right, he shouldn’t cost me 50 quid.”

She looked at me, horrified.

"How much??" she shouted.

Within seconds, the little jeep had been pulled from the sea and onto the sand.

"Thank you," I shouted towards the farmer.

He nodded his head.

I walked over to the driver's door and opened it. Water and bits of seaweed poured out onto my feet.

*Shit, it's a mess.*

Meanwhile, Doris was observing the rear.

"I'm going to see if it'll start," I shouted.

"I don't fancy your chances," she shouted back.

I turned the key, and remarkably, it started on the first go. This was a result - we could at least drive it back to the rental place.

"How the hell has it managed to start?" she asked.

I shrugged my shoulders.

"Duno, luck of the Gods, I guess."

"You're not a lucky bloke, Dave."

"Dam right I'm not. I'm on holiday with you, for starters."

"Dave, we're having a lovely time."

The farmer watched from his tractor.

"Right, I'll be seeing you then," he shouted.

"Thanks again, mate, much appreciated," I shouted back.

I then proceeded to walk round the back of the vehicle, but seeing the concerned expression on her face, I knew the outcome wouldn't be pretty.

"Shit - the bumper and rear door have been royally shafted. It will need a new bumper and door, by the looks of it."

"That bad?" she asked.

"Yeah, it's beyond panel beating that Doris."

"How much will it cost, Dave?"

I shook my head.

"I can't see much change out of a grand of any man's money to put this shit right,"

She looked concerned.

"We can take her to a valet, blast her clean, try to get the carpets sorted at least, and then we'll take her back to the rental place and *pray* they don't bill us hard," I said.

"We could do a runner," Doris suggested.

"Nice idea, Doris, but they know where we're staying."

"Why did you tell them that?" she asked, her face creased like a paper bag.

"Bloody hell, you do actually have to fill in a few forms, Doris, ID, that kind of thing."

"Agh, I see," she nodded.

"See? Yeah, see what shit we're in now because of you."

She looked upset.

“Listen, I’m sorry. I didn’t mean to raise my voice; it was an accident,” I added, putting my arms around her to give her some comfort.

“So, you’re not angry with me then?” she asked.

“No.”

“Despite everything, Dave, we’re having a nice holiday, aren’t we?

“Wonderful,” I said.

“We haven’t exactly committed any crime,” she added.

“We won’t be on Interpol’s database anytime soon, Doris.”

“Inter .. who?” she asked

“I’m not *‘inter’* this Doris, that’s for sure!!”

“Interpol, what’s that?” she asked.

“What does it matter? We need to get this jeep cleaned.”

“I’m just curious,” she asked.

“They are a crime agency. They look for people on the run and specialise in finding elderly criminals.”

“Really?” she asked

“Especially old ladies,” I added.

“You’re full of shit, Dave.”

A few hours later, we had the jeep carpets valeted at a local garage, and the result wasn’t too shabby.

The carpets didn't look "showroom" condition, but they'd do. I also kept a few air fresheners in the cabin.

"We'll have to ask them to inspect it with their eyes closed," I said as I stuffed the last few wet wipes in the bin.

"Yeah, but they won't be able to see it then," she said, like I was serious.

"Jump in then, Doris. Let's get this over and done with."

I climbed in, stuck the key in the ignition, and looked at her.

"Can you imagine if it didn't start?" I said with a grin on my face.

"Don't tempt fate, Dave. This isn't a time to joke; we're about to be seriously out of pocket."

I turned the key and the engine turned over, but it wouldn't start.

"Shit," I shouted.

"I bloody told you, look what you have done. You've cursed it now," she shouted.

"Chill."

I took a deep breath and tried again.

The little engine fired. I pressed the accelerator to rev it a few times, and it rumbled to life.

"You lucky bugger, Dave."

"Lucky, I bloody wish," I said.

"Right, let's get out of here," I added.

We spoke a little on our way back to the rental place, but I contemplated a lot.

"Doris, best case, £500; worst case, we get a quote, bung some extra on top, and it comes upto £1000 ish," I pondered with a sigh.

"I agree with you on that one, Dave."

*As if she has any idea of the gravity of what might happen.*

Moments later, we pulled up outside the rental shop entrance, and I switched the engine off.

She looked at me, and I looked at her.

"Listen - let me do the talking. Whatever the outcome, we'll go halves. We're a *team*, after all," I said.

"I can't expect you to pay half Dave. It was my fault."

"We're in this together, chill; what happens, happens."

She had a half smile.

Suddenly and without warning, a car smacked into the back of our jeep – and with a thud, the impact sent me and Doris jerking forward in our seats.

Doris screamed.

"Fuck," I shouted.

I looked behind me and saw another car attached to our rear bumper.

I looked at Doris, "You okay?"

"Good job I left my seat belt, eh," she said.

"You okay?" I asked again.

She nodded.

"Good job I wasn't holding a box of eggs, eh Dave."

"My thoughts exactly. Wait here."

I unclipped my seatbelt, got out, and walked over to the rear of our jeep.

I then made my way to the driver in the other car.

I looked in through their window, smiled, and suggested she put her window down.

"What happened?" I asked

The lady in the driver's seat was in shock, with her head in her hands. She looked up at me and burst into tears.

"I'm terribly sorry, I hit the accelerator instead of the brake," she said.

Her partner in the passenger seat looked over and smiled apologetically.

"She normally drives an automatic," he said, shaking his head.

"Listen, are you both ok?" I asked.

"Yes, but look at the damage I have done to *your* car," she said.

I glanced at the rear of the jeep and looked back at them.

"Ouch, fragile bodies on these jeeps," I said, shaking my head.

"Listen, it's not a problem; accidents happen. On a positive note, no one's hurt, and that's the main thing," I said.

The man leaned across, "Listen, we'll pay for the damage to your car. It's obviously our fault," he said.

"That's *very* kind of you," I said with a sympathetic smile.

"We just need to explain what happened to the front desk and let them sort the paperwork," I said.

"I just need to go and check if my friend is ok."

"No problem," said the lady, now looking a little more composed.

I walked back to our jeep and got in. Doris looked at me.

"Are you sure you're ok, Doris?"

"I'm fine, but this bloody nightmare just gets worse. How much will it cost us now?" she asked, her face contorted with fear.

I nodded my head and then smiled, but Doris looked confused.

"How can you be so bloody laid back about everything, Dave?" she asked.

"Because- I think it'll cost us a whole lot less than we had first thought, Doris."

"What are you up-to? I know that look, that cheeky smile!" she asked.

"Well, it would appear they hadn't seen the damage to our vehicle before she drove into the back of us, so in summary, Doris, it would *appear* that we have got off with a potentially expensive repair bill."

"But Dave, that means you're letting them pay for the damage that was already there?"

"Correct," I said.

"But that's morally wrong, Dave. You can't do that," she said, clearly aggrieved.

"You're right. We'll just have to pay £500 each then to fix it ourselves, and that's our beer tokens for the rest of the holiday - gone," I said.

"We won't have any more nights out. We'll be eating beans on toast, basically," I added.

"And no bingo money for you and Betty."

She looked at me.

"They have bingo on the island?" she asked, all serious.

I nodded, "Yep, they do."

They didn't, but I needed to enhance my pitch.

"Well, when you put it like that, Dave, they *did* crash into us, so in principle, they *should* pay."

"If we were in England, you'd be claiming whiplash, Doris."

Her eyes lit up.

"Eh, you're right. How much compo could I get for that?"

"About two grand, I think."

"Two bloody grand, let's put in a claim," she shouted.

"Calm yourself, Doris - let's just consider ourselves fortunate that we aren't paying for any repairs."

She nodded.

"I knew you'd come round to my way of thinking."

She smiled, "Dave, you are *terrible."*

"Terribly good, I agree."

# Chapter 6

The following day, Doris and I agreed to keep it low-key.

My blood pressure couldn't take much more. People talk about the risk of too much fat, salt, and sugar, resulting in high blood pressure. I watch what I eat, but seriously, you could be as fit as a flea, yet just a few hours in the company of Doris would be harmful to anyone's health.

We found ourselves hanging out in a charming little bar by the sea. It was mid-morning, and the sun was already hot. Doris sipped and slurped from her coffee cup, and I polished off the remains of my breakfast.

"Dave, I've been *thinking*," she said.

"Careful, Doris, I suggest you keep it to *just* thinking and *less* of doing. We can't get into any more scrapes, can we?"

"No - listen, my friend Betty, you *know* the one, she really likes to drink."

"Never heard you mention her before," I said.

"Anyway, she told me about a time she went wine tasting on a Greek Island, and well, I was thinking, wouldn't it be nice if we did a bit of that?"

She cunningly slipped a "wine tasting evening" branded leaflet in front of me.

I finished the last drop of my coffee and reached for my reading glasses.

She looked at me and smiled.

I picked up the leaflet and began to read it aloud –

*"Naxos wine tasting at its finest. Come and visit us at our splendid vineyard and share in the delights of our fine wines. Just 30 euros per person, inclusive of BBQ and live music,"* - doesn't sound half bad that Doris."

"Well, what do you think?" she asked, all animated.

"Where did you find this?" I asked.

"It was on the floor when we walked in."

"Hey - *listen*, I don't want to find *you* on the floor after this wine-tasting evening."

"Oh, so you approve then?" she asked.

"It has to be better than a night of Scrabble with you, Doris."

"*That's* because I'd beat you at Scrabble, Dave."

"You couldn't *beat* an egg," I said, shaking my head, "But don't get pissed," I added, pointing a meaningful finger at her.

She sat back and laughed, "Oh Dave, listen, I'm many things, but one thing I'm not, is a drunk."

"Ok - enough said, I'm sold. Let's give them a call and make our reservation then, eh."

"We can't mess about Dave, first come, first serve."

"Calm yourself, Doris."

"Well, look, there's a number on the leaflet we can ring," she said, panicked, as though the last two slots were about to vanish.

"I'll ring them now - oh, and apparently, according to this, they'll even pick us up at 4 p.m. outside the town hall," I said.

"Can they not pick us up from our villa?" she asked.

"Bloody hell, Doris, would you like them to send a limo?"

"Does it have that as an option?" she asked.

"Come on, let's pay the bill and get back to the villa," I said.

"We have plenty of time," she said, shrugging her shoulders.

"Yeah, we do, but by the time I shower and deliberate over what shirt to wear..."

"Oh, Dave, you're such a tart."

We made our way to the pick-up point at the town hall and stood about waiting.

Looking around, it was obvious that this tour was popular. We were accompanied by a dozen or so other willing participants. A real mixed bag of ages, but nobody I would observe as a potential suitor; no one on the right side of 40.

"No potential totty for you here, Dave, I'm afraid."

"No *shit* Sherlock."

"You'll just have to hang out with me, eh," she said while laughing; she was enjoying this.

"And – you've worn your best shirt."

"Alright, Doris, pipe down. I'm not doing this for a bus load of single 30-somethings; I'm doing this for the culture, the wine, the experience, and above all else, the good company."

She looked at me and sighed, "You're full of shit, Dave."

The bus arrived, and people began to get on.

*Shit, this bus has seen better days.*

It had more holes than your average watering can. Some of the rust was crudely painted over with white paint to match the original, and other bits had black gaffer tape holding the rust together.

"Mind where you put *your* feet, Doris. I'd be surprised if this bus even has a floor in it."

"Looks fine to me," she said, all jolly.

"I hope the food and entertainment aren't as *rusty* as the transport," I added.

"Hello, hello, welcome, welcome," said the driver, all smiley and animated.

He wore a smile that grew wider as people crossed his palms with cash. Once the last few stragglers got on, he got out of his seat and closed the door. It didn't look easy, as he needed all his strength.

"Shit, if this thing crashes, remind me to make my escape through the window," I said, looking at Doris to get her attention.

"Why do you say that?" she asked.

"I think it'll be faster."

With everyone on board, the driver fired up the engine, and after a brief struggle with the gear stick, he found a gear of sorts, and off we went with a splutter.

"Just 30 minutes to the vineyard, ladies and gentlemen," the driver shouted over the noise of the engine.

He glanced in his mirror and smiled. He was having a good day; the bus was full, and so was his wallet.

We made our way up the traditionally Greek, dusty road with no barriers, no health and safety. If the driver drove into a ditch at sea level, we'd be fine, but where we're going, hitting a ditch up here means only one thing: a tumble down the rocky hill and into the sea. The thought made me grip my seat even harder.

*I hate shit like this.*

"It's times like these, Doris, when I think a blindfold should be mandatory."

"Why?" she asked.

"I'd rather not *see* where we're going," I shouted.

I had to shout to make myself heard over the tank-like noise of the engine, which seemed to get louder with every gear change.

"Agreed, Dave - I might take a nap."

Only she could take a nap under these circumstances. It was a unique skill.

The views en route were spectacular. Olive groves, pine forests, and churches of all shapes and sizes could be seen on the hilltops.

Small villages dotted about in the distance where locals sat idle, drinking tea, playing cards, and doing as little as possible.

An odd dog or a cat sits in the shade of a tree, and an occasional lizard is seen scampering across a cluster of rocks. Goats by the roadside happily chew on dry grass, a donkey drinks from a watering hole; these little details are why I love Greece's charm so much.

I glanced at Doris. She was leaning back in her seat with her mouth open, snoring away and catching flies.

We eventually arrived at the gate to the vineyard.

Peering through the window, I could see a lady dressed in all white, head to toe. She waved at the driver as she opened the gate. The driver, again, doing his best to find a gear, slowly drove into the entrance of the grounds.

All I could see were vineyards, from the valley floor to the hilltops, as far as the eye could see. I gave Doris a nudge.

"WOW, look at this, Doris. Get your drinking boots on; we have arrived in paradise."

The bus came to a halt.

*"Welcome,"* the driver shouted.

As we all got off the bus, we were greeted by a lady and what appeared to be her husband. He was less present, more hanging at the back behind her shoulder. He was dressed in black, so they looked like a pair of piano keys.

"Hello and welcome to vineyard Stavobabsa", the Greek obsession with the name "Stavros" was even reserved for vineyards.

*Let me guess. I bet he's about to introduce himself as Stavros.*

"Let me *introduce* myself. My name is *Stavros*."

*You couldn't write it.*

"And my wife's name is *Barbara*."

*Barbara? Next, he'll be telling us that she's from Wigan.*

"Hi everyone, I'm *Barbara*, or Babs for short, and as you can probably guess, I'm not Greek."

Her revelation was met with a few chuckles.

"I'm from a small town in the North of England," she said, smiling.

"Hi, luv, which town is that then," shouted Doris, her arm aloft.

"*Wigan,* do you know it?" she asked.

"Eh, we're from Wigan luv, small world eh!" said Doris, all animated.

*I don't bloody believe it.*

"Is there anyone else here from Wigan?" Babs asked.

I was still in shock, rooted to the spot with a total inability to speak.

No one spoke.

"We're from Billinge, near Orrell, about five miles from Wigan," shouted Doris.

She had now reverted to local Wigan lingo, and I reverted to mute mode to not draw any attention to myself.

"Oh, do you know Betty from Green Lane, near the school?" Babs asked.

"I do. She's good friends with me. We go back years," Doris claimed.

*Will this take long*, was the expression on everyone else's faces, including mine.

"Well, you're in luck. Betty is here with her husband and some of her friends. They're in the first group tour of the vineyard, so you'll probably see them later," Babs added.

Doris was jubilant, but I wasn't.

"Ok, before the tour, let me escort you to the farmhouse courtyard, where you'll find some refreshments," said Stavros.

*Bloody hell, Babs has done alright for herself. She's living the dream here.*

We all began to walk towards the farmhouse, so now was a good opportunity for me to have a word in her ear.

"So, if you don't mind me asking, which part of Wigan are you from, Barbara?" I asked.

"A place called Beech Hill luv, top of the road near the traffic lights, near Greggs," she said.

"From rags to riches, eh? Not that people from Beech Hill are rag wearers," I said, putting my shovel away.

I chose my closing comment carefully - I want the glass of wine *handed* to me, not thrown at me.

"Hahaha, that's right, luv, you can't polish a turd," said Babs, beaming with teeth straight out of a Colgate advert.

Doris began to walk beside me.

"Do you know what, Dave, I've always wanted a vineyard," she said.

"My cat Mog knows more about wine than you do," I added.

"You don't give your cat wine, do you, Dave?" she asked.

"Don't be daft, Doris - she prefers a gin & tonic."

"My cat *occasionally* has a beer, you know," she said.

"I was joking, Doris, obviously."

"Well – I'm not. Mine likes a Stout at Christmas," she added, very matter of fact.

"Doris, seriously, you do worry me. Next, you'll be telling me you're partial to cat meat yourself?"

"Well, I did run out of *tuna* once in 2009 when we had that bad winter, so I had no choice. I didn't leave the house for a *week* or more with all the snow we had," she said with a deadpan expression.

"Now you're scaring me, Doris".

"It was quite *nice,* actually. Well, once you remove the jelly from the meat, it's really rather tasty."

"I'd rather eat my own toenails than cat food," I added.

"Oh, Dave – don't be so vulgar," she said.

The group continued to make their way to the farmhouse. I looked at Babs to get her attention.

"So, is it just the two parties of people then today?" I asked.

"Oh no, we collected a party of six at 2 p.m. - so they have finished their tour."

"Oh, right," I added.

"Busy then?" I asked.

She looked at me and smiled.

"Very busy!" she added.

"You'll meet them now; lovely party of girls," she said, smiling.

"Girls?" I asked.

She looked at me and smiled.

"Yes, from Sweden."

"*Sweden,* you say," I said, doing my best not to look overly impressed.

"Good job, you wore your favourite shirt then, Dave," said Doris, her face creased with a wrinkled smile.

I nodded my head.

One thing was certain; the day had just gotten a whole lot more interesting.

# Chapter 7

Stavros pushed open the old cast iron gate and beckoned the group to follow.

Immediately, we saw a group of six ladies, all sitting on a large wooden table. They were all giggling and chatting with wine-infused banter. They didn't look very *Swedish*; there wasn't one blonde amongst them. I looked at Babs and pondered.

"Babs, can I ask a question?" I asked.

"Yes, luv."

"The group of girls over there…they don't look very Swedish from where I'm standing."

"What do you *mean* by that?" she asked, confused.

"You said they were a bunch of girls from *Sweden?*" I queried.

Babs smiled.

"Oh, *sorry*, my mistake. I meant they're from *Swinton*," she said, with a face of apology.

She could see my disappointment.

*Swinton, is she having a laugh? So we have a bunch of grannies from Swinton, a suburb of Manchester, not a bunch of girls from Sweden?*

I felt deflated.

"Oh well, close, eh," I said.

The last time I felt this gutted was when I failed my driving test for the third time.

Babs laughed, clearly amused by my disappointment.

Well, at least Doris will have some more company.

I had another question for Babs, "Don't tell me the evening's entertainment is provided by a bloke from Barnsley?"

She laughed.

"No, I'm afraid not. I did try, but he had a prior engagement."

She then turned to address the rest of the group, "Ladies and gents, your tour guide will meet us here shortly."

"How long, I could murder a glass of wine," shouted Doris.

I gave her a nudge.

She looked at me, bemused.

*"What?"*

"You *know* what, calm yourself."

Doris shrugged her skinny shoulders, and Babs laughed.

"She's *just* about to return with the other group, which should be any time now."

Babs used a hanky to wipe the sweat from her forehead and swigged from a bottle of water. It wasn't a pretty sight - she had removed most of the fake tan in the process.

Suddenly, the gate opened, and people from the other group started to walk through. It was another mixed bag of interesting-looking characters, all very Swinton and unsuitable in terms of talent.

"Oh *Dave*, look, there's my friend, Betty," said Doris with a beaming face.

There was an instant recognition between the two of them, all waves and animated smiles.

"*Doris,* my love, fancy seeing you *here,* eh."

Betty was of a similar age and appearance to Doris. She waved her arms about like she'd just won the lottery. She was less lottery and more bingo and sported wings to match.

"Well, *hello* stranger, fancy seeing you here, eh," said Doris.

She had returned the recognition with a beaming smile and an equally animated wave.

I shook my head and continued to observe the people coming through the gate. I was willing, just one fit girl to walk through…even a half-fit girl…just a girl. I'd take one with a pulse right now; things were getting desperate.

It was *then*, that someone caught my eye.

In walked the guide.

She was a tall lady, in her 30s, I'd have guessed, dressed in shorts and a baggy T-shirt, although she would have looked elegant wearing a bin bag from what I could see. She was a local, maybe a family member. If she was, then she was definitely from the Stavros stock, just without the beer belly and the tash.

My gaze was transfixed; she was stunning.

*"Dave,* come and meet my friend Betty."

"Eh, what? Yeah, I will; just give me a moment, Doris."

"Oh, I see. A new shiny object has caught your attention, has it, Dave?"

"Doris, listen, she's about to speak."

"Hello, my name is *Sofia*; I will be your guide for the next vineyard tour."

*Guide? She could guide me to the bedroom if she liked.*

She was a rocket fit, and I was in love. I remember when I was a kid, maybe seven or eight, and my dad had a friend who visited. He drove a 911, and in that moment, I was in love. This was one of those moments, and *she* was *that* car.

I looked at Doris.

"Are you ready?"

"Born ready, Dave."

Moments later, Sofia stopped the group.

“Okay, everyone, we will have a short walk up the path to collect our transport for the tour of the vines.”

Her English was excellent, almost as good as Barbara’s, only less fake tan and more a lovely olive colour.

“Follow me, please,” she instructed.

Like sheep, we followed her up the path to what appeared to be a series of large, almost industrial-scale, outhouses.

Some of the blokes had pushed to the front of the group, and I could imagine what would happen should she drop her pen. At least ten blokes would all reach down to the floor at the same time to pick it up. It was embarrassing, and I wasn’t like that. I was playing it cool.

I could see a number of golf-type buggies.

*This could be interesting.*

I’d often contemplated taking up golf just so I could drive about in one of those things.

“Okay, everyone, I would like to split the group up into smaller groups. I count twelve of you, so we have three groups of four per buggy, please.

Everyone seemed to approve with some grunting, and others nodding their heads.

“Has anyone driven a buggy before? It's really easy, just an accelerator and a break?” she asked.

A few hands were raised.

“Do we have any *volunteers*?” she asked.

Three of us put our hands up almost simultaneously like kids in class who wanted to answer the teacher's question first.

"*Excellent*, so we have three drivers. Ok, I will take the first buggy and lead the way," she said.

"And please, take it *slow*? Keep a safe distance between each buggy at all times," she added.

I wasn't used to such health and safety in Greece. It was like being back home.

"Any hi-viz vests?" shouted the man standing next to me.

*Is this guy for real?*

"No, sorry, but I think we will be okay," she said.

She was clearly amused by the historic first request.

"*Well,* I think it would *ensure* we are all *visible* at all times," he continued.

She looked speechless; we all did, and I had to intervene.

"Do you work for a Council by any chance, pal?" I asked.

"*Yes,* I do, actually. Why?"

"I don't see any first-aid boxes on any of the vehicles either. This could be a problem for you," I added.

"Well, yeah, I might have to walk then; can't be too careful," he said.

I raised my arm to get her attention.

"I think this gentleman would *prefer* to walk."

She shrugged her shoulders.

"I am afraid you won't keep up with the buggies unless you run," she shouted.

I looked at him. He was 5ft nothing, early 60s, and looked like he liked a sandwich. He couldn't run a bath, let alone run a few miles along a dusty road in 35°C heat.

"No – it's fine. I will take my chances," he shouted.

"Before we go, can I take a quick toilet break?" I asked.

The rest of the group looked suitably pissed off with yet another delay. I didn't need to go, but I wanted to check my hair and make sure I was looking my best.

"Yes, no problem, it's just over there on the left," she said.

I returned to be greeted by just one buggy. A buggy with three French tourists and an empty driver's seat reserved for me.

*Ok, no problem, so the rest were in a hurry? They could have bloody waited.*

I looked towards the bottom of the hill and saw the rest of them racing along. With no time to hang about, I climbed into the driver's seat.

"Don't worry. We will soon catch up to them?" I said.

They just sat there, expressionless. It was like a buggy full of mannequins. I quickly removed the hand break and pressed the start key. The battery pack powered up the electric motor, and my right foot propelled us forward.

“Hold on tight, folks. These things are deceptively quick,” I said.

I glanced at the French man sitting in the passenger seat; his face was contorted with fear.

“I’ve always wanted to drive one of these,” I shouted over the noise of the motor.

He looked at me with horror.

“I thought I heard you say you had driven one of these before?”

“That’s right, but if I’d been honest, I wouldn’t be sitting here now, would I?”

I laughed out loud, doing my best to provoke more fear. I was enjoying this, but he wasn’t amused.

“Look, they have stopped. They are waiting for us,” he said.

I could see his relief.

We all bobbled along the dusty track alongside field after field of lush green grape vines. Fruit pickers could be seen harvesting the grapes into large baskets and hurling them into the back of old red massy Ferguson tractors. It was a lovely sight.

Suddenly, Sofia brought her lead buggy to a halt, and the rest of us applied our brakes.

Then suddenly, the buggy directly behind the lead jolted forwards, pushing the lead buggy out of the way. It then accelerated down the track.

We all looked on.

*What is happening? What kind of nutter is driving that buggy?*

The path was narrow and rocky, and judging by the lack of interest in anyone wanting to give chase, I decided to jump out and began to run towards it.  As I got closer, the passengers began to scream. Two managed to leap out, but a couple had remained in their seats and were clearly hanging on.

"*Brake, brake, brake,*" everyone shouted. I continued to run, gasping for breath with every stride. Getting closer, I could see it wasn't one of the designated drivers; it was *bloody* Doris sitting at the wheel.

"*DORISSSSSSSSSSS,*" I shouted.

"*Doris - brake*, put your foot on the *bloody* brake," I shouted.

Sofia was now also running alongside the vehicle.

*Shit, this girl can shift.*

She reached out, managed to grab hold of the door frame and climbed in. She then wrestled the wheel off Doris and brought it under control.

I was spent. I stopped and crouched to my knees, gasping for breath.

I looked up and watched as the vehicle was brought to a stop. *Wow - She was impressive,* but in that moment, I felt more like zero than a hero. My first attempt to impress her had failed.

My chest was heaving while walking toward the drama, like a man who smokes forty fags a day.

Doris sat at the wheel, head in her hands and shaking, while Sofia comforted her with an arm around her shoulder.

"It's ok, no harm done," her words of reassurance appeared to offer Doris some comfort at least.

I leaned on the buggy door frame, peering in at Doris. She removed her hands from her face and looked up at me.

"Doris, please explain why you replaced the designated driver?" I asked.

She sheepishly looked at me, her face a mixture of fear and guilt.

"I persuaded the driver to let me have a go," she rambled.

"You can't even walk straight. What makes you think you can drive one of these things?" I asked.

"I know, I know, I'm really *sorry*, how stupid of me," she said.

I wasn't impressed, an emotion that's never far away when in the company of Doris.

She looked at me again and then looked at Sofia.

"I'm ever so sorry; these vehicles are a bit of a handful," she said, shaking her head.

"You're a bit of a bloody *handful*," I said.

Sofia looked at me and smiled.

"Can I apologise - this really wasn't meant to happen? I will ensure she remains under my *close* supervision for the rest of the day," I said.

She smiled and then laughed.

*"Listen*, no harm done. Let's just get this buggy back up the hill so we can join the others," she added.

"Doris, that means you're in the back seat," I instructed.

"I will drive it," said the man sitting beside her.

*Some help he was; he could have prevented this drama in the first place.*

"Ok, let's get the other buggies up the hill," she said.

"Sounds like a plan."

She looked at me and smiled again.

"Thank you for helping," she said.

We eventually joined the rest of the group outside the entrance to a large gate. The gate leads into one of the many vineyards spread across the valley.

I gulped from my water bottle as the sun beat down on our heads. Doris had made a makeshift hanky and placed it on her head. She looked like a cross between Roland the Rat and Alf Garnett.

"Are you alright, Doris?" I asked.

"I'll be a lot bloody better with a glass of wine in my hand, Dave. What are they expecting us to do here, crush our own grapes?" she said, all frustrated.

"Just roll with it. This won't take long, I promise."

"Yeah, Columbus said that when he was trying to find America," she said.

The guide walked to the front, and we all gathered and waited for further instructions.

"Ok, now I will take you into the vineyard," she pushed open the gate, and we followed.

I watched Doris as she removed one of her sandals and began itching her feet. She then pushed her fingers between her toes and removed bits of grit; she proceeded to do the other foot as well.

"Doris – you're *gross*," I said.

She looked zero bothered.

The guide beckoned to a man on a tractor. He wiped his brow and made his way over.

"Hello, everyone, welcome. My name is Marco. Would you like to try some grapes?" he asked, offering a basket to Sofia, who then passed it around the group.

I leaned towards Doris.

"Let me grab some for you to try," I said in her ear.

"I'm quite capable of grabbing my own."

"No you're not - I've just seen where your hands have been!"

Sofia continued to talk and point and referred to the grape growing and harvesting process. Occasionally, I would nod and pretend I was listening, not unlike the people who pretend to observe the flight crew when they are doing the customary inflight demo on a plane.

I wanted to be interested, but if I really wanted to know more, I would just google it.

Eventually, we made our way back up the hill and into the processing compound. Once more, we assembled in the courtyard and waited.

"Okay, so here we are at our processing sheds. We will now have the opportunity to sample some of the wine directly from the barrels. I am sure you have all been looking forward to this moment," she said, looking at us with a big smile.

I thought the moment would never come.

"It's cooler in here, Doris. Take your hat off," I said.

She removed the hanky from her flat head and pushed it into her pocket.

"I will now hand you over to my father - Stavros, who will introduce you to the fine selection of wines we have available here."

"Can we buy some?" shouted Doris.

“Of course, and at a very special price,” she said with a smile.

I loved her smile.

It was a real shame that she was leaving us so soon, as she was far easier on the eye than Stavros.

“I will see you all later for the BBQ and don’t forget, we have live music this evening,” she said as she made her exit.

*“I will look forward to it,”* I whispered to Doris.

Doris looked at me, “You’re such a tart.”

“I was only being sociable.”

“Yeah, right, Dave. I see the way you look at her.”

“I am only being my charming self, nothing more. I’m a good egg, you know that.”

“If you get *anywhere* near her, Stavros will make sure your eggs get scrambled!”

I looked at her and laughed.

“I think you’re probably right, Doris. Though, jokes apart, she’s well out of my league, and I’m not about to make a fool of myself; anyhow, she won’t be single.”

She nodded her head and smiled, her face creased with a big grin.

“We both know what a tart you are; you’ll try and catch a big fish with a small worm,” she said, laughing so loud that others began to look over.

“Less of a small worm, Doris. That’s a bit personal.”

We all entered the large, expansive building, greeted by a smiling Stavros, his arms aloft as though he was about to perform something operatic.

*Surely he isn't about to sing?*

"Welcome, welcome, follow me, please. Allow me to show you the *business* end of winemaking," he turned to face our group and smiled.

"This is where it gets very *interesting*," he added.

He was a very jolly chap, but then I would be the same if I had pockets as deep as his.

The interior of the building was a vast expanse of fermentation equipment, large tanks, pipes, tubes, you name it, and, more importantly, plenty of barrels of wine.

They were all horizontally stacked on large wooden shelves that seemed to go on for miles.

I did my best to listen to him talk about wine, but it was all a bit dull, like being surrounded by wine and not a drop to drink.

I looked at Doris. She looked back at me and rolled her eyes. It was clear that we were on the same wavelength.

"Correct me if I'm wrong, but aren't we supposed to drink wine at a wine-tasting event?" she said, shaking her head.

"Should I ask if there's a fast-forward button?" I said.

"That said, we might just *learn* something. Maybe we should listen to what he has to say?"

“Did you just say *those* words Doris?”

“Dave, listen, it’s actually rather interesting.”

“So what have you learned so far then?” I asked.

She looked at me, bemused.

“Go on, humour me!” I added.

“Well, white wine goes in the fridge, and red stays at room temperature,” she said, doing her best not to smile.

“You’re full of shit. Everyone *knows* that.”

“No, I didn’t. He just mentioned it now,” she insisted.

He hadn’t; she was full of shit.

“I know my wine, Dave.”

“Words from a lady who drinks lambrini,” I said.

“It’s only £1.99 a bottle in Asda,” she insisted.

“What, *that* much? You’re being robbed.”

Stavros continued to address the group with his infinite knowledge.

“Ok, *so* - Sofia would have explained how winemaking has been around for thousands of years. It is not only an art form; it is also a science. Wine-making is a natural process that requires very little human intervention. The wine-making process has five basic steps: harvesting, crushing, pressing, fermentation, and clarification. Then, we age and bottle our wines. It’s that simple.”

I looked at Doris, “I’ve got a feeling this guy likes the sound of his own voice.”

Stavros continued, "Step one is Harvesting. As you saw, this is the first step in the wine-making process."

He continued to talk, but it was debatable how much of this information any of us could absorb. I was willing his next word would be his last.

"Is step *five* drinking it?" I shouted.

Stavros laughed, "*Yes*, I have now concluded my talk, so let's grab some glasses and try some wines."

*Thank fuck for that. Talk about spitting feathers.*

He began passing wine glasses to the group. People practically charged toward the tasting barrels.

*"Wait* - take only enough wine in your glass for one or two sips. Look, watch me, like this," he said, raising his glass aloft with purpose.

He filled his glass only a quarter full and then placed his nose to the rim of the glass and swirled the contents. He then pressed his nose against the rim of the glass again and inhaled.

"You see, let the wine move around in the glass, let it find its note, allow it to breathe, let it flirt with your senses. What do you smell, oak, vanilla, and fruit?" he continued.

I looked at Doris, and she looked at me, our glasses a quarter full.

"Doris, are you with me? Count to three and down in one?"

She laughed, "Hmmm, I'm not waiting that long, Dave," and at that moment, she swigged the lot, raised her empty glass, belched, and laughed.

"You classy lady," I said, quickly following her by doing the same.

"Why thank you," she said.

"Doris, it's a marathon, not a sprint. You'll be pissed before we get to the BBQ at this rate. Pace yourself, woman."

She belched and laughed again.

"I will drink *you* under the table, Dave; just watch me."

"That's where I'll probably *find* you in about an hour."

"Oh Dave, *relax,"* she then put her nose to the empty glass.

"Why have you got your conk in the glass?" I asked.

"I'm finding its note."

"You *need* wine in the glass, Doris. That's the idea."

She grabbed another glass and filled it to the brim with white wine.

Stavros, the current world champion of liking the sound of his own voice, meanwhile, continued to engage with the group. I helped myself to another glass of red. It was rich, full-bodied, smooth, and rather quaffable.

*Greek wine has clearly improved over the past 10-15 years.*

Doris swigged her wine like a teenager tasting alcohol for the first time. Then, suddenly and without warning, her teeth fell into her glass; this was becoming a habit.

"Doris, you *seriously* need to change your fixative."

She swirled her spindly fingers around the bottom of the glass, popped her teeth back in her mouth, and continued to drink her wine like nothing had happened.

"I think you need to drink a bit faster, Doris. You've only had about half a dozen glasses."

She moved the now-empty glass away from her face and belched.

"I think I'll have another, please, Dave."

"I think you *bloody* won't. I'll be peeling you up off the floor at this rate."

I grabbed her empty glass before she attempted to go for a refill.

Stavros then took centre stage again and addressed the group with his arms held aloft; it was a biblical moment.

"Ladies and Gents, I think *now* would be a good time to join the others."

Maybe this was a tactical move to avoid people peaking too soon, although, judging by how some of the group were now staggering, I think he was a tad late with his judgement.

We arrived at the courtyard gate and were greeted by Babs and Sofia. They looked like an interesting combination, both visually and in terms of personality. They're both birds, like comparing a white dove and a pigeon, but that's where the comparison ends.

"Hi, welcome back, everybody," Babs stood with her arms open, like a school teacher gathering her kids.

My gaze was again transfixed on Sofia, who had changed into a white linen dress and looked exquisite.

"Dave, put your tongue back in your head."

"Doris, I am just admiring the view."

She looked at me and laughed.

"Out of your *league,* Dave, remember?"

I nodded my head in agreement, "Yep, you're right. Come on, let's get another drink."

# Chapter 8

The band was in full swing. It was everything I had hoped it would be - a traditional Greek band playing native songs.

The evening was further enhanced by the presence of Barbara and Stavros, who encouraged people to participate in the merriment by dragging them up from their seats to dance badly.

"*Doris*, what do you think of the singer?" I asked.

"He's no *George Michael.*"

"God bless George, what a man, what a singer, what a loss," I added.

"Why, where's he gone?" she asked.

"Have you ever read a newspaper?"

"No, not really. I prefer a good book, though."

"I thought so."

I needed a cigar, but somewhere out of the way, alone, where I could chill.

"Are you ok if I go have a smoke for a bit?" I asked.

"I'll join you if you like?"

"No, I wouldn't."

*"Charming."*

"Don't be gone *too* long, Dave. I may need you as my dance partner later."

"How could I resist?"

*I won't hurry back.*

I walked to the back of the courtyard and found a small empty table. It was the perfect vantage point. I was able to see without being seen.

Striking a match, I lit a cigar, took a drag, and leaned back to observe the stars in a clear night sky.

I could see Doris doing her best to dance. Her arm was wrapped around Betty so tightly that she was practically strangling her, while I just sat, people-watching. I lifted my bottle of red to check how much was left and topped up my glass.

This was good; Doris was distracted, and it gave me time to gather my thoughts.

I leaned back in my chair on two legs, lifting both feet up on the table, and rocked gently back and forth. It was just me, a glass of wine, and a cigar; it was bliss.

"*May I join you?*" A voice came from the darkness behind me.

I jumped out of my skin, falling backwards in my chair and crashing to the floor behind me.

"*Oh my god, I'm so sorry*. I didn't mean to startle you," she said, helping me to my feet.

"Are you ok? Nothing hurt?" she asked.

"Just my ego."

"*David, isn't it?*"

I dusted myself down and sat back in my chair.

"It is, yes. Sofia, isn't it?"

"Yes, hi."

She stood before me like an E-Type Jaguar with flawless bodywork and such beautiful lines.

"*Are you having a nice time?*" she asked.

"Hmm, yeah, *amazing,* thank you," I said.

I was still a little flustered.

"Your glass is empty. Would you like a refill?" I asked.

"Sure."

I grabbed another chair and placed it by mine.

"*Please, take a seat,*" I insisted.

"Good, I'm glad you're enjoying it, and it appears your Mother is too."

We both looked at Doris swaggering about as she grasped a glass in one hand and her friend Betty's neck in the other.

"*Oh no*, she's not my *Mother*. She's my *neighbour* from back home. It's a long story."

She smiled, "I'm intrigued, tell me more."

"She had no one else to take on holiday with her. None of her friends were available, so I volunteered my services as a *holiday companion*."

"Wow, that was very *kind* of you."

I could see from the expression on her face that she probably suspected it was kindness combined with insanity.

We just sat back, drank, and chatted for what seemed like ages. It was the most normal time I had spent since we arrived, and I didn't want it to end.

Doris was pissed, but I didn't mind; at least I could keep an eye on her from here.

"Oh bugger, looks like she's coming over," I said.

She laughed.

"I didn't think she would find me sitting back here," I said apologetically.

"It's ok. I would like to meet your *friend*," she said.

"Really?"

"Sure, she looks like a very interesting character."

"Yeah, she's definitely something," I added.

Doris staggered over to our table and pulled up a chair, but just as she proceeded to sit, she missed the chair and fell backwards onto the floor.

*"SHIT - Doris – you alright?"*

We both raced from our seats in a bid to rescue the now horizontal Doris, who lay on her back in fits of laughter.

Grabbing an arm each, we helped her up.

"*Doris*, there you are. I've been looking for you," shouted Betty.

My charm offensive was officially ruined when Betty appeared at the table.

Within seconds, Doris and Betty were engrossed in a drunken conversation, sprawled across our table. Their eyes glazed as they talked shit about nothing.

Sofia looked at me and laughed.

"Would you like another bottle of wine? I need to put some more bottles on the tables, so it's not a problem."

"Yeah, sure, thank you," I said.

*"Would you like to help me?"* she asked.

*How could I refuse?*

A cunning plan was beginning to unfold in my head, but what I didn't need was more distraction, which meant that once she had done her wine duties, we then needed to escape through the gate before Stavros spotted us. He looked like a protective father who might not take too kindly to an Englishman cavorting with his daughter.

We were within a few feet from the gate when a voice was heard shouting in our direction.

She turned and replied in Greek. It was Stavros.

"What did he say?" I asked.

"He just asked where we were going."

Within moments, he was standing in front of Sofia like a troll protecting his cave. He then looked at me, frowned, and made his way through the gate and up the path.

She looked at me and laughed, "My father is a little protective. He has gone to get the wine."

"Hey, no problem, I'm cool with that."

I wasn't, but I had little choice.

"He also thinks that I need to spend more time with the other guests."

She smiled again, almost in apology.

This opportunity was fast slipping away, and I had to think; I had to find some balls.

"*Listen*, would you like to go for a bite to eat one evening? Provided your father approves, of course, and…if you'd like to?" I asked.

She laughed.

"I won't be offended if you are busy," I added.

She smiled; I was in love.

"Don't worry about my father. He means well. Yes – I would *love* to," she said.

I froze. Had she just said yes? I was gobsmacked.

*"Are you ok?"* she said, laughing.

"You look a bit surprised?" she added.

"No, I mean yeah, I mean great, that'll be great."

"The wine is working then, yes?" she asked.

I was confused.

"Wine working?" I asked.

"It has given you courage?" she asked.

"Agh, yes, well, I guess," I said, looking at my glass.

She laughed.

"Yeah, *very good wine.* It's definitely having an impact on me."

"Great, so how should I contact you?" I asked.

She handed me a business card.

"There you are, you see, you can call my mobile, call the house, fax or email."

I looked at the card and smiled.

"Thank you for this," I said.

"Though, maybe don't call the house, just in case my father should answer," she said, laughing.

"*Absolutely, agreed.* Okay, I will call you tomorrow."

She nodded and smiled.

"Ok, I had better go. I will see you later," she said.

"You shall."

While Sofia went off to mingle, I decided to go and find Doris.

I could see she was still sitting and chatting with Betty, so I grabbed some more wine and went to join them.

*"Do you mind if I join you ladies?"*

They both looked up at the same time. On a scale of 1-10 from sober to smashed, they both scored an 11, so this was like having a conversation with a couple of mutants.

"*Hello* Dave – Doris *tells me you might be gay?"*

Betty's voice was loud, so I looked around to see if anyone was looking.

"And *why* would she tell you I'm gay, Betty?"

"She just did."

"I didn't say you were *gay,* Dave. I just said you were 43 and lived alone with a Cat called MOG," said Doris.

"Why don't you shout the word *gay* a bit louder? They can't hear you in the main town," I said.

I looked at Betty.

"How does that qualify me as being gay?"

"Well – I think any man living alone in his 40s must prefer the company of a man and just wants to be discrete about it."

"Oh really?" I asked.

"I'm sure I read somewhere once that most gay men who live alone, normally have a cat as a pet of choice," said Betty.

"Oh, well, I had better give the cat away then Betty, as I wouldn't want people thinking I'm *gay* now, would I?" I said.

"So, are you *gay* or what?" she said.

She couldn't have shouted it any louder. Sofia was now looking over, as were several other people from neighbouring tables.

Not that I have any issues with the sexual preferences of others, but I don't personally condone the behaviour of bigoted grannies.

*"Hey*, I'm *gay,* by the way - but I wasn't aware we had some homophobes among us," came a voice from another table.

*"You two, enough!"* I glared at them both.

I had no choice but to go and apologise to the man, "Please accept my apologies on behalf of my friends. They do get a bit colourful with their language, and they're not always terribly PC."

The man sat alone. He took a drag of a thin cigar and exhaled smoke circles. He sported a pink shirt, undone by at least five or six buttons, and he had chest hair that any man would be proud of. He took a big gulp of his red wine, held the glass in his hand, and looked at me, all without a word.

*Shit this apology is proving harder than I thought. He's keeping me in suspense.*

"No offence taken, darling. I just don't do *bitching,* that's all. There's only one person around here allowed to be a *bitch* … and that's me, darling!!"

He smiled and took another drag of his cigar.

He glanced to where the ladies were sitting, looked back at me, and smiled.

"I never had you down as the *older* lady type, darling," he added

"I'm not; she's just a friend," I said.

He took another drag and exhaled more smoke circles.

"*Friend,* you say, I count two ladies," he noted.

"You're a *frisky* fellow, aren't you?"

He laughed.

"Trust me, they're *just* friends."

"Do you normally hang around with grannies?"

"It's a long story," I said.

"That sort of thing turns you on, does it, darling?" he asked.

He looked at me and smiled.

"Well, you are a dashing chap."

"Really?"

"Oh darling, you're such a gentleman, quite a catch; the caring type. I like that in a man, and such a handsome fellow. I'm sure you would attract lots of attention from both men and women alike," he said.

"You're too kind," I said.

"You ever swing both ways?" he asked.

"I like *birds,* mate. It's not something I have ever considered."

"Such a shame, nice chap like you. Well, if you ever change your mind, darling, you know where I am."

"*I'll let you know, mate*," I said, laughing awkwardly.

"Oh, this boy isn't for turning, is he?" he said, laughing loudly.

"No mate, no offence."

"That's what the last boy said, then a few hours later, he was as frisky as a sheep."

"Are sheep noted for being frisky?"

"Of course they are. The sheep near me are always shagging."

"Really?" I said, laughing.

"*Gay as a lord*, the sheep near where I live."

He flicked his hair to one side and took another drag of what was left of his cigar.

"I accept your apology. Although, tell your two *golden girls*, anymore chat, and I'll give them a bitch slap."

"I will, yes. Enjoy the rest of your evening," I said.

I returned to our table and sat down. Grabbed the first bottle I found and poured half a glass.

"Ladies, as stimulating as this conversation has been, I will leave you alone to *further* discuss my sexuality. Could you do your best *not to offend* anyone else while I'm gone?"

"I think he likes you, *Dave*," said Betty, chuckling away with Doris.

*"Doris*... have a word with your friend, please."

"What did the gay guy want?" asked Betty.

"He said he will bitch slap you if he hears you offending gay people again, so you have been warned, Betty."

"Maybe he's not gay?" said Betty.

"Why do you say that?" asked Doris.

"Because I have just seen him chatting up Sofia."

I turned my chair to get a better view, and there he was, chatting away with her.

"Maybe he bats for both sides?" said Betty.

"He won't be chatting her up, ladies. He's probably complaining about you two."

"I will wait until she's free."

"Well, now's your chance. He has just walked away," said Betty.

I wandered over.

"Sorry to interrupt Sofia, could I have a quick word?" I asked.

"Yes, of course."

*"Great band,* by the way."

"Thank you, David, glad you like them."

"Listen, about the gay man. I can explain everything."

She looked puzzled.

"Betty suspected I was gay because I am single, living alone, and in my early 40s, but I can assure you, *I am not gay*, not that I have a problem with people who *are gay*. I'm just not *gay* myself."

She still looked puzzled.

"Thank you for letting me know, David," she laughed. She then paused and laughed again, putting her hand to her mouth to contain her amusement.

"So, please accept my apologies."

She smiled, still confused.

"I don't understand. What are you apologising for?" she said, confused.

"The gentleman who you were just talking to, I assume, has put in a complaint about my friends?"

She laughed.

"Hmm, not that I am aware of. No, he was just saying how much he was enjoying himself. Why has your friend offended him?"

"Yeah, it was nothing, she knocked his drink over, and they exchanged a few words. He got a bit upset, nothing more."

She laughed.

"Upset?"

"Yeah, it was a full glass of wasted wine. He wasn't too impressed."

"But what has that got to do with him being gay?" she asked.

"Hmm, must have been the pink shirt. My friends took offence."

"Well, it's a good job we have plenty to spare then," she said.

"Shirts?" I asked.

*"No wine*," she laughed.

"Ok, I'll go back and make sure they're not knocking anymore wine over," I said.

"Also, tell them not to offend any more men who might be wearing pink," she laughed.

*This was way too random.*

She laughed again, "Okay, see you later, David."

I smiled.

"I live in hope," I added.

I returned to our table and sat down.

I lit another cigar, took a drag, and then grabbed a glass and poured some more wine. I sat back for a moment and observed them both absorbed in conversation like I hadn't been noticed.

It was more slurs and distorted sentences; none of it made sense, but it humoured me nonetheless.

"Betty, what are your plans for tomorrow evening?" I asked.

"Listen – you don't need to ask me out on a date, *Dave*, just to prove your sexuality, and anyway, what would my husband think?" said Betty, her laughter bellowing.

"Damn, a missed opportunity, eh *Betty*," I said.

"I thought you might like to spend some time with Doris tomorrow evening, that's all?" I said.

Doris looked up, "Dave – are you trying to get rid of me?"

"What makes you think that?" I asked.

"Because I know you, Dave. You're a dog with a bone with that Greek girl," she added, her face all disappointed.

"I bet it's not the only bone he's thinking of, *Doris*," Betty said, followed by more laughter.

She didn't take it well. She slammed her glass down so hard that she snapped the stem.

"Shit, Doris, be careful," I said.

I grabbed the broken stem and removed the glass from her hand with a napkin.

"Don't panic. I will grab you another glass," said Betty, about to leave her chair.

"Betty, she needs water, not *more* wine."

Doris looked at me, her eyes fixed on mine.

"What am I going to do while you're on a date, Dave?" she asked.

"At this rate, you'll be sleeping off your hangover. That's what you'll be doing," I added, gesturing to Betty to grab some water.

"*She's out of your league, Dave, remember?*"

"I agree, but sometimes in life, you get to drive a sexy car that you'll never own," I said.

*"He will wipe the floor with you,"* she said, her face all serious.

Stavros had made eye contact with me from a distance, and his gaze remained fixed. I looked back at Doris.

"He's just given me the snake eyes."

"Dave, if you go on a date with his daughter, the only eyes you'll be having are two black ones," said Doris.

I nodded my head; she was right. Taking Sofia out would be like taking a motorbike out with a sidecar attached to it. No matter what, the sidecar will still be there. Stavros was the sidecar.

"You're a brave man," said Betty.

I nodded my head.

I looked at them both.

"Nothing ventured, nothing gained, ladies."

# Chapter 9

Doris and I agreed to hang out by the pool the following day. I'm not a poolside junkie by any means, but nor am I a Doris junkie, and I'd had enough scrapes over the past few days to justify some poolside loitering.

Doris sat in the shade of an umbrella, deeply engrossed in an assortment of trashy magazines. I was reading a book by Bear Grylls, his latest, and it was very apt: a book about survival, and that's *exactly* what I was doing with Doris.

"I need to go and get ready for tonight. You hanging out here for a bit?" I asked.

She peered over the top of her oversized 1980s sunglasses.

"I may see you later, Dave."

"Oh really? I wasn't planning on bringing you on a date with me."

"That's not what I meant."

"Go on then, I'm all ears."

"Betty and I will be taking a walk into town for a few cocktails later, that's all, so we may see you."

"Listen, I don't want you two following us, understood?"

She peered over the top of her sunglasses and smiled, "Dave, stop panicking. Even if we see you, we'll pretend we haven't."

"Good, keep it that way. I need this date to be a success."

"Do you not think you're punching above your weight?" She asked.

"We've had this conversation. Yes, I do, but are you telling me that every good-looking girl has an equally good-looking partner?"

"Well, the blokes that aren't are normally rich."

"Well, maybe she's an exception; she goes for personality over looks."

"But Dave, you have neither," she laughed.

"Do you know what I really like about you, Doris?"

She looked up, "No?"

"Absolutely nothing," I said with a smile.

She continued to flick the pages of Bella. She wasn't one for reading the content; she pretended to read when I knew she was just looking at the pictures.

"Enjoy your trashy magazines."

"So I'll see you later then, Dave".

"Not if I see you first."

I hatched my plan back in the bedroom.

I finished the finer details in my quest to look at least half decent. Grabbing my aftershave, I splashed it on with a similar vigour as the man in the Old Spice aftershave advert from the 1980s, although without the dramatic music and with a notable absence of a chiselled jaw or striking good looks.

I looked in the mirror and checked my nose and ears for impromptu hair growth. Such attention to detail didn't exist in my world ten years ago, but now I'm in my 40s, and if I didn't do this shit, I'd look like Bill Oddie.

Doris soon returned to the room, sporting a red nose. I will never know how she managed to burn whilst sitting in the shade.

"Dave, before you leave, I need to ask a favour."

There was a lump in my throat in anticipation.

"I'm listening," I said.

"Could you drop me and Betty off in town before you go on your date?"

"I will drop you off at the other side of the island."

"You bloody won't. The town centre will do just fine, please, Dave."

"Do I have much choice?" I asked.

"Great – I will take that as a yes then," she said.

She then disappeared to get ready.

I opened the fridge, grabbed a beer bottle and went to sit on the balcony.

Not one to hang about, she soon reappeared sporting another one of her 80s dresses, with more gold bling than a Snoop Dog Convention.

"Doris, thinking out loud, to drop you off in town would mean that I'd have to go back by myself to pick up Sofia, so it would make sense if we pick Sofia up first."

She mumbled some words of approval whilst applying her red lipstick. I could see her pouting her thin lips in the mirror and checking her teeth. She then grabbed her gold leather bag and flung it over her shoulder.

"Well, what do you think, Dave, will I do?"

"Doris, *look at you.* Maybe I'm taking the *wrong* girl out?"

"You're such a charmer, Dave."

"Just let me finish this beer, and we'll go," I said, swigging the last of my bottle.

"Right, come then, let's get out of here," I said.

It was only a short drive to Sofia's house, AKA the vineyard!

"Right. Can I trust you not to play with any of the switches this time?" I asked.

"I still can't believe the rental shop let you take another jeep after the state we handed the last one back in," she queried.

I looked at her and smiled, "It wasn't our fault, remember?"

She shook her head.

"You're a bugger, you Dave."

*Was she for real?*

"Doris, listen to me. Under no circumstances are you to even *look* at that hand-break. I will be back in a mo."

"*Whatever*," she said like some moody teenager.

I made my way up the path and arrived at a large sky-blue front door. It had a cast-iron knocker that I grabbed with purpose. My heart was beating fast, and my palms were sweaty.

The door opened with a dramatic creak, like the type you would see in a black-and-white horror film.

Stood before me was Stavros. Now, my bottom was rumbling in my pants. It was times like this when I wished I could pop an Imodium tablet just to be safe.

He looked bemused by my presence but not surprised, so at least he was expecting me. He was probably hoping I wouldn't show at all, so it was a shame I had to disappoint him. He didn't speak a word, just looked at me for what seemed like an eternity. He then looked back over his shoulder and shouted into the house.

Thankfully, the steely silence was rescued by Sofia, who quickly appeared at the door. She had a beaming smile and looked divine.

Doris was right; I was clearly punching above my weight, and the look on her father's face suggested that he thought the same. She kissed her dad on the cheek and exchanged some words in Greek, then closed the door behind her.

"You look fantastic," I said, doing my best not to burst with pride.

"Thank you, David, so do you."

"Well, you know, I do try," I said.

"Oh, is Doris joining us for dinner then?" she asked, spotting the unmistakable Doris peering out the passenger window.

"*No,* don't panic - I offered to drop Doris and Betty in town, but don't worry, I'll make sure I drop them somewhere where they won't find us. Do you know of any deserts around here by any chance?"

She laughed, "No, sorry, there's no desert in Naxos, but there are mountains and forests. Will that do?"

"It's an option," I said.

Doris climbed onto the back seat, and Sofia sat beside me in the front.

"Seat belts, please, ladies," I instructed, knowing that Doris had a habit of pretending to wear one in a bid to preserve her outfit from creases.

"Doris, do you have the directions to Betty's?" I asked.

She handed me a crumpled bit of paper with an address on it, and I showed it to Sofia.

"Do you know this area?" I asked.

"Yes, it's not far. I will show you."

It was a short journey to Betty's villa, no more than a couple of miles. This was going just as I'd hoped. I was optimistic.

"Should I honk the horn or go and knock?" I asked Doris.

"Just honk. She will know it's us."

Moments later, the door opened, and Betty stood on the doorstep and waved.

"Oh look, she's holding a dog. I hope she's not bringing it with her," I said.

Doris leaned forward between the two front seats for a better look.

"No, it's her handbag," she said, sitting back down.

"Doris, when was the last time you had your eyes tested? It has four legs and a tale," I added.

"Yeah, it'll be one of those Radley bags. She loves her bags," she said, all matter of fact.

Sofia looked at me. She was finding this all very amusing but had decided not to comment just yet.

"She will probably leave it in the villa. I wouldn't worry?" said Sofia, now struggling not to laugh.

"It's a dog, Doris, a dog, not a bag," I insisted.

She looked again, "Oh yes, so it is."

"I believe it belongs to an English couple who live next door. She's probably looking after it for them."

We watched as Betty closed the door behind her, with the dog still under her arm.

"Looks like the dog is coming with her, Doris," I said, shaking my head.

Betty walked towards the jeep, waving with her other free arm. She approached my window and stuck her head in.

"Hi, everyone. Thanks for picking me up. Would it be possible to bring Poppy with us?"

"Do we have any choice?" I asked.

"Oh, I love Jack Russell," shouted Doris.

*Bloody hell, is this actually happening?*

"Well, Cath and Brian are away for the night, and the dog doesn't like being left alone?"

"Dave, be nice. Of course, it's not a problem. What a charming little dog," Doris added whilst reaching out to stroke it through the window.

Sofia put her hand to her mouth in a bid to stifle her laughter.

"Oh Dave, it's so cute," Sofia said, all animated like how girls are around small animals.

Doris and Betty sat on the back seat whilst Sofia volunteered to have the dog on her lap.

I started the engine and looked at it again. It was a nervous-looking thing that began to shake. It made *me* nervous. I could feel a trickle of sweat on my brow, and my shirt began to stick to my back. If it wasn't bad enough having two grannies in the back seat, with their own animal-like behaviour, I now have to contend with a nervous dog.

I looked at it again, and it looked back at me. It looked all smug, as though it knew I was on a first date, and yet, it was closer to my date than I was; the little shit was enjoying it.

*Little shit,* I wanted to poke it in the eye.

I moved my hand towards it and patted it on the head to show my willingness. It instantly growled and snapped at my fingers, catching the tip of my middle fingers with its teeth.

"Bloody hell, that hurt," I retracted my hand and looked at my finger.

"What was that all about?" I asked, looking in the windscreen mirror for Betty's attention.

“That’s very odd. She doesn’t normally snap at people,” she said, leaning forward to stroke it through the gap between the seats.

“She’s nervous, that’s all,” Sofia added while giving the dog a reassuring stroke.

I notched through the gears, and the little jeep gathered speed up the hill. The dog didn’t look so smug now. It had nervous eyes and began panting and shaking, sticking its tongue out.

“Does it need some water?” I asked.

“No, don’t worry, it’ll be fine,” shouted Betty.

I took deep breaths and focussed on the road ahead. I looked at the dog again. Its eyes looked spooked, and its tongue flapped about as it panted hard.

“Betty, this dog doesn’t look right.”

“She will be fine. She just gets a bit car sick,” she said.

“Have you been in a car with it before?” I asked.

“No,” said Betty.

I shook my head.

Suddenly and without warning, the dog vomited violently over Sofia’s lap. It then proceeded to vomit onto the dashboard, like a scene from the exorcist. Vomit was now splattered everywhere.

Sofia was instantly repulsed. Holding her mouth, she struggled to contain her disgust, but within a matter of seconds, she vomited over the dog. The dog yelped and barked and jumped off her lap onto the floor by her feet.

The smell was rancid; we were all retching at this point.

"*Don't* panic, everyone," I will pull over.

I looked at the road ahead for somewhere to turn around, but it was narrow, and to complicate matters, a truck was now following closely behind us. Its headlights helped to illuminate what looked like carrot and potato chucks that littered the interior.

"What has this dog had for its tea?" I shouted.

The smell was like nothing on Earth. Then, more vomit sounds came from the rear. I looked in my rearview mirror and saw Doris now vomiting by her feet, bent double; she retched and groaned.

*Shit, fuck, bollocks, this can't be happening.*

"Don't panic, Dave, just keep your eyes on the road. Take some deep breaths and count to ten," Betty advised.

"Deep breaths, Betty. Are you for real? I'm holding my breath!" I said.

Sofia was now sticking her head out of the passenger window.

"Deep breaths, everyone," Betty shouted again.

"That theory might work when giving birth Betty, but not in a jeep at 40mph, with more vomit than your average club 18-30 piss-up and a truck up your arse," I said.

"We need to get back to my villa and fast, Dave," shouted Betty.

I managed to turn the jeep around at a small roundabout, and we sped back up the road. Sofia bundled the dog onto the back seat. It yelped and barked with distress.

"Why didn't you keep the dog on your lap? The last thing we need is more vomit on the back seat," said a distressed Doris.

Her lipstick had smudged, and her eyeliner had begun to run. She now resembled Batman's Joker in drag.

I glanced at Sofia; she was remarkably calm. She handed face wipes around.

"Good job, you had those in your bag, eh?" I said.

"I never leave home without them," she added.

"David, it's fine. Let's just get back to the villa and clean ourselves up," she said.

"Betty – did you feed the dog before you left the house?" I asked.

"I *did,* yes, why?"

"What the hell did you feed it? Bombay potatoes?" I asked.

"Just some leftovers from last night's curry," she replied.

"Curry!! That'll explain it. Since when does a dog eat curry, Betty? We're in Greece, not Mumbai," I shouted.

"Listen, nobody panic. Once we clean ourselves up, we can get straight back out again," said Betty.

I had to admire her optimism.

"What about the vomit on the dash?" I asked.

"We can clean that up in the morning," Betty advised.

"It'll be dry and horrible by then," I said.

"What, as opposed to wet and horrible? I know which I'd prefer," Betty added.

I looked at Sofia; she was doing her best not to come into contact with any more of the vomit by keeping her hands close to her chest. It was all in vain; I could see she hadn't noticed the bits of vomit hanging from her hair. Her face was creased with a repulsed frown, yet even in her compromised state, I still bloody fancied her.

"David, this is so gross. We have to get to Betty's and fast," Sofia insisted.

"Can we put the air vents on and get some clean air into the car by any chance?" Doris asked.

I turned the heat button to cold and pushed the vent button to max power. Within seconds, bits of vomit flew out of the gaps in the vents and into the cabin. Everyone screamed in disgust.

"Turn it bloody off, turn it bloody off," shouted Betty.

"Blame Doris. It was her idea," I shouted.

"Maybe just bring your handbag next time and leave the dog home, Betty," I shouted.

"Listen, don't panic. We'll all be cleaned up in no time," said Betty, the only one of us who appeared to be unscathed and untroubled.

I glanced at Sofia's dress. It didn't look like it was about to be wiped clean with a flannel anytime soon.

"We'll be cleaned up in no time," shouted Betty.

Her optimism was now in overdrive.

"Yeah, we get the message, Betty. I know we'll get clean; it's how clean I'm worried about," I said.

"What about the Jeep? It won't clean itself, and what about the dog? Oh, and what if we can't clean the mess off our clothes? What then? Or do we walk into town in our underwear on the off chance we might buy some replacement outfits?" I asked.

"Calm down, Dave, you're such a drama queen," said Betty.

I looked at Sofia, "I'm really sorry. This wasn't intended to be a first date from hell."

"It's okay, don't panic," she said, half-smiling.

How could she remain so calm? It was a trait I had to admire, but only time can tell how sincere she is.

"I would have suggested we went to my house first so I could change my dress, but I'd rather not have to explain to my father why I'm back so early."

I wasn't about to argue.

We arrived at Betty's villa and made our way into the kitchen. Betty flicked on the light, and we all stood, looking at each other while inspecting the damage.

Remarkably, both Doris and Betty were spotless.

*How the hell did that happen?*

However, if Sofia's dress had a voice, it would be shouting for help right now. It seriously looked like it wanted to walk to the washing machine, climb in and slam the door behind it. I hadn't escaped either. I had bits of vomit on my shirt and on the right leg of my jeans.

"Is there a dressing gown Sofia can wear while she waits for our stuff to be washed and dried?" I asked.

"Sofia, you come with me. Dave, you wait here. We'll have your clothes washed and dried in no time," Betty said.

"I admire your optimism, Betty," I added.

"Stop panicking - I'll put them on a fast cycle,"

"How fast?" I asked.

"20 mins max," she added.

Betty oozed confidence; she was the captain of a sinking ship but still relished the challenge of keeping it afloat. I just hoped she was right. She was now a credible rival for Doris in how to get in and out of a fuck up in record time.

I was waiting in the kitchen when Doris suddenly appeared and handed me a pair of trousers and a jumper.

"Bloody hell, Doris, they're size 46" with a 28" leg. Betty's husband must have a body like a space hopper."

I looked at the yellow v-neck Lyle & Scott jumper. It was an XXL, and I wanted to cry. The trousers were some 80s throwbacks made of nylon. Good job, I've got a belt.

"I'll look like Ronnie Corbit wearing these. Hardly great for what little is left of my street cred, is it?" I moaned.

"I wouldn't worry, Dave. She won't know who Ronnie Corbit is."

"That's not the point. I will look like a right knob wearing this. Do me a favour and suggest to Betty that it won't be a bad idea for her to keep Sofia in the bedroom until my stuff is dried. She can't see me wearing crazy shit like this," I said.

"You're only wearing it while your other stuff dries. Take a chill pill."

"Do you have any?" I asked.

"Have what?" she queried.

"Doesn't matter. I look like a deflated balloon."

"Dave, calm down. It's hardly a crisis. Relax."

"Not a crisis?"

She looked me up and down.

"I always did have a soft spot for Ronnie Corbit," she said.

"Doris, the only soft spot is in your head!"

## Chapter 10

We all sat having a drink and making small talk whilst Betty loaded the washing machine.

Sofia was seriously struggling to contain her amusement at my compromised fashion.

"Eh, up, we're out of wine, folks. Dave, won't you be a love and nip to the shop for some supplies," asked Betty.

She waved her empty glass at me with a daft smile.

"In case it had escaped your attention, ladies, but these trousers are a foot too short, and my belt makes them look like I have lost about ten stone and shrunk by four feet. Oh, and the jumper, it's not only enormous, it's yellow and yellow really isn't my thing," I added.

"Oh David, you are funny. You look fine," Sofia said, struggling to contain her laughter.

She had clearly spent too much time in the company of these two, but at least she was softening and adjusted to just how chaotic they could be.

"Listen, who will see you and more importantly, who will *know* you in Naxos?" asked Doris.

"So you want me to go to the shop then?"

"Yes," came all three voices in sync.

"Right then, it looks like I'm off to the shop, ladies."

I grabbed my wallet and made my way to the door. I could hear chuckles of laughter from behind; they were enjoying this.

The local supermarket was rather large and not what I expected. That was a positive in terms of choice but a negative in terms of the number of people that would see me. I saw my reflection in the window as I walked in. It did nothing but add to my fear.

I quickly found the alcohol section, grabbed several bottles and then proceeded to add some crisps, chocolate and nuts. I then made my way to the till.

I noticed a sign above the till. The "ten-items-only" policy had made its way to Greece.

I waited for the chap in front of me to pay for his items and then took my place. The woman at the till looked at me as I placed my items on the belt. She had a face like a slapped bottom (a jobsworth face), and she spoke with a voice of total disdain.

"You do know I could *object* to serving you?" her sense of empowerment continued as she *bleeped* my items through.

"Really, why would you do that? Is my outfit that bad?"

"It's a *ten* items or less till, and you have exceeded *ten* items."

"Surely, you can make an exception?" I asked.

She *bleeped* a bottle of wine through and looked up at me.

"Twelve items are *not* ten items. It's two more items," she said while *bleeping* another item through.

"Well, arrest me at once and send me to the supermarket jail," I said.

She looked at me, and I looked at her.

"I think you'll find I have six items: a case of wine and five loose items. Unless you're counting *each* of my six bottles? Surely these would be classed as a bundle and, therefore, classed as one item?"

She shook her head and tutted.

"Perhaps you're new and still need to learn about the vast product range and the definitions of what is considered a single item and a bundle. My math, therefore, suggests I have, in fact, six items in total. Maybe you should work on the till for six items or less, as it'll be *less* stressful for you".

She was speechless, a bit like when Marco Van Basten scored that wonder goal in euros 1988. The crowd was speechless then, and so was she now.

I grabbed my bits and made my way towards the door. Suddenly, a voice could be heard from behind me. I had almost forgotten what I was wearing for a moment and how crazy I looked, but I was a man on a mission, and I began to walk faster towards the door.

*"Dave*, is that you?" shouted a voice from behind.

*Keep walking. I don't know anyone in Naxos, remember? Keep walking.*

"*Dave!"* the voice was even louder.

I looked behind me and dropped my bags.

*Shit, fuck, bollocks.*

It was Stavros; the Greek mountain man was standing before me.

I was shaking like a shitting dog. My mouth was dry, and my head was empty of speech. I was an empty vessel, so I stood there, awaiting my fate.

# Chapter 11

"Where is my *daughter?* I thought you were taking her for *dinner?*"

My mind was blank. I was rooted to the spot, speechless. I wanted to run, but my shoes were nailed to the floor.

"I asked you a question."

"We decided to stay in, and I would cook."

He wasn't buying it, and I was now struggling to contain my panic.

"Cook?" he asked.

He looked at the two plastic bags hanging off my trembling arms.

"It doesn't look like you'll be doing much cooking to me?"

He stepped closer to inspect the contents, his enormous hands shuffling about in my bags.

"Is all this wine to help you *seduce* my daughter, huh? Why is she not with you now? You better have some answers."

I was a boxer on the ropes with many problems and no solutions. His raised voice was now drawing attention, so I began to make my way towards the exit.

"I said you had better start *talking.*"

He wasn't so much following me, but more me following his huge frame.

"She preferred to wait at the villa, so I'd better get back, as she'll be wondering where I am."

I was now frog-marching myself out of the store with Stavros just off my left shoulder. He was so close that I could practically feel his breath on my face. I could pretty much tell you what he'd had for his dinner.

"Why are you wearing these *silly* clothes?"

There was me thinking he hadn't noticed.

"If I told you a dog vomited on my shirt, would you believe me?"

His face looked confused. It then switched to looking angry.

"Enough of this bullshit – take me to see my daughter now."

I had tried to defuse the bomb as best I could, but the fuse had already been ignited the moment he spotted me, and it was now fizzing uncontrollably.

*"How far is this villa?!"* he shouted.

"Not far, 10-15 minute walk, maybe less".

"No, you can come with me. My car is just over there," he wasn't asking; he was telling.

Judging by its dilapidated appearance, he had a Fiat Panda from the mid-80s.

There's no way that thing has an MOT. There wasn't a straight panel on it, and the wheels looked like he'd borrowed them from something agricultural.

Surely, a man of his wealth would drive a nicer car, but then it reminded me of a lot of people I had met in business over the years: rich but penny counters, not spenders. I knew one such man who had worn the same coffee-stained t-shirt for years yet had a Swiss Bank account.

He opened the boot for me to put my bags in and then went to his driver's door. He opened it with such force that I thought the thing would come off in his hand. I stood back and waited for him to open the passenger side.

*What's he doing now? He's taking ages.*

"The door is jammed; you will have to get in through the boot and onto the back seat".

He said it in a way like it was completely normal to enter a car via the boot and under such circumstances.

*Do I really fancy climbing in the boot of a potential murderer?*

"*Hurry up, come on,* I haven't got all night", he shouted.

I somehow managed to clamber past the boot contents, which consisted of my shopping, some straw and scattered feathers, making the boot resemble a mobile bird's nest.

As I forced my way onto the back seat, I suddenly felt a cold, wet sensation on my trousers. I didn't want to look; I just needed to get my arse out of the boot and onto the back seat as fast as possible.

The back seat wasn't much better either, with more shit than your average skip, and if that wasn't bad enough, there was a distinct lack of seat belt, a device I might need should Stavros be no exception to the Greek norm and drive like a fucking idiot.

"I hope you didn't crush the *eggs*", he shouted over the noise of the engine.

I looked down at my trousers.

*Oh, bollocks.*

"No, I didn't."

He glanced behind me. We soon set off, and his driving skills didn't disappoint. Every gear change was a painful grind of cogs on metal.

*Who needs a radio when you have that to listen to?*

Our conversation wasn't exactly flowing, not that I could hear much of what was said over the noise of the engine rattling like a tin of spanners.

"Can't go wrong with these old Fiats, eh Stavros? They go on forever."

He made no comment.

"They were never that popular in the UK. I recall that they weren't fond of the rain," I added.

Still no comment.

"They rusted a lot," I further added.

"Which one is it?" he shouted, with reference to the villa.

"It's just a bit further, mate," I said, peering through the dusty side window.

"There, it's that one on the left," I said, taking a deep breath.

I was just relieved the journey was a short one. I walked into the villa first, with Stavros breathing down my neck.

The first thing we saw was all three of them dancing around in just their underwear to the backdrop of what sounded like music straight from Club Ibiza.

They hadn't even noticed us standing by the door, as if we were shrouded in an invisible cloak.

I glanced at Stavros; he stood speechless. I could see a bottle of port, which they'd clearly cracked open. We both looked at each other, me with a face that begged for mercy, and he had a face that wanted to strangle me.

He reached over and whispered in my ear.

"I thought you said *dinner*? This doesn't look much like *dinner* to me?"

His anger was notching through the gears again, and his voice was raised over the music, so it was only a matter of seconds before we were finally noticed.

"Ladies, may I have your attention, please," he shouted, like he was about to do a king's speech.

All three of them stopped and looked like rabbits in the headlights. Their expressions were priceless.

"Father - *what* are you doing here?" Sofia placed her glass on the coffee table and slowly stepped forward.

*Had they forgotten they were in their underwear?*

"I was about to ask *you* the same thing. W*ho* are *these* people, and where are your *clothes?"*

His voice bellowed across the room with a deep rumble that practically shook the foundations.

"*Please,* allow me to explain," an unflappable Betty decided to interrupt.

"No, let *me* explain. I want my daughter to get dressed and come home with me right away."

"Father, I am *not* a child."

"No, you are not, but you're *not* spending any more time with these perverts either!"

"Excuse *me.* I think you need to wash your mouth out. We won't have language like that round here," shouted Doris.

Her outburst even caught Betty by surprise.

"Father, let me explain."

Sofia's voice begged for reason. I couldn't see this ending well. We were soldiers in the trenches, knowing that the loud bangs around us were about to get a whole lot louder.

They both ranted at each other in Greek while the rest of us stood and watched in fear. Suddenly, Stavros turned and made his way out the door with not so much as a glance in my direction.

*I guess that means I won't be on his Christmas card list anytime soon.*

The door slammed shut, shaking the frame.

I looked at Sofia.

"Will he be ok?" I asked.

"Of course, he's always grumpy when he eats late."

"I hope he's not having an omelette," I said.

She looked confused.

"I sat on his eggs on the back seat."

She laughed.

"Ladies, are my clothes dry yet?" I asked.

"Dave, *where have you been*?" asked Betty

"I went to Mecca bingo with Stavros. Where do you think I've been?"

"I thought we had sent you to get some wine?" Doris piped up, hands on her hips, all attitude.

"I bumped into Stavros, and we got chatting. You know how it is; we lost track of time. I was pleasantly surprised how much we had in common."

Sofia laughed.

"He's such a control freak. I'm ever so sorry, David. He likes you, honestly, he does," she said, all smiley and slightly pissed.

"I would shudder to think what he's like when he doesn't like someone?" I added.

Sofia laughed.

They all looked at my trousers and laughed.

"Turn around, Dave," shouted Betty.

"What?" I asked.

I looked down, "Yes, I know. I was just telling Sofia about the egg drama."

"Normally, my father doesn't keep eggs in the back seat of his car. Do you think it was a trap just for you, David?" she asked.

She was enjoying this.

"Probably."

"Ladies, I feel a tad overdressed. Should I get down to my underpants?"

"Oh *shit,*" Doris shouted.

"*Dave* – look away," said Betty, grabbing anything that might help hide their blushes.

“I blame the Port,” said Betty.

“I think your next *port* of call should be the bedroom and getting some clothes on, ladies,” I added.

“Oh, David – this shouldn’t be happening,” she put her hands to her face to defuse her laughter.

“What shouldn’t be happening? Seeing you in your underwear?” I asked.

I was doing my best to act cool but quickly remembered what I was wearing.

“No, leaving it this late before we eat,” her face was never far from a smile and a sense of cheekiness. I liked it a lot.

# Chapter 12

Finally, it would seem that normality had been restored. I didn't know what that felt like anymore; the calm and the storm kind of rolled into one in my world.

However, Sofia and I had finally escaped the grip of the grannies. We sat in a charming little restaurant by the sea, and life was looking up for once.

"My clothes look a little creased," I said, inspecting my shirt.

"We better make sure we sit in a dark corner somewhere then, David?"

I nodded with approval.

"Can I just say thank you for agreeing to still come out with me this evening, especially after everything that's happened. I wouldn't have been offended had you changed your mind."

Sofia finished chewing on her prawn linguini and looked up.

"Hey, listen, I like you, David. You're different and certainly know how to entertain a girl, even if some of the entertainment wasn't intended."

She continued to twist the fork in her pasta, taking another mouthful. Pasta on a first date; it was a brave move, but she managed it effortlessly.

"Well, I obviously really like you too, Sofia. You're very attractive and funny, and that's a rare combination to find in a girl, I think."

She smiled and nodded.

It was a calm evening, loosely speaking. The sea could be heard teasing the rocks a short distance away. The moon was full, and the buzz about the place was right on point.

I pushed my fork into another piece of calamari and forced it into the pot of garlic mayo which accompanied it. I glanced around the room and observed other people doing their thing.

Some flash bastard had just ordered lobster; there's always one. The platter it came on was so big it needed its own entourage. Then, from the corner of my eye, I could spot the unmistakable in the distance.

Two silhouettes against the moonlight.

"Oh *shit*"

"What's wrong?" Sofia asked.

“I think I’ve just seen Doris and Betty. I hope they don’t spot us. Just keep your head down and look like you’re captivated by my every word, like we’re two lovers. I know it’s a big ask on a first date, but just try.”

Sofia just laughed.

“Do they have the *dog*?”

“Yes, I think so.”

“Do you prefer David or Dave?” she asked.

“I don’t mind. Whatever you are comfortable with?”

“Ok, I like Dave more, I think, but I may change my mind.”

“I’ve been called worse,” I added, “But yeah, I see a dog with them.”

“Then there’s no problem. They won’t allow dogs in here, not in a restaurant. Relax, it's fine.”

I took a gulp of wine to calm my nerves.

“More wine?” I asked.

“Of course,” she said, gently pushing her glass towards me.

“Well, *hello,* you two lovers, fancy seeing you here. What a coincidence,” said Betty.

She stood before us with the four-legged handbag under her arm. Doris was just behind, flirting with the waiter, all jokey and laughy in her usual exaggerated way.

“Betty, I’m *really* sorry, but you can’t bring animals in here. You will have to eat somewhere else,” I said.

“I could say it’s my guide dog, Dave. What do you think?” she pondered.

“I think they’ll be guiding you off the premise; that’s what I think.”

“Seriously, Betty, they won’t let you bring a dog in here, but I’m sure we will see you later?” I added

I smiled with my best “get the fuck out of here” expression.

“Oh, don’t worry. The waiter said it was absolutely fine. Provided it didn’t bark or do any poo poos,” Betty had an answer to everything.

Sofia’s smile was less convincing on this occasion, but she was as diplomatic as ever.

“Would you like to join us?” she asked.

“I’m sure you’d prefer to eat *alone,* eh ladies?” I asked, hoping the frown on my face was enough to get the message across.

Doris put her neck in.

“Well, we wouldn’t want to impose, especially considering you’re on a first date,” she said.

They were enjoying this. Betty smiled at Sofia, all jolly and daft.

“Well, we wouldn’t want to impose,” she said.

Sofia smiled.

“No, not at all,” she said.

Sofia looked at me and laughed.

“We had just been saying how nice it would be to see you guys again tonight,” Sofia added.

I nodded and smiled.

“Of course we had.”

“Before I get settled, I need to powder my nose. Mine’s a large dry white if I miss the waiter,” Doris said before making her way toward the ladies.

This was an opportune moment for me to leave the table and follow her.

“Do you know what? That makes two of us,” I left the table in hot pursuit.

“Doris, can I have a quick word?”

“Oh, hello, stranger. If I didn’t know you better, Dave, I would think you’re avoiding us”.

“Avoiding you, bloody hell, *I wish.* In case you hadn’t noticed, I am trying to have a *date,* and how can I have a date when you and Betty are following us everywhere we go?”

“Oh, Dave, I’m not sure she’s the *right* girl for you. I think *we* need to spend some more time in her company before we can make an accurate judgement,” she added.

“What do you mean *we*? Listen, when you return from the ladies, please make your excuses and give us some space. That’s all I ask, Doris.”

“Ok, point taken, Dave. You’re right. We shouldn’t be crowding your space.”

*Bloody hell, finally, she is seeing sense.*

I returned to the table and sat down.

"Everything alright?" asked Sofia, clearly observing *the will to live* draining from my face.

"Absolutely, I just needed to have a word with Doris about the shoes she's wearing. They gave her blisters the last time she wore them, so I suggested she might need to go back to the villa and change them."

"Oh, Dave, you're so thoughtful," said Betty.

Sofia smiled.

"Oh, David, that is very sweet of you," Sofia said.

I sat down and smiled at them both.

"Ladies, it's the kind of guy I am."

Moments later, Doris returned to the table.

"This dress I'm wearing is a bit tight, Betty. I could do with going back and changing it. Would you mind coming with me?" she said.

"I thought it was the shoes that didn't fit?" Betty looked at me with suspicion.

"No, they're fine, they're from Clarks these. I could run a marathon in them," she said, lifting her left leg to reveal her shiny new shoes.

Betty looked at me.

"If I didn't know you better, I would suspect you're trying to get rid of us, Dave."

Betty's normal radiant smile was now replaced with a frown. Sofia laughed. She was enjoying this.

Out of nowhere, a small, chubby waiter appeared at the table and pointed at a sign on the wall a short distance away. It read *no dogs in the restaurant, thank you.* As though the dog knew its fate, its eyes momentarily fixed on mine.

*Nice try*, but it wasn't getting any support from me this time.

"I have a suggestion," said Betty, with a more perky expression.

"Dave and Doris, take the dog back to our villa, and Doris can change into something more comfortable," she looked at me with a smirk.

"Why would I need to go with her?" I asked.

"Dave, you can't let a lady walk alone at night," said Betty.

Sofia looked at me, "She's right, Dave."

"To be honest, I think the dress is okay now. It must have been the tag rubbing or something," said Doris.

"Listen, ladies, can I make a suggestion of my own? Let's do a deal. Dave and I will take the dog back to the villa, while you two stay here and enjoy yourselves, and we *might* see you later. How does that sound?" said Sofia.

I liked the emphasis on *might*. In fact, I was totally bought.

Betty and Doris looked at each.

"Okay, *fine* by us. Here is the front door key, Dave, don't lose it," said Betty.

"We'll see you later," added Doris.

"Have you paid for your food and wine, Dave?" shouted Betty.

I walked back and put some euros on the table.

"That should cover it and whatever you ladies would like to drink."

We left the restaurant and stood outside, looking back at them from a short distance. Sofia had the dog under her arm. It looked quite happy, smug, in fact, and I hated it.

"Right, let's get that thing back to the villa," I said.

Sofia attempted to attach the lead, but it wouldn't sit still, wriggling and jumping about all frantic.

"Just hold it a second while I tie my shoelace."

She put the dog on the floor and had another attempt at attaching the lead, but it just wriggled and barked.

"Let me have a go," I said, grabbing its collar.

"Are you sure?" she asked, as though I'd never held a dog before.

"Trust me, I'm very good with animals," I added.

"Yes, but it did snap at your fingers earlier," she said.

"I think it probably mistook my fingers for sausages."

She laughed.

“Right, come here, you little bugger,” I said while grappling with the dog.

But, within seconds, it had escaped my grasp and bolted up the road.

Sofia looked a little frantic.

“*Shit,* Dave, what are we going to do?”

“Wait here, don’t panic, I’ll catch it, don’t worry,” I said.

I gave chase for a few hundred yards while Sofia stood and watched, but it was all in vain. It ran through some shrubs and disappeared out of sight.

“No dog, then?” she asked, with a face of despair.

“It would appear we have a *problem*,” I said, my hands on my head.

“What now?” she asked.

“Plan A: we panic, plan B: we … “

“What’s plan B?” she asked.

“I haven’t thought of one.”

# Chapter 13

"Dave, what are we going to do?"

"Panic a bit more?"

"No, seriously", she added, her face contorted with fear.

"Worst case, we buy another dog. I mean, black and white terriers are easy enough to find."

She laughed.

"You can't find the one you've just lost," she said.

"Not easy then, eh?" I asked.

"Not in Naxos they're not, so you might have to come up with a better plan, I'm afraid."

"Okay, let's keep calm. Take a look around the square; it won't be far. It's probably a bit spooked and hiding somewhere."

She nodded.

"Okay, I guess it's our best option so far."

"Sofia, don't worry, we'll find it."

We began walking up the road, looking left and right and occasionally holding our gaze for any kind of movement in the bushes, all of which amounted to nothing more than the odd cat in search of an evening meal.

Greece has more cats than shrubs, and Naxos is no exception. We soon arrived at the main square and continued to look in all directions, like tourists without a map.

"What are we going to do? We can't just walk around aimlessly, hoping that we might stumble across the little bugger," I asked.

"Listen, I have an idea. There is an internet café on the other side of the square," Sofia suggested.

"What do you think the dog might be in there, looking up its address online?"

She laughed.

"I like you, Dave. Even in a time of crisis, you never lose your sense of humour. Listen, we can find a picture of a similar dog on the net, make some flyers and then hand them out in all the shops and bars -  what do you think?"

"Brilliant idea. I'm really beginning to enjoy this date. Who needs candle-lit romance? It's so overrated," I said.

She smiled.

"*Listen*."

Sofia raised her voice ever so slightly.

"We get the dog, hand it back, and go on *our* date. Ok, it'll be a bit late, but better late than never," she said.

I liked this girl. She'd just downed a pint of optimism.

At that moment, my thoughts turned to Betty and her reaction should we not find the dog. We needed to stay focused. I didn't want to entertain the idea of the worst case, not yet, at least.

The internet café was more of a bar, which wasn't bad, as we could at least grab a few beers for our troubles.

Sofia's fingers typed away on Google, and within seconds, the screen was filled with images of black and white terrier-type dogs in various poses.

"Ok, what about this one?" she asked, pointing at one example in particular.

"They all look the bloody same. Yeah, it'll do. I mean, what are the chances of there being another dog like the one we've lost?" I said.

"I will print a hundred, fifty each - that should be enough, or is that too many?" she asked.

"It seems a lot?" I said.

"You think less?" she asked.

"I just thought we were mailing bars and shops around Naxos town, not all of Greece. At this rate, we'll be mail-dropping from an aeroplane!"

"Okay, maybe fifty in total would be a safe number," I suggested.

She pondered, “No, let’s do 50 each, Dave, just to be safe.”

“Ok, go for it,” I agreed, “We aren’t going to have time for a drink, are we?” I asked.

She shook her head.

“Time is of the essence, Dave. We can’t hang around.”

We both looked at the mailer and then looked at each other. At any moment, there could have been laughter or tears.

“We need to give people an incentive to look, maybe a reward?” I said.

Sofia stopped; she was thinking.

“You’re right. How about two hundred euros?” she asked.

“Shit, not that much; maybe one hundred will be enough, that’s plenty,” I said.

She typed away and amended the current version.

100 euro reward

Please help us find our lost dog, Poppy

Call David on 07789071330.

“I reckon we split up for an hour in opposite directions and agree to meet back here at 9 p.m. Do the bars, restaurants and shops first, then just hand them out to tourists, locals, anyone? What do you think?” I asked

“Sounds *good,* but be careful,” she warned.

“Why, do you think some unsavoury person might mug me for my hundred euros? I’d better not stick a flyer on my forehead then.”

“The only forehead I’m concerned about is yours. Betty is likely to use it as target practice with her handbag,” she said.

She was right.

“Also, we don’t want them seeing us, so keep an eye out for them!” I said.

“With a bit of luck, they’ll stay put where we left them,” she added.

“Agreed”, doing my best to remain cheery and upbeat, but my mind was never far away from imagining the look of horror on Betty’s face should we have to confront her with the news that we’d lost her neighbour’s dog.

We hugged each other and went our separate ways. It was all very cub scouts rather than a passionate embrace.

I walked in and out of bars and cafes, leaving flyers on tables, smiling as I handed them out to locals and tourists; it was done quickly and like a man on a mission.

I didn't have time to stop and make small talk. No matter how fast I went about my business, the pile in my hand didn't seem to be getting any smaller.

There was still a bit of time to kill before I needed to make my way back to our meeting place. I sat on a wall and looked at the "self-replenishing" pile in my hand. I could only hope Sofia had had better luck than me.

I sent her a quick text. I sat back, took a swig from my water bottle, and watched people going about their business. The aroma coming from the fish restaurants all around me was divine. My stomach rumbled.

Just across from me, I could see a couple of Greek kids using their skateboards as seats. They sat devouring their kebabs, and I watched with envy. I checked my phone, but still no reply from Sofia.

I got up and continued to walk around, aimlessly handing out flyers to anyone who would take one.

"Excuse me, mate," came a voice from behind me.

I turned to look. I would say it was a young lad, British, and in his 20s. He had my flyer in his hand.

"You lost your dog?" he asked, all serious.

"Yeah, have you seen it?" I asked, all hopeful.

"Is it small?" he asked.

"Yeah, about this big."

"Black and white?" he asked.

"Yeah."

“No mate, sorry,” he said, walking off with a fit of laughter.

*Arsehole.*

I began making my way back to our meeting point in the square. I could see Sofia in the distance; her slender figure was unmistakable. She was like a piece of sculpture.

She was early. I glanced at my watch.

*Shit! No, she isn’t*; I was late.

“*Sofia”*, I shouted, waving the last of my flyers above my head.

She turned and smiled.

“No luck then!” she said.

“I tried to ring you, but my battery was flat,” she added.

“*Shit,* this is getting serious now. I’m half expecting a call from Doris to see where we are.”

She looked as defeated as I felt.

“Should we grab a coffee and have a re-think?” I asked.

Suddenly, my mobile vibrated in my pocket.

“Told you, that’ll be Doris texting me.”

I pulled the phone from my pocket and looked at the message.

“Oh, it’s not a number I recognize. It could be in response to the *flyer.*”

I clicked and opened the message in anticipation.

“What does it say?”

"Eh, what the .. "

"Dave, what's the matter?"

I read out the text content.

*"Hello, we have your dog Poppy. She is safe and well. You do not need to worry. We would like to return the dog to you, but it will cost five hundred euros. Please accept this request and await further instructions."*

"It's got to be a windup, surely?" I said.

My heart was in my mouth, and my wallet was in the gutter.

"What are we going to do?" she asked.

She looked as stressed as me.

"Well, what choice do we have? I could try and negotiate a better deal?"

"How much does a Jack Russell cost in the UK?" she asked.

"I'm no expert. Maybe fifty quid?" I said, shrugging my shoulders.

"So, little Dave, are *you* sure?"

"Are there any pet shops in Naxos?" I asked.

Sofia looked confused.

"Why?" she asked.

"I'm thinking, worst case, we can buy another dog," I said.

"What if we can only find a white one?" she asked.

She was clearly amused by my suggestion.

"We buy some black paint," I said.

My face was deadly serious.

"Now I know you're *joking,* Dave," she laughed.

"What are the chances of us finding an identical dog, Dave," she said, laughing.

"I should be asking you the same question. Permission to swear?" I asked.

She laughed.

"Bastards."

"Do you feel better after that?" she asked.

"No."

"Dave, it could be a couple of kids playing a joke. They may not even have the dog."

"I will see if they'll take two fifty. Meet them in the middle."

I began typing my reply.

"Ok – message sent. I have suggested two fifty would be a more reasonable offer."

Moments later, my phone vibrated again.

"Shit, I don't think I can take any more stress," she said.

"What have they said this time?"

"They've said 'it's five hundred, that is the deal, take it or leave it. If you take it, we will meet, and exchange. If you don't, then you never see your dog again.'"

"Could be a bluff, Dave?"

"Can we take that chance?" I said.

"Should I ring the number? See what idiot answers?"

Then my phone *bleeped* again, and I read the content out loud.

"Do not try and call me. All communications will be done by text. Now make your decision, yes or no?"

"Oh my God, they are probably somewhere watching us. They must be," she said, all exasperated.

"Just agree, Dave. We have no choice."

I replied, and we waited, then another *bleep*.

"What have they said?"

"Hmm, they have just said to wait for further instructions."

Sofia shook her head.

Then came another *bleep*, and we both looked at each other again.

"Go on, open it," she said.

"Oh – it's Doris."

I don't know what was worse. I read the content out loud.

*"Hi Dave, hope you two are having a fab time. Betty and I are having one more for the road and then heading back to Betty's. See you later."*

"Shit, Dave, what are we going to do?"

Another *bleep*. We both looked at each other in anticipation. I opened the message and read the content out loud again.

*"Leave the money in a plastic bag in the bin opposite the clock tower. Do this thirty minutes from now. When you have left the bag, please turn around and walk away. Do not look behind you; just keep walking. I will text further instructions on where you will find your dog later."*

"How do we know this isn't some scally tying it on? They might be blagging us," I said.

"Dave, may I ask a question?"

"Sure!"

"What is a scally, and what does 'blagging us' mean?"

It was Sofia's first introduction to native slang.

"Ah, scally is a kind of bad person, you know, the type that takes things that don't belong to them, and blagging, that means not telling the truth."

She nodded her head with a half-smile.

"We'd better get to a *bank* then, Dave, and fast."

"*Shit*, could this get any worse?" I added.

*Bleep*; another text. It read - "*Your time is running out.*"

We walked with speed through the square and up the hill to the crossroads where the bank was located. I had plenty of euros in my wallet, but I prayed I could draw out what I needed to make the difference, or we'd be fucked.

"Dave, you grab the money, and I will pop into this shop to get a plastic bag".

I inserted the card into the machine. My palms were sweaty, and my hands were shaking. I was slowly imputing my PIN in fear that if I typed any faster, I'd cock it up, and my card would be gobbled.

Sofia appeared with a white plastic bag, and I stuffed the money inside.

"Ok, let's get to the clock tower," I said.

## Chapter 14

*Bleep, Bleep* – another text and another heartbeat missed.

Sofia looked at me, her face urging me to grab my phone. I slid my finger across the screen and opened the text.

*"Drop the bag in the bin located outside the clock tower as instructed earlier. Then, walk away in the opposite direction. Do not look behind and await further instructions on where to find your dog."*

"Shit, well, no time to mess about then, Dave. Let's go."

We walked briskly, darting in and out of tourists.

"Sofia, you really don't need to hang about. I wouldn't be offended if you wanted to get off home and let me sort this out."

She looked at me and smiled.

"Thank you, Dave, but seriously, I've come this far, and I really need to see it through with you."

"We make a good team then, eh?" I said.

She smiled again. I loved that smile. It was very addictive.

"Well, there is potential, Dave. I won't lie. Just drop the bag in the bin and hurry back to me."

I wasn't going to argue. I snapped back into mission mode and walked towards the bin, leaving her to watch from a short distance.

The bag of cash left the palm of my left hand, and I watched as it dropped into the bin and disappeared into the darkness. Five hundred quid, I sighed with despair.

If I wasn't with Sofia, I'd have told these scumbags to whistle dixie, called their bluff, told them to do one and find some other mug.

It was as close as I was ever going to get to play James Bond, albeit a budget version, because I was shockingly incapable most of the time and only half as attractive, but nonetheless, I was kind of enjoying it in a bizarre way.

I walked back towards Sofia and quickly grasped her hand. She looked at me and gave me one of her smiles; a smile that would melt the hearts of a thousand men.

We didn't hang about, did exactly what the text had instructed, and began to walk away, not daring to look back.

I have to think of the goal, the ultimate prize.

We had been walking for what seemed like a matter of yards when my phone *bleeped* again in my pocket. We both stopped and once again, I opened it and read the message out loud.

*"Your dog is tied to the leg of the same bin. Thank you for your cooperation, and enjoy your evening."*

"That dog is going to get a .. "

"A *big hug,* Dave, you were about to say?"

"Well, exactly, I have really missed that little dog, to be honest."

"You are *so* sweet, Dave. Despite spending all that money, you still wouldn't wish any harm on the dog."

She couldn't see the pain behind my fake smile; it was agony. I really wanted to strap the dog to a rocket and fire it to the moon.

"Listen, it's just money, no big deal. You can't put a price on the welfare of a defenceless animal, Sofia."

"Dave - that is such a lovely thing to say."

We both turned around and looked back at the bin in the distance. I could see what looked like a little black and white four-legged mutt standing next to it.

*Bleep, Bleep* – "Shit, what now? Why are they texting me again? to gloat in their glory?" I said.

I grabbed my phone from my pocket. We stopped for a moment, and I opened the text.

"Oh, it's Doris. *Shit!* I had almost forgotten about them two."

"What is she saying?" she asked.

*"Hi Dave, it's Doris. We are on our way to the square. Where are you two? Fancy meeting us for one by the clock tower?"*

"Shit - let's just get to the dog, and then I'll reply."

I grabbed Sofia by the hand and practically dragged her towards the bin. As we got closer, the dog spotted us and began to jump about, all giddy, tail-wagging frantically. Sofia left my grasp and ran towards it, getting down on her knees and letting the dog lick her face.

*Lucky sod, it gets to bugger off for hours, costs me a small fortune, and gets to snog Sofia too, little shit.*

"Oh, Dave, look, she's so pleased to see us and seems unharmed."

I watched as the two of them embraced like long-lost lovers.

"I'd better reply to Doris."

"*We are here already, outside the clock tower. Where are you? Meet us at Zano's. You can't miss it.*"

"I've suggested they meet us at Zano's."

"That's great, Dave, but aren't we supposed to have taken the dog back to *Betty's* villa?"

"Shit, I'd forgotten about that. We won't have time to do that now. I'll think of some excuse before we see them."

"I admire your confidence, Dave".

Sofia picked up the dog and placed it under her arm.

"Come on then, let's go grab a well-earned drink," I said.

I was gasping for a beer, a sit-down, and a few moments to adjust and reflect before the onslaught of head noise that would come from Doris and Betty.

"Dave, look, it appears Doris and Betty are already there."

"How, that's not possible?" I added, bewildered.

"Well, hello strangers, long time no see," said Doris.

She was all smiles and waves and already half cut, it would appear.

"Correct me if I'm wrong, but isn't that Poppy under your arm, Sofia?" asked Doris.

"Why haven't you taken her back to the villa?" asked Betty, looking bemused.

I felt the need to control the conversation before these two started notching through the gears.

"We ended up taking her for a walk on the beach, and before we knew it, we had lost track of time," it was a good, solid improv.

"That's right," Sofia added.

Betty smiled, "That's very odd, Dave. Poppy hates the sand," Betty smirked.

Sofia looked lost for words; she was letting me punch our way out of trouble. Doris looked deadpan, with no emotion. She was clearly waiting for Betty to take this interrogation to the next level.

"We didn't technically walk on the sand. We just walked on the road by the beach," it was a good recovery.

"That's very odd, Dave. She hates walking on roads and is practically terrified of traffic," Betty continued.

"We actually carried her for most of the walk," Sofia added.

"That's very odd, Sofia. She hates being carried," Doris added, a big smirk on her face.

"Bit of a fussy little fucker then, isn't she?" I said.

"Sit yourselves down. I'm sure you're both gasping for a drink?" asked Betty.

She had a daft smirk on her face. I really wanted to slap her, but I'm not sure if it would enhance my charm offensive with Sofia.

The waiter appeared at our table. He was a welcome distraction that would allow me a few moments to gather my thoughts and stock up on ammunition for the next chapter of interrogation.

"Hello, how are you? What can I get you?" the waiter looked about ten years old.

*I've got underpants older than this guy.*

Doris looked at Betty.

"Well, I'm feeling rather brave, Betty. I think we should live it up. What do you think, maybe a bottle of champagne?"

I looked at the wine section. She must be pissed at these prices.

"Feeling flush? Have you been playing on them scratch cards again, Doris?" I asked.

Betty interrupted, "Even better, Dave. A very generous man treated us."

Doris took control of the drinks menu.

"What choice of champagne do you have?" she asked, looking up at the waiter.

"We have Moet, Taittinger and Bollinger, all very nice, madam, all at very special prices."

He sounded like Del Boy from Only Fools and Horses; someone must have bought him the box set for Christmas.

"Which one is the most expensive?" asked Betty.

"The Bollinger, madam, very special," he said, with a degree of awkwardness.

"One hundred euros, that's *very* reasonable. Well, as it's Dave's treat, I'm sure he won't object, will you, Dave?" Doris asked.

How could I refuse? I was on the charm offensive with Sofia, and these bloody women were exploiting me to the max.

"Very good, madam. I will bring four glasses," said the waiter.

Out popped a wedge of euros from Betty's handbag, and she placed them on the table in front of us.

"I wasn't aware Naxos had a casino. You ladies been getting lucky?" I asked.

Betty took two fifty euro notes from the cash and pushed the rest across the table to me. I looked at the wedge. It was in a bundle with an elastic band around it.

"What's this for?" I asked.

"Count it," Betty asked.

I quickly counted it: 400 euros.

Sofia looked equally bemused.

"That's to pay for the Bollinger. The least you can do for l*osing* my neighbour's dog, Dave," she said, pointing her finger at me with conviction.

Doris pushed a familiar-looking flyer across the table.

"*All* this time, it was *you* two, you *little* sods," I said.

Sofia laughed.

"It's a good job we have a sense of humour, ladies, or *you* two would be in a lot of bother right now."

"Not half as much trouble as you would be in Dave if you'd lost *that* dog," Betty said, always keen to have the last word.

Doris laughed like a witch who had just cast a spell, whereas Betty laughed with a deep rumble, almost manlike; it was an interesting combination. People at the other tables began to glance over in amusement.

"Oh, here comes our bubbles," said Betty, clapping her hands with delight.

"Bottle of Bollinger ladies," said the waiter.

"Oh yes, please," Doris and Betty's faces beamed; they were loving this.

"May I?" I asked, looking at the waiter and reaching out to grab the bottle.

"Of course, sir."

I grabbed the bottle and looked at the label.

"Oh, it's a 2010 vintage, a good year apparently," I said.

I looked at Sofia to grab her attention. I had to at least sound like I had the foggiest idea.

"I will leave you to enjoy your drinks," the waiter returned to the bar.

"So, go on, tell us, how did you find the dog?" I asked.

Betty laughed, "It found us where it left us, at the restaurant," she said with another smug smile.

I removed the foil and metal clasp to reveal the cork. Everyone was waiting patiently with flutes in their hands.

Don't fuck this up; maximum pressure. I then slowly began to remove the cork to reduce the risk of exciting the contents. *POP* – and no matter how hard I tried, the contents still bellowed over the top and down the side of the bottle.

Doris grabbed the bottle and put her mouth over the top to stop the flow.

"Doris, don't be so gross," I said, grabbing the bottle and removing it from her mouth with her false teeth still wrapped around the rim.

Everyone was grossed out, silenced by the horror they saw before them. Doris grabbed the bottle, removed her false teeth from around the rim and put them back in her mouth.

"*Bloody hell*, sort your fixative out, woman," I said.

"Rude to waste it, Dave," she claimed with her granny grin.

We all pretended not to watch as she thumbed to straighten her teeth.

Betty wiped the bottle with a napkin, doing her best to remove Doris' DNA while struggling to contain her own amusement.

"Right, well, you've had your fill. Now, for everyone else," I said.

I began to fill the other flutes, ensuring a now semi-reluctant Sofia had the first shout.

"Let's have a toast," shouted Betty.

We all raised our glasses.

"To absent friends," said Betty.

"I wish you two were bloody absent," I shouted against the backdrop of Sofia's laughter.

# Chapter 15

Doris and Betty walked ahead of us, and I felt the need to hold Sofia back to give us some space.

The warm breeze was doing its best to make me continually sweat, but on an emotional level, I felt cool and back in control again. Right now, in this moment, life was good. I had a beautiful girl on my arm and not an obstacle in sight.

The whole evening had been like playing in a football match, where we were five-nil down at half-time, knowing only a miracle would turn things around. Right now, this was the "second-half miracle" I had been hoping for. The game was now five all, and in the 89$^{th}$ minute, we'd been given a penalty.

I looked at Sofia. She smiled, leaned in and kissed me on my lips, softly but briefly, as though to tease me. This was my moment; I stepped up to take the penalty. I wanted to smash the roof of the net by giving her a big snog.

Just as I leaned in to make my move, we were interrupted by shouts from a short distance away.

"Where's that coming from?"

"Sofia .. Sofia .. Sofia, is that you?" came a voice from nowhere.

We both stopped and looked around, and then suddenly, a bloke stood before us.

"Sofia, it is *me*, Luigi," he spoke English, which was rather odd when surely he was supposed to speak Greek? He certainly looked Greek.

I had been waiting to take my penalty kick and win the match – plant the kiss, get the girl – but this arsehole has made me miss; I've hit the post.

"I don't believe it, Luigi. Is that really *you? My God, it is you. How long has it been*?" she asked.

"Too long, my lovely, too long," he repeated.

"Dave, this is a friend I knew from school. We used to hang out in our early teens. His family is from Italy. If I recall, they came to live in Greece in the early 80s but then returned in the late 90s?" she said, looking at him for confirmation.

"Hello, I'm David."

"Hi, I am Luigi."

He looked at Sofia and smiled.

“We moved back to Italy not long after we’d left school. My parents wanted to return home,” he added, glancing at me briefly.

“What are you doing *here* anyway?” she asked.

“I am visiting friends.”

At this point, I was invisible. He looked tall, dark and handsome, and I didn’t. Even with my best Greek tan, I suddenly felt very pale.

“It has been a *long* time since we saw each other last. We were practically kids,” she added while glancing my way.

“Well, we weren’t exactly friends, more *lovers*,” he gloated with a big, handsome Italian smile, his teeth as white as the white-washed walls behind us.

Even in this light, his eyes were as green as emeralds, and he bore an uncanny resemblance to Paulo Maldini – an Italian footballing icon and arguably the best-looking man in the world.

*Fuck*, this was a Lada competing with a Ferrari; I was spluttering, and he was revving with a raspy exhaust note.

Sofia reassured me, “It was a long time ago.”

“It was, but do you know something? It feels like it was just *yesterday*,” he said, gloating some more.

He was full of the lay-it-on-thick charm, and my legs began to wobble.

“Hey, it is so good to see *you.* You look just how I remembered, as beautiful as the flowers on that tree.”

*Shit, is this really happening?*

Sofia looked at me again with an awkward sense of embarrassment.

"He always was a charmer."

"Are you staying long?" she asked.

"I have an open ticket."

He looked at me with a smug grin.

"I will see how it goes, maybe a few weeks."

He was centre stage, and I was in row Z right now.

"My friends moved from Athens to Naxos a couple of years ago," he said with his hands on his hips, looking me up and down as if to suggest I was punching above my weight.

I was. I just didn't need him to remind me.

Her hand, which had been so firmly placed in mine, was now removed as she reached over to Luigi to hug him. The kind of hug you'd give a long-lost friend or lover, who knows, but either way, it hurt.

"It's so good to see you after all this time. I hope you enjoy the rest of your stay in Naxos," she said.

"Let's not leave it so long next time, my darling. I will be hanging out with friends in the Square most evenings, so I'm sure I will see you again before I return to Milan."

He was oozing confidence like a peacock in mating season. I was more like a pigeon, no different to any other pigeon.

"You live in Milan? Oh wow, I have never been to Milan. I hear it's so amazing."

"It's pretty special, yes."

"What do you do for work?" she asked.

He paused, glanced at me, then back at her and smiled. I knew what was coming. He was hardly about to tell her he worked in a shoe shop, and I couldn't help but feel his pause was more about keeping *me* in suspense, as though the next words were about to blow us away.

"I work for PRADA as a designer," his face, once again, had a smile that revealed his perfectly formed teeth, on his perfectly formed face.

I wanted to vomit on him.

Sofia looked at me, then back at him.

"Oh my god, you are a designer? Wow, that is so cool. I love Prada. I am so envious. I remember you being creative at school, so it doesn't surprise me."

I felt sick; every word spoken was nauseating. I had to try and pull her away from this man before he proposed, and she accepted.

"Well, I *do* okay. To be precise, I work as a shoe designer," he added.

His credibility had just been elevated into orbit. He was a rocket I couldn't catch.

"Wow, that is so *amazing*. I *love* Prada shoes. They are my favourites."

"Do you design men's shoes, then?" she asked.

"Both. I design ladies too."

She looked at me, her jaw on the ground.

"OMG, you design ladies too?" she said, swooning like a puppy with its new owner.

He looked at me.

"What do you do?" he asked me.

He knows full well, I won't be able to beat that whatever answer I give, but I didn't want him to have the upper hand. I had to think fast.

I looked at Sofia and smiled. Then I looked at him and fixed my gaze.

"I'm a car designer."

*There, have a bit of that, you arsehole.*

His face creased with a shocked expression, and he raised his eyebrows. Sofia looked at me and smiled.

"Dave, you are a car designer? Wow, why didn't you tell me this?" she asked.

"Well, I don't like to shout about these things. It's no big deal."

"What kind of cars do you design?" he asked.

I had to take this up a notch. I had to blow him away.

"Maserati."

There, have a slice of that. I've told him I design for an Italian icon - that should kick him into the long grass.

"Wow, Dave, I love Italian sports cars - that is so impressive," she said, her face beaming.

He nodded his head with approval.

"So you're based in Modena, Italy, then?" he asked.

He might probe deeper into my Italian geography, so I needed to sound credible.

"No, I am an international consultant, so I base myself in the UK, but I travel extensively, which does include Modena occasionally, yes."

*Shit*, I have more or less convinced myself that this bull-shit was real.

"Dave, you are so cool. I am so impressed," she said, her face lit up.

She now looked at him more out of sympathy. This was one nil to me, no question.

"But, being a shoe designer is also very impressive, Luigi," she said.

"Well, there's a very good chance you may wear some of my own designs then," he fought back; he wasn't done yet.

"Sofia - I will have to take you out for a drive in my Maserati sometime?" I added, "When you come and visit me in the UK, I mean."

She looked at me, her face all impressed.

"One I have designed, of course."

He was on the ropes, and he was done. His legs had gone.

"It's been lovely meeting you, Luigi, but we need to catch our friends."

He looked at me with an expressionless face. He then looked at Sofia and smiled.

"Maybe I will see you around then?" he told her, his face fixed on hers with not so much as a glance at mine.

He leaned in for a kiss on both her cheeks. I wanted to vomit on his shirt.

"Yes, I'm sure we will bump into each other again," she said.

He slowly walked away towards the Square, looking back to wave. I looked at her and smiled. I had to play it cool.

"What a lovely bloke," I said.

She laughed.

"Is there anyone you don't like?" she asked.

"It's the kind of guy I am, Sofia. I'm a people person."

"*Come on, you two*. I thought *we* were slow," came a distant shout from Doris.

I reached out to clasp Sofia's hand again. She wasn't reluctant as she wasn't swooned by him yet.

Her hand felt soft and warm. I wondered how many more times I would feel this hand in mine, knowing an "Italian Stallion" was sniffing around.

"I can't believe how *long* it has been since I saw him," she added.

*Shit, he really has had an impact on her, hasn't he.*

"He seems very nice," I said.

It was painful just saying those words.

"He was cute, and I liked him, but then his parents returned to Italy, and although we wrote to each other for a while, it fizzled, and I guess that was that."

She smiled, but her eyes told me that it had bothered her a lot at the time.

Okay, so he was an action man, and I was a rag doll, but as far as Sofia is concerned, I'm a rag doll that works for Maserati. I had to maintain that profile, at least for now.

We were soon reunited with Doris and Betty at the entrance to Betty's villa. I glanced at my watch.

*Shit, it's 1:26 a.m.*

Betty turned to face us.

"Right then, does anyone need a taxi?" she asked.

"Could you order one for me and Doris, and we can drop Sofia back off at her house on the way."

I didn't want to give Sofia the impression I was expecting more on a first date. I had to play the long game.

"Come in then while you wait. I'll make us some coffee," Betty suggested.

While Betty and Doris sorted the drinks, Sofia and I walked through to the back of the villa and onto the balcony.

We sat at the plastic white table, illuminated by nothing more than the moonlight and the distant lights of the town.

"So, despite everything, have you had a nice evening?" I asked her.

I was nervous as my confidence had been knocked down after our earlier encounter.

She swiped her hand across her face to fend off a fly.

"I had an amazing time, Dave. Despite everything, I did *enjoy* myself. It was one hell of an adventure."

"Would you like to go on another *adventure* with me, maybe without Doris and Betty and any craziness?"

She laughed.

"There's a charming little fishing hamlet not far from here with a table and our names on it," I said.

She smiled.

"Of course, Dave, I would love to."

"*Back of the net!*" I shouted, with my fists clenched and my arms in the air, as though waving to the imaginary crowd.

She laughed at my animated state.

"So does that mean you're rather pleased I said yes?" she asked.

"More relieved, I think."

She laughed.

"I like you, Dave. You're quirky."

"What's the shouting all about?" asked Doris.

She appeared at the door, holding two coffees.

"Put the light on somebody," shouted Betty.

"Dave was just expressing his happiness at me agreeing to another date," she said.

Doris smiled.

"Excellent news, so he should. I did say Dave was punching above his…"

I interrupted Doris before she could finish.

*"Doris*, Betty has just called you," I said.

"Did she?" she asked, all bemused.

"Best go check, eh?" I suggested.

"Check what?" said Betty, appearing at the door.

Sofia took a sip from her coffee.

"Coffee, alright?" asked Doris.

"Perfect, thank you," said Sofia.

"Wonderful. I *knew* you two would hit it off," said Betty.

Doris smiled more out of politeness, it seemed.

"Well, what a great idea, so where are we all going next then?" Doris asked.

"*Doris,* this is a date for *two* this time, no Doris, no Betty and *most* definitely, *no dog*."

"We wouldn't want to cramp your style, eh Dave," Betty added.

It was as though my suggestion was an outrage and that these two buggers would love nothing more than to be glued to our hips, like something you would see on the program "Undateables" where daters are always accompanied by a chaperone.

Suddenly, our conversation was interrupted by the *beep* from our taxi.

"Right, come on, drink up, ladies," I said, polishing off the last of mine.

Doris and Betty hugged at the door.

"I'll text you tomorrow, Doris," said Betty, followed by a hic-up.

She then grabbed me and planted her lips on mine. It was wet and horrible and totally unforeseen. I did my best not to wipe my face for fear of offending her. She then embraced Sofia, with her "baggy bingo wings" wrapped around her like a wrestler.

"Come on, I don't have all night," said the waiting taxi driver.

Betty waved us off, then closed the door behind her. I looked at Sofia with an inquisitive face.

"Doesn't that taxi driver's voice sound familiar?" I asked.

She laughed.

"It does. That's because it's my father," she said, covering her mouth to contain her amusement.

*I don't bloody believe it.*

This man is like a fungal infection on your toenail, impossible to get rid of.

"Come on, he hates waiting around," Sofia added as we made our way down the path.

Doris looked either pissed or confused, but probably both.

"So he runs a taxi firm too?" I asked, bewildered.

"Yes, and *don't* forget to be nice and tip him!" she added.

"Tip him? I'd rather kick him," I whispered in Doris' ear.

# Chapter 16

I turned over in my bed and squinted at my watch to read the time. It was 7:02 a.m. The sun was already bright enough to render the thin curtains redundant.

I've never been an early bird at the best of times, but I somehow knew I might struggle to get back to sleep because all I could think about was my next date with Sofia.

I rolled on my back and stared at the ceiling. The light fitting was a 1980s relic with no less than eight protruding light bulbs from an era when energy conservation didn't exist.

I could hear Doris switching the kettle on and the click of her zippo lighter as she lit her customary first fag of the day. I then heard the distinct sound of a spoon being tapped on the lip of her cup, followed by the sound of her rinsing the spoon under the tap and putting it on the side.

Although I couldn't hear it, I knew she had put the teabag in the sink, despite the bin being only a few feet away. I also knew she was using an empty cup as an ashtray; she always did, despite the fact there was an ashtray provided.

*"Are you awake yet, Dave?!"* she shouted.

Her shout was followed by a deep rumbling cough as she made her way onto the balcony to finish her fag.

I didn't answer. I never did, but she asks the same question every morning at about the same time. I need coffee before I can even contemplate talking to anyone, let alone Doris.

I closed my eyes and let my thoughts return to the day ahead. I reached for my glass of water, but it wasn't there.

*Why do I make the same schoolboy error every time?*

"*Dave*, are you awake?' she tapped loudly on the door.

"Well, if I wasn't, I am *now Doris.*"

"Can I come in?" she asked, despite already pushing my door open and putting her head through the gap.

"You alright?" I asked.

"Not *exactly*. I have a *bit* of a problem."

This was hardly front-page news.

"Why am I being filled with dread already? Go on, spit it out, what now?"

"I have run out of fags," she said.

"Is that it? I was expecting something a bit juicier?"

"I don't like that man in the local shop. He's a pervert," she added.

"Why is he a pervert?" I asked.

"He always looks me up and down."

"That might have something to do with the fact that on the last few occasions you have been in there, you have either been in your dressing gown or forgot to put your teeth in, or both."

"Anyway, he gives me the creeps."

"I think you're paranoid, Doris."

"Can I ask a favour; just go get me some fags, please?"

"On one condition, you and Betty will not gate crash my date with Sofia tonight under any circumstances."

She smiled.

"You're rather taken by this girl, aren't you?"

"That's the deal. Take it or leave it."

She laughed, shook her head and left the room.

I took a shower, grabbed my shorts, tee and flips and left the villa. Walking down the path towards the main road, I stopped for a moment to admire the view of the valley. I took a deep breath, not unlike a hiker, just before climbing the hill. I just wanted to let the smell of the morning breeze fill my lungs.

*Bloody hell, It feels great.*

Tonight couldn't come quickly enough for me. The road to the shop was bustling with mopeds and cars going about their business as normal. The smell of fresh bread lingered in the distance; there was no better smell.

*I'll get her fags and then go get some pastries. I'll treat her.*

Just before I arrived at the shop, a van pulled alongside me and slowed to match my walking pace.

It was an LDV Pilot.

*Shit, do they still exist.*

It had been white once, in a previous life, back in the factory maybe, but now had more rust than your average farm bucket.

The van then accelerated and stopped a short distance in front of me. The man in the driver's seat wound his window down and stuck his head out in my direction. He had a baseball cap on and large oversized sunglasses. He sported a big head of hair and an unruly beard. He was definitely Greek.

"You *English*?" he asked.

"I am."

*Surely he's not about to ask me for directions?*

"Are you lost?" I asked.

"No, I need a hand to carry some watermelons into the shop if you don't mind. It won't take long," he added.

"Do I get a free one if I help?"

"Yes, sure."

He smiled, got out and led me to the back of the van.

"I haven't got long, mate. How many are there?" I asked.

"Not many," he assured me.

He inserted the key in the double doors and opened them wide.

"Get in," he said.

I turned and looked at him.

"Eh?" I grunted.

*Smack* - His fist met with my face, and I was out cold.

I woke up dazed and confused. My heart was racing, my mouth was dry, and I needed water, but I couldn't see properly. I had a sackcloth or something similar over my head. It was big enough to allow enough air to circulate, but the air was warm and stuffy, and judging by the smell of the material, it had been used to store onions.

I had no concept of how long I had been here. I know I hadn't come out with my mobile, so Doris wouldn't have been able to call me. I could see a tiny amount of daylight through the tiny gaps in the woven material, but that was it.

Thoughts raced around my head.

*This must be a mistaken identity case, that's it. They've got the wrong guy?*

However, I had the sudden realisation that either way, I had been abducted.

I just lay on the floor. It felt wet, maybe greasy, as I slid around when the van changed direction. My hands were tied behind me, and my feet were bound.

*This definitely isn't one of my better starts to a day.*

I once watched a Bear Grylls episode, where he said that most mistakes occur when you panic, so it was imperative that I remained calm.

I jolted from side to side as the van sped along. I couldn't hear any passing traffic, which made me think we must be on some back road somewhere remote.

*Am I in the van alone?*

I squinted and tried to peek through the tiny holes in the sackcloth, but the light wasn't great, as though the van had no rear windows or maybe they had blacked them out to conceal their crime.

We suddenly hit what must have been a pothole; it jolted me onto my side, and I banged my head on the metal floor.

*Shit, that hurt.*

I wanted to cry but had no time to feel sorry for myself. Then another pothole appeared, and my body jerked again, making me slide towards the other side of the van floor. One thing was certain; there were no melons, *just* me in here.

I wriggled my fingers and toes and moved from side to side; nothing hurt or broken.

Suddenly, the van began to slow down and then stopped. Two doors slammed shut.

*So the driver has an accomplice?*

Two sets of foot steps approached the rear of the van. The doors opened, sending in a gush of light. I could just about make out their silhouettes.

"Gentleman, may I suggest you swap your LDV for a Ford Transit for your next abduction? The ride quality would be much smoother for the captive," I said.

"Quite the funny guy, aren't you?" one of them said.

He had a mature voice with a deep rumble, maybe the Greek's answer to Barry White.

"Listen, I don't want to alarm you, but my friend Doris is waiting for her cigarettes and trust me, she hates waiting."

They grabbed me and dragged me out of the van. One had my legs, and the other grabbed my arms. They stood me up against the side panel, with the back of my head pressed against the metal. I didn't object, and I moved like a rag doll.

I didn't feel panicked. They had clearly got the wrong guy, so I did my best to remain calm. I knew that, at any moment, they would realise their error, dump me, and drive away.

"Do you know my mother is Irish?" I asked.

"What?" asked one of them.

"The potato sack you have over my head reminds me of home," I added.

"Shut up," said the other man.

He, too, had a mature voice, but a higher pitch, a much higher pitch.

*Shit, I've just been abducted by the Greeks' answer to Barry White and Barry Gibbs.*

They grabbed an arm each and dragged me along. Dust and gravel scattered as my feet bobbled about helplessly.

"Hey, these were expensive flip-flops, you know. Show some respect," I shouted.

It was all happening too quickly. I couldn't see much, but I could sense I was being taken to some room somewhere, some building, a warehouse, maybe?

One of the men kicked open what sounded like a wooden door. It creaked on its hinges as he forced it open. They then stood me upright while the other man removed the rope that held my ankles together. I was then marched forward a few feet and pressed down onto a hard plastic chair. I sat upright, squinting to see whatever I could.

"*Hello, David,*" came another voice, a new voice.

This guy sounded more normal, a bit more refined. I could just about make out the shape of someone sitting at a desk before me.

"Let me guess, you're good at guessing names, or you have my wallet and ID in your hand?" I asked.

"Do you know *why* you are here, David?" he asked, his tone unchanged, calm, collected, with no emotion.

"Let me guess, I was about to buy the last pack of cigarettes available on the whole island, and your guys *needed* them more?"

"No," he said, again without emotion.

"Let me guess again. This is an audition for the next Mission Impossible film?"

"No," he said.

"Jack Reacher?" I asked.

"No," he said.

"*Tonight*, you and your friend will be boarding a plane back to the UK."

"I don't have a friend; you must have me mistaken for someone more popular," I replied.

"Tonight, you and *your* friend will be boarding a plane back to the UK," he said again.

"Well, that's very kind of you, but that won't be happening for two reasons. Reason one, my holiday isn't over yet, and reason two, I have a *date* tonight."

"*David*, listen to me carefully. Your date will not be happening, and you *will* be leaving the island tonight."

"Do you understand?" he added.

His tone was now cold and direct.

"Okay, so what if I *agree*? What next?"

"We take you back to where we found you, drop you off, and you go back and pack. Our driver will be waiting to take you and your friend to the airport," he concluded.

"And what if I *disagree*?" I asked.

"What we say goes. It's as simple as that. We ask you to do something, and you do it."

"You would make a great *diplomat,*" I added.

There was no comment. I squinted through my mask again and saw the shape of the man who had spoken. He sat at the table in front of me, and his heavies stood on either side of him.

"Has anyone ever suggested you should work in *sales*?" I said.

"Don't try anything silly, David. My colleagues will help you pack your things if you like."

"Make sure I don't forget anything, eh?"

"Correct."

"How do I explain this to my friend?"

"You'll think of something, David. You're a smart guy."

"Listen, you have the wrong guy. This is clearly a mistaken identity case; let me go, and I will say nothing."

He rose from his chair and pushed it under the table. The metal legs squeaked against the floor.

"How do I explain the potato sack over my face? I'm no David Beckham in the looks department, but a bag over my head is a bit extreme, don't you think?" I asked.

"My colleagues will explain what happens next."

"How nice of them."

"Nice meeting you, David. Have a safe flight," he said as he got up and left.

I sat and waited for the next sequence of events. One of the shadowy figures walked towards me and gripped my shoulder.

"Time to go, *arsehole*," the voice whispered in my left ear.

His breath was warm and smelt like stale tobacco.

"You should *seriously* consider a job in hospitality," I said.

## Chapter 17

They dragged me like a rag doll back to the van. They opened the door and forced me inside head first. I dropped to the bare metal floor with a thump. They then pushed me forward by my ankles, like a roll of carpet being forced back on the rack. The doors slammed shut behind me, sucking out what little light I had.

The engine started, followed by the grind and a crunch of the gearbox, and off we went down the bumpy road again.

The van came to a stop after what seemed like ages. Both doors slammed shut, and footsteps approached the back of the van. The creak of metal could be heard from the hinges as though they hadn't been greased since the van had left the factory.

"Ok, *arsehole*, you're here."

"Come on, get up," said his side-kick, his voice pitched even higher than before.

This guy was more excitable than ever. He laughed and sang the words to some Greek song under his breath.

"You sound happy?" I said.

"Shut up," he commanded.

One of them removed my leg ties and dragged me forward by my feet. I sat upright. The other removed the sackcloth off my head and un-tied my hands. I squinted my eyes as they adjusted to the bright light.

I could see our villa; it was a short walk away.

*Shit, I am back from the brink.*

"Gentleman, I hope you don't expect a tip," I said.

I could finally see my captives. The guy with the high-pitched voice was tall and thin, and the guy with the deep voice was short and fat, just how I had imagined them to be.

"This is the next stage, funny guy. This is when we escort you to your villa to help you pack," said the skinny guy.

"Well, that's very kind of you, thank you, and what do I tell my friend?" I asked

"Tell her you have to abandon your holiday early due to work commitments, and we are your taxi to the airport," came a deep rumble from the fat guy.

"What if I run?" I asked.

"If you try, then we might have to shoot you," said the skinny guy, pointing his skinner finger at me.

He looked like a guy who wanted to mean it, but I wasn't convinced. He had arms like rags; he would do well to hold a cigarette without his arm hurting, let alone have the strength to hold a gun.

The skinny guy put his left hand in his jeans pocket and pulled out what looked like the handle of a gun. There was no way of knowing if it was real, and it was clear he wasn't about to take the whole thing out to show me either.

*Is he bluffing?*

I really wasn't arsed, which probably meant I wasn't convinced. The skinny guy walked up to me and stared right into my face. His breath was stale, and his teeth yellowed by years of smoking fags.

"Do exactly what we say, you understand?"

"I wouldn't want to mess with *you*. You look like the sort of guy who works out," I said

The fat guy laughed, but his skinny friend wasn't amused.

"Listen, *funny* guy, don't tempt fate. It won't end well for you," warned the skinny guy.

"Which one is yours?" the skinny guy asked.

He pointed in the direction of the villas.

"Hard to tell; they are so alike, I normally just knock on each one and see who answers," I said.

The fat guy stepped forward and slapped me across the face. It hurt but just a little.

"Which one?" the skinny asked again.

I pointed to the villa next door to ours, and we began to walk towards it.

They walked a few yards behind me and talked in their native tongue. High pitches and deep rumbles, they had a proper chat, as though they were talking about what they were having for tea or who won in the football, like all this was normal, like I was just another parcel who had gotten lost and was now being dispatched to the correct address.

I had to think; the only way to buy time was to walk slowly, pretending my stiffness made me walk like a robot.

"Can you not *walk* any faster, funny guy?" said the fat guy.

I stopped and turned around to face them.

"I can hardly walk. That might have something to do with the fact you bound and gagged me and let me slide around a van for however many miles. That kind of shit hurts; hence, I can't walk any faster."

"Less of your shit, and keep walking," shouted the skinny guy.

We arrived at the villa next door to ours. I took out my key and pushed it into the lock.

"There seems to be a problem. My key isn't working," I said, twisting and turning the key in an exaggerated fashion.

"What do you *mean* it isn't working? Then knock," the fat guy said, clearly agitated.

I knocked. No answer – I prayed that the occupants were out.

"Let's go around the back," the skinny guy suggested.

"I don't have a key for the back door, sorry," I added.

I had managed a sneaky peep at the skinny guy's watch earlier, so I knew I'd been gone for over two hours at least. Doris will probably think I've gone for a walk into town.

"Gentlemen, may I make a suggestion? It looks like my friend Doris has gone out, so I need to call her from my mobile," I suggested.

They both looked at each other and spoke in Greek.

"Listen, we have a plane to catch, right? So the sooner I make that call, the sooner my friend can get back, and we can get packed," I insisted.

The skinny Greek pulled out my phone and handed it to me.

"I thought I had left that back at the villa?"

The skinny guy looked at me, confused.

"We found a wallet and a phone in your pocket, arsehole. This is your phone, right?" he asked.

"Yeah."

"What about my wallet?"

"You don't *need* your wallet to make a call," the fat guy insisted.

"No funny business, funny guy, just make the call," he added.

I looked at the phone: several missed calls from Doris and one text from Sofia.

*I bet Doris is frantic, two hours without a fag.*

I quickly opened the text. It read, "*Hi Dave, looking forward to seeing you later. Sofia xx.*"

My heart raced.

I quickly went onto Google to look up the number for Naxos Police and pressed dial.

"Yes, hello, it's only me. I am locked out of my villa; come quickly. We must leave the island, and we must leave now, so get here now. I need your help," I said.

The voice on the end of the phone was a man. He spoke back to me in English, which was a relief.

"I am sorry. W*hat* exactly do you want us to do? This is the *police*. Do you have the *right* number?" he asked.

I had to keep babbling, making no sense, enough to at least tempt the policeman to come and investigate.

"What do you *mean*, you are in town? Get a taxi, then. You know our address. It's Villa Stavros, the other side of town," I said, praying the guy didn't hang up.

"Villa Stavros, I know where it is, but how can *we* help you? If you're locked out of your villa, call the holiday rep," he said, his tone dismissive.

"No, listen arsehole, get your fat arse here now, or I'm going to beat the shit out of you. You get here now, or I will smash this place up."

I looked at my captives. They stood back, gobsmacked.

*"Shit* – do you always talk to your friend like that?" asked the fat guy.

I looked at my phone again, checking he hadn't hung up, and the call was still connected.

"You fucking *dumb fuck*, I will burn this place down if you don't get your fat arse over here now," *that should do it.*

The phone went dead. They both stood there looking at me. The skinny guy looked at his watch.

"Your friend better get her arse here and fast," he shouted.

He took out a pack of cigarettes from his top pocket, pulled one out, placed it on the tip of his lip and offered one to his fat friend.

"How long will she be?" The skinny guy asked.

"She'll be here in five minutes. She was out shopping, and you know what women are like; they love *shopping*."

The skinny guy dragged on his cig like it was his last. He exhaled, picked at a tobacco flake stuck between his teeth, and spat it out. He was a poor man's Clint Eastwood.

The fat guy was playing on his mobile, like he was passing the time with some stock phone game, maybe snakes, as his phone looked at least ten years old. It was held together with black tape like he'd dropped it many times. He tapped away with his fat fingers, his face transfixed.

"So, did you have a nice time, funny guy? Good holiday?" asked the skinny guy.

"You should get a job in customer services; you're wasted on this shit?" I said.

He smiled, taking another drag of his cig.

"Answer to your question, of course. The best bit was meeting you two clowns.

"*Clowns*, and what makes you think we are clowns?" he shouted over to Fatty to get his attention.

"Hey, funny guy thinks we are clowns."

Fatty looked and laughed.

"Because only a couple of clowns would be daft enough to hand back my mobile phone, so I can call the police," I said, my turn to be smug.

"You're bluffing," said the skinny guy, his hands moving from his pockets to his hips.

He spat his cigarette on the floor and squashed it with his left shoe.

"Nice try, funny guy," said his mate as he finished his game of snake and put his phone back in his pocket.

"Ring her again," said the skinny guy, pointing to the phone in my hand.

"I don't need to," I said.

Looking to my left, I could see Doris walking towards us, but too far away to recognise me yet. Both of them looked, their eyes fixed on the spindly figure in the distance.

"Doris!" I shouted.

She looked up.

"Where have you bloody been? You've been gone for ages. I was *gasping* for a fag."

"Oh, have you met some new friends?" she asked.

Doris put her bag down and stood there with her hand on her hips.

"Well, aren't you going to introduce me? I do apologise. My friend Dave has clearly forgotten his manners."

Skinny and fatty stood side by side, speechless, occasionally glancing at each other, as though both were now aware this was off the script, not part of their plan, and they were devoid of ideas or solutions to get this shit back on track.

"Doris, meet the Greeks' answer to Barry White and Barry Gibb. They are a tribute act and very good by all accounts. They are here to personally escort us to their gig tonight, aren't they kind?" I said.

"I thought you had another *date* tonight?" she asked, all confused.

"There *won't* be any date. I thought we told *you* to tell your friend that you had to go home early due to business commitments," said the skinny guy.

"What's going on, Dave?"

"Don't worry, I will let them explain everything to the policeman," I added.

"What policeman?" the fat guy asked, whilst laughing.

I pointed to a police car heading towards me from a short distance away. They both looked at each other, emotionless.

The police car stopped just in front of us. It had seen better days. The car was a blue Fiat Panda with white stripes on the doors and a half-broken blue light on the roof. The cop looked snug, not because the car was small, but because he was twice the size of the vehicle.

It looked like he'd need a tin opener to get him out. The policeman popped his head out of the window and grunted.

Doris looked bewildered.

"Dave, what's going on?" she asked.

My Greek captives didn't say a word. They stood rooted.

"Are you the English guy who rang about the villa?" he asked.

"I am," I said.

"Do you normally shout abuse down the phone at a policeman?" he asked.

"*Always,*" I said; I couldn't resist.

"So you're not about to set fire to your villa then or smash it up?" he asked.

"Dave, what's going on?" said Doris, agitated.

"Officer, it was a ploy to get you here - these clowns kidnapped me, took me to some random warehouse and told me and my friend here that we had to leave the island tonight. These heavies held me captive for over two hours, with no explanation."

Doris stepped forward.

"Heavies? Well, he looks *heavy,* but that one looks like he needs a good meal inside him," she shouted.

The skinny guy looked at the policeman and smiled.

"This Englishman is crazy. He has been taking drugs," he said, while he made some kind of hand gesture towards his nose in an attempt to mimic snorting.

"Dave, I have the key to the *villa.* It's here," Doris interjected.

The cop looked at me bewildered.

"So you are saying these men kidnapped you, and you are saying this guy is crazy on drugs, and you lady are saying he isn't locked out of his villa. Is this a joke?" the cop was now in a mild rage.

He scratched the stubble on his fat, sweaty face and contorted his features as though thinking about what to do next.

The two guys looked at me as I took my mobile phone out.

“Smile, guys," I said, pointing the phone towards them and taking their picture.

I’m not sure why or what for, but it might be useful later.

“None of this makes any sense to me. I think you all need to go about your business and stop wasting police time. You understand me, Englishman?”

The cop then looked at the two Greeks, who nodded and exchanged some words in Greek.

“What about my wallet?” I asked the Skinny guy.

He looked shifty.

“I don’t have your wallet? What are you talking about?” said the skinny guy.

The cop looked at the skinny guy.

“Do you have this guy’s wallet?” he asked.

“He does, and I want it back,” I asked.

The cop opened his car door, unfastened his seat belt, and exited.

“Stay where you are,” he told the skinny guy while the fat guy stepped to one side and watched.

The skinny guy pulled my wallet out of his pocket and handed it to me.

“Why have you got his wallet?” the cop asked.

“I saw him drop it and picked it up,” he said.

"Why didn't you hand it back?" he asked.

"I was just about to when you arrived," he said.

"Is there anything else of his in your possession?" the cop asked.

"No!" he said.

"Please go about your business and do not waste any more Police time."

Fatty and skinny slowly began to walk down the road, exchanging rants in Greek.

The cop sat, watching them walk away. He looked at me and smiled.

"You ok?" he asked.

"Never better, and thank you," I said.

"If they give you any more trouble, just call me."

"You know them?" I asked

He nodded his head.

"I have seen them about," he said.

"Are they trouble?" I asked.

"We have lifted them a few times, petty theft, the odd brawl, nothing major."

"They did kidnap me, you know, tied me up and tossed me in the back of a van."

He looked puzzled.

"Then why didn't you say that?" he asked.

"My word against theirs, no witnesses," I said.

"I don't see any cuts and bruises on you. If they did what you say they did, there is not much evidence," he added.

"Bastards," I said.

"Keep away from them," he added.

"Dave, can we get indoors now, please?'

The policeman squeezed back into his car, started the engine and stuck his head out the window.

"Listen, stay out of trouble."

He then drove away.

I looked at Doris.

"Well - Did you get my fags then or what?" she asked.

"Oh *shit,* sorry."

"Where *have* you been, Dave?" she asked.

I shook my head in disbelief.

"I went for a drive in the country."

"You do *worry* me, Dave. Your head has been in the clouds since all this Sofia stuff. You need to get a grip," she added.

"I've already been gripped once today, Doris. I will pass on that suggestion."

She looked at me, her face blank.

"You smell of *onions,* Dave."

"Do I?"

“If that’s your aftershave, Dave, I suggest you buy another before taking Sofia out.”

“I think you might be right, Doris.”

“Come on then. Let’s run you a bath. You can’t be *stinking* for your second date.”

# Chapter 18

"Which pair of shoes should I wear, Doris?" I shouted from the bedroom through to the balcony, where she was sitting quietly having a fag.

"*I'm having a fag,*" she shouted.

"Yeah, I *gathered.*"

*"I had to get my own fags in the end, Dave, and you know I hate going to the local shop; the man who owns it is a pervert."*

"Yeah, you told me."

I made my way to the balcony and put a selection of shoes on the table.

"I'm wearing jeans, so which ones do you think work best?"

She took another drag on her fag and flicked the ash into the empty cup. Her face was pensive as she looked at the selection.

“Well, what do you think?” I asked.

She took another drag on her fag and looked at another pair.

“Why do you never use the ashtray provided?”

She looked up and tutted.

“Do you want my opinion or not?”

“No rush. It’s not like I’m getting ready for a date or anything.”

She took another drag.

“What do I *think* – I *think* you have too many shoes, that’s what I think,” she said.

“Don’t apply for a job in a shoe shop anytime soon, Doris.”

“I think you should go casual.”

“How casual?” I asked.

“Well, when I spoke with Sofia yesterday, she mentioned your next date. She said she wanted to do something low-key, maybe even just hanging out on the beach,” she said.

“So no shoes then, maybe just flip-flops? Is that what you’re suggesting?”

“I think just shorts, a T-shirt and your flip-flops, Dave. Seriously, she was suggesting very casual, so no point dressing up.”

“Just a bit strange; she never mentioned anything to me.”

“No, that’s because when she mentioned it to me in passing, I said I’d make sure I’d let you know,” she said.

“You’ll be on the payroll next, Doris!”

“What do you mean?”

“As my PA,” I said.

“As long as you pay me the going rate, Dave, I’d even wash your underpants,” she added with a cheeky laugh.

“Keep your hands off my underpants if you don’t mind, and I wear boxers. This isn’t 1980; fashion has moved on,” I said.

“What would you pay me?” she asked.

“The going rate for a walking liability is about ten pence an hour, Doris.”

“Ten pence - they pay more than that to those Polish tomato pickers.”

“Polish?” I asked.

“Them tall, skinhead types from that cold part of Europe,” she added.

“Not all Polish people are skinheads, Doris,” I laughed.

“The men are,” she said, all serious.

“What about the women?” I asked.

“Yeah, them too,” she said.

“I’ve been to Poland, Doris, but I don’t recall seeing either.”

She shook her head while taking another drag on her fag.

“Right, I’m off for a shower.”

“Remember, keep it causal, Dave.”

I looked back at her, “Yeah, I heard. I will.”

About half an hour later, I was ready.

I walked back onto the balcony and stood before her.

“What do you think?” I asked.

“I think you have horrible feet, Dave. That’s what I think,” she claimed.

“Everyone has *shit* feet, Doris.”

“I bet Sofia doesn’t,” she said.

“Listen, nobody looks at your feet,” I added.

“Well, I hope so, for your sake,” she said, chuckling to herself.

She was sitting reading a magazine, or at least pretending. She took her glasses off her face and looked me up and down.

“What you smiling at?” I asked.

“Oh, Dave, you always make me smile,” she flicked another page.

“Will I do then? This isn't *too* casual?”

“No, it’s perfect,” she said with another big smile.

“So, dare I ask, what are *your* plans for this evening?” I asked.

"Betty is out with her husband tonight, so it looks like I'm on my own."

"Will you watch the tele?" I asked.

"It's all in bloody Greek, Dave. What good's that to me?" she said, shaking her head.

"You can just look at the pictures. You don't need to know what's going on," I added.

"What use is that?" she asked.

"Well, it's no different than pretending to read your magazines when we both know you just look at the pictures," I said, smiling back at her.

"You cheeky bugger, of course, I *read* the content," she insisted.

"Give it here," I put my hand out, grabbed the mag, and looked at the page she was on.

"Okay then, what's this article about?"

She looked lost.

"Hmmm – well, it's about, you know, people's lives," she said.

"What are their names?" I asked, "Yeah, their names, it tells you here, so who are they, and what's it about?" I added.

"Oh, Dave, I don't bloody know," she said.

She reached out to try and snatch it back.

"Shouldn't you be going?" she asked.

"You're right, Doris! Right, I'm off, don't wait up."

"Enjoy!" she shouted as I closed the door behind me.

I walked to the end of the road and grabbed the attention of the first taxi I could see. It pulled over, and I got in the front seat.

"*Where you want go*?" the bloke asked, his English a bit broken.

"Stavros vineyard, do you know it?" I asked.

He nodded, "Yeah, yeah, I know it - will be about ten euros, okay?" he asked.

"Fine, mate, no problem."

I sat back and reflected on the recent abduction.

*He, too, could be one of Stavros' heavies.*

I pondered again about the two clowns I'd encountered earlier and their possible connection with Stavros. What I couldn't do was just assume; I needed more evidence.

"You *know* Stavros?" I asked.

He glanced at me.

"*Yeah*, I know Stavros. He's *good* man. I like him. He does a lot for community," he said.

I nodded my head.

I thought, *that doesn't sound like someone who goes around arranging the kidnap of tourists, but then I'm sure Pablo Escobar did a lot for his community too.*

I had to maintain my suspicion.

We soon arrived at the gate to the house, I paid the man, and he drove away. I pressed the intercom on the gate and waited. There was no response, but then the electric gates suddenly opened, and I walked through tentatively.

I stopped outside the familiar-looking blue door and took a deep breath. I lifted the cast iron knocker, tapped it thrice, stepped back, and waited. The security light came on, and I could see some movement through one of the windows.

The door opened slowly, and to my relief, Barbara stood there before me, all smiley.

"Hi Luv, you are here to take Sofia out, I presume?"

"No – I'm here to take your husband out for a pint," I said.

She laughed.

"He'd *love* that," she said, her face all serious as if to suggest he actually wouldn't.

"Well, don't just stand there, Dave. Come on in, luv, take the weight off your feet. Would you like a drink?"

She was the perfect host, as always.

Closing the door behind me, I followed her into the kitchen. I looked around nervously, but there was no sign of Stavros.

"Sofia is still getting ready, luv. Sit down, relax," she said.

She opened the fridge door and took out a bottle of beer.

I could hear the distant sound of a hair dryer.

"Is that Stavros I can hear getting ready?" I asked.

Babs laughed.

"He actually scrubs up rather well, you know," she insisted, handing me a bottle of Mythos.

"Is your husband out t*onight,* then?" I asked.

"No, I'm *not* out," came a deep rumble from the room next door.

*Bloody hell, this guy could hear a pin drop.*

He walked into the kitchen and made his presence known. Babs sat at the table, and Stavros stood beside her. His face, as always, was expressionless.

"Is this some kind of joke?" he asked, looking me up and down, "Do you always make such little effort on a date?" he asked.

Suddenly - Sofia appeared through the other door.

"Oh, hi Dave – oh, you're casual," she said, her face confused.

She was wearing an elegant black full-length black dress, heels to match and an expensive-looking leather handbag.

*Oh fuck.*

"So when you take my daughter to the casino, you dress like a tramp, do you?" he asked.

Babs didn't say a word.

"But I don't understand. Doris told me you told her earlier that you wanted a low-key evening, a 'dress casual' evening, maybe even hanging out at a couple of beach bars?" I said.

"That's interesting, Dave, because she told me you had told her you would be taking me to the casino tonight," Sofia said.

I looked at Stavros.

"You see, it wasn't deliberate. My *friend* Doris appears to have an interesting sense of humour."

Sofia laughed.

Babs laughed.

"Sounds like Doris has set you up, Dave," she laughed again.

"Listen, it's cool. I don't mind. I will go and change into something a little less glam," she said.

"Hey, no, you look amazing. Let me go back to the villa and get changed."

"No, it's no *problem,* Dave. It won't take me long."

Sofia made a quick exit up the staircase.

*I could strangle Doris.*

"Don't worry, luv, stuff happens, wires crossed," said Babs.

"Wires crossed? I'll be wrapping Doris up in wire when I see her," I said.

Stavros wasn't amused. He looked at Babs and then back at me, his face creased with confusion.

"Don't have a go at him, *Stavros*. He's done *nothing* wrong," said Babs.

He was incapable of making any kind of positive conversation with me.

"*Listen* to me; she is a good girl. You look after her, you hear," he pointed his fat finger at me.

He meant every word.

"How long have you got left before you go *home*?" he asked.

"Do you know, I very nearly had my holiday cut short," I said.

Babs looked confused, "Oh, why was that then?" she asked.

"Some guys didn't want me hanging around, it would seem. It got messy," I said.

"Oh my god, what happened, luv? Did someone try and mug you?"

"No, just a few guys looking for trouble. I sorted it."

"Locals?" Babs asked.

"Greeks answer to the chuckle brothers," I said, smiling at Babs.

Babs laughed.

I watched Stavros' body language just to see if there was the slightest inkling that he was behind my abduction.

He didn't even flinch, no emotion.

"Sit down. You make my home look untidy," he said.

I sat opposite Babs, grabbed my beer, took a nervous swig, and smiled.

"Lovely evening, isn't it," I said, looking up at Stavros.

"It *was*," he said.

He looked over towards the staircase as though he expected Sofia to walk in at any moment. Babs sipped from her glass of wine.

"David, unfortunately for you, my husband is very protective of his daughter."

"Really - I hadn't noticed," I replied, taking another swig of beer.

I put my beer back on the table, looked at them both, and smiled.

"You haven't put poison in this, have you?" I said, looking at Stavros.

Babs laughed. He said nothing. His face was deadpan as ever. I grasped my neck with both hands and mimicked the effects of choking.

She laughed again, louder.

I was doing my best to break the ice with Stavros. It wasn't working. He walked off into the next room and closed the door behind him.

Babs smiled.

"Listen, he'll come around. It's not that he doesn't like you; he does."

"Oh, I know. I can feel his warmth," I said.

I took another swig from my bottle. Babs laughed.

"He's a big softy, really."

"I'm sure a grizzly bear is, too, from a distance, but it's not something I'd want to cuddle," I said.

"No, *seriously,* he's a real people person," she insisted.

"I'll take your word for it, Babs."

"Another bottle of beer while you wait?" she asked.

She opened the fridge door and pulled out another.

"Thanks, Babs, you're very hospitable."

"You're welcome, luv."

I took the opportunity to digress while we still waited for Sofia.

"I guess with such a large-scale business and all the land that goes with it, you'd need to employ *security*?" I asked.

Babs was a little surprised by the topic shift.

"Yeah, we employ a few chaps who patrol the perimeter at night, but Stavros sorts all that out," she said, helping herself to another glass of wine.

“Do you meet them from time to time?” I asked.

“I see them occasionally in passing, and they seem nice enough. As far as I know, there are only two or three of them. It’s hardly protecting the crown jewels; it’s only a few grapes,” she said.

I was about to ask more questions when Sofia returned to the kitchen.

“Dave, I’m so sorry. It appears it takes just as long dressing down as it does dressing up,” she said.

“Darling, you look fab,” Babs said, raising her glass to toast her attire.

She was wearing a pair of hot pants, a long, baggy T-shirt with some brand I didn’t recognise splashed across the middle of her chest and a pair of Converse pumps. Her hair was thick and curly and hung down over her shoulders. She wore next to no make-up but still somehow looked insanely attractive.

In my opinion, some girls are like cars; they only look good when washed, waxed and polished, but she was different. She could do absolutely nothing to her exterior and still, somehow, look a million dollars.

“Right then, are we ready?” I asked while standing up from the table.

Babs gave us her best “Bee-Gee” smile.

“Listen, you two. Play safe and stay safe, eh,” she instructed, as though we were a pair of eighteen-year-olds.

"You don't want to bump into the chuckle brothers again, do you?" she laughed.

"Who are the chuckle brothers?" Sofia asked.

"I'll tell you later," I said.

"Stavros!!" Babs shouted.

"Can you be a *love* and drop these two off in town?" she shouted.

"I'm *busy*," he shouted back.

"It won't take you more than *ten minutes*," she shouted.

Moments later, he walked back into the kitchen and grunted.

"I'll grab my keys," he said, as happy as ever.

I looked at Sofia.

"He'll probably put us in the back of his *tractor*," I said.

"No, he likes his cars, Dave," she replied.

"Eh, I've seen his car. I sat in the back of it, remember?"

She laughed.

"We made our way out the front door and into the courtyard. There was no sign of Stavros and his clapped-out Fiat.

"He won't be long," Sofia suggested.

Out of sight, round the corner, came a deep rumble. It was loud - it sounded like a monster, whatever it was. Then, it appeared to get closer. I could hear the sound of tyres on loose gravel. Within moments, there before us, in all its glory, was an Aston Martin.

"What happened to his Fiat?" I asked.

She smiled.

"He only uses that to grab stuff from the supermarket."

*What's such a nice car doing, being driven by such an arsehole?*

"I'm impressed."

*"See*, I told you he *likes* his cars," she said.

I opened the passenger door and leaned my head in.

"Lovely car, Stavros," I said.

There was no comment, not even a look in my direction.

"You get in the back. Sofia can sit in the front," he said.

I didn't argue. I just clambered over the front seat and into the back. It was sardine-tin-tight back here. Even a hobbit would complain about the lack of legroom.

We made our way out of the grounds and onto the main road.

"So, Sofia tells me you like your sports cars?" I said.

"Yes," he replied.

"It's his pride and joy, Dave. He loves it," Sofia added.

"It doesn't come as a great surprise, Sofia. I can see your dad is a man with great taste."

I was just filling the gaps in the conversation with bullshit; he didn't like me, and no amount of compliments would change that.

"The engine makes a lovely sound, Stavros."

No comment.

Sofia then began to speak to him in Greek. That was fine by me as it meant I didn't have to make any more small talk.

"There's a nice little beachfront bar I'm taking you to, Dave. It's not far."

"Sounds like a plan," I replied.

I peered out the window and saw a cluster of bars straight ahead; it looked busy.

"I'm sure we can find a dark little corner somewhere in one of these bars," I said.

Stavros made his face visible in the windscreen mirror. He was doing his very best snake-eye impression. Good, it was just the reaction I wanted.

"Dark little corner?" Sofia said, laughing.

"I'm an English romantic, Sofia. I can't help myself."

I made eye contact again with Stavros in his mirror. His face creased with a frown.

"Oh, Dave, why can't Greek men be as romantic as you?" she asked, laughing again.

The road narrowed and suddenly we were hit by traffic. Noisy mopeds weaved in and out, and Stavros beeped his horn.

Suddenly, I could hear some shouts in our direction.

I peered to see who it was. A man started to walk towards our car. He looked vaguely familiar. In fact, as he got nearer, the more familiar he looked.

*Shit, no way. It's skinny guy! Well, what a coincidence.*

Stavros put his window down and stuck his head out. He shouted something in Greek. The skinny guy kept walking towards us.

Sofia looked back at me.

"He works at the vineyard," she said.

"Oh, I thought I recognised him. Is he a fruit picker?" I asked.

"No, he looks after the *security*," she said.

If Stavros wanted him to go away, it was having the opposite effect. Suddenly, the skinny guy appeared beside the driver's window and looked in. He waved at Sofia but didn't notice me sitting in the back.

I had two options: make myself known or stay out of the way and hope he doesn't spot me. I opted for the latter. If he spotted me, it could all kick off, and my evening would be ruined. I made myself as small as possible and kept my head down.

The conversation was brief, not out of the skinny guy's choice, but because the traffic was moving, and our car also began moving forward.

They waved him off, and Stavros put his window back up.

"He seemed like a nice man," I couldn't help myself.

No comment from Stavros.

"Yeah, he's practically a member of the family. He would do anything for us," she added.

"I'm sure he *would*," I said, "He looks like the sort of guy that works in pest control," I couldn't resist.

Sofia laughed, "Funny you should say that. Yes, he does put down rat traps from time to time."

I was pressed into the seat with a sudden burst of acceleration. Stavros was clearly rumbled; he just wanted to get me out of his car as fast as possible.

The car then slowed and stopped outside a bar.

"Ok, we're *here*," she said.

Sofia spoke to Stavros in Greek. She opened her door and stepped out, then leaned in and pulled the seat forward to help me out.

I looked at Stavros, but he made no eye contact.

"Thank you, Stavros, you are a true gent," I said, looking back at him.

“Dave, you’ll make my dad blush with all these compliments,” she added.

She walked round to the driver’s side and leaned in the window to kiss him on the cheek.

He then looked across at me. I waved and smiled. He showed no emotion; he just flawed the throttle and sped off up the road.

“Right then, Mr. Englishman, are you going to show this Greek girl a good time?” she said, all smiley.

“Well, I’ll certainly do my best.”

## Chapter 19

The bar was a blend of white-washed stone walls and wide plank flooring, blue-painted rectangle wooden tables and nautical-themed lighting. Long white linen curtains hung from deep recessed windows. They gently moved and flickered with the evening breeze.

The front was lively, but the rear was more intimate. The tables were spaced apart to allow for a more intimate setting without knocking elbows with fellow diners. I liked it; Sofia had good taste.

“What about that table over there?” Sofia said.

She pointed to a dark corner, lit by the faintest of flicker from a lantern; it looked perfect.

We both slumped back on the sofa and looked at each other.

“Good choice, Sofia. I like your style.”

“Romantic, don’t you think?” she asked.

"*Very*."

"Only *one* slight problem," I stated while picking up the drinks menus and handing her one.

"Problem?" she asked.

"I have many talents, but reading a menu in the dark isn't one of them," I said.

"I know what's on the menu. You need to take my hand and let me guide you," she said.

She grabbed my hands in hers and smiled.

"You can guide me anywhere you like," I said.

She laughed.

"So, may I suggest a cocktail? They make the *best* here, seriously," she said.

She raised her arms aloft to get the attention of a passing waiter. The waiter approached.

"*Hello*, how are you?" he asked.

"Dave, do you like rum?" Sofia asked.

"What are you thinking? Mohettos?" I asked.

"You have *read* my mind," she said.

She turned to the waiter and ordered two drinks in Greek.

The place had a great vibe. A gentle backdrop of melodic trance music, instrumental and ambient mixes set the mood. It was loud enough to be heard, but not too loud to be intrusive.

The waiter returned with our drinks.

"Try that," she said.

I grabbed the straws and tucked them in.

"*Bloody hell*, that's strong, but very nice; perfect choice," I said, taking another slurp.

"Are you *trying* to get me drunk?" I asked.

She laughed again.

"I might be? Why, you don't like the idea of a Greek girl taking control?"

"I'm not so sure your father would approve," I said.

"He *does* approve, Dave. He likes you," she said.

"It feels like a cat stalking a mouse. I'm not so sure I would use the word 'like' quite so freely?" I said.

"He doesn't see the point in a *holiday* romance," she added, taking another sip of her drink.

"I'm sure when he met Barbara for the first time - it was *just* a holiday romance?" I said.

"*Exactly,* Dave."

She smiled, taking another sip from her drink. I was playing it cool, but ultimately, inside, I was beaming.

"It's nice just to spend some time together without any distractions," I said.

"I *know.* It's been quite a challenge, wouldn't you agree?" she said.

Something had caught her attention. I looked but couldn't see what.

“What?” I asked.

“I don’t want to *worry* you, but look over there,” she said.

I looked.

“It’s Betty at the bar with her husband,” she said.

“She won’t see us sitting here, don’t worry about it,” I assured her.

“It’s not that I don’t like Betty, I do, but I’m not so sure I could cope with her tonight,” she added.

*I couldn’t agree more.*

“Excuse me, sir, would you like another lantern?” a waiter's voice appeared at our table.

He placed another lantern next to us, smiled and walked away. Our table was now lit up like a football pitch.

“Maybe Betty asked him to bring one over?” I said.

“I think you might be a little paranoid, Dave?” she said, laughing.

“I’ve got a reason,” I said.

“Don’t worry, I’ll fix it.”

She lifted it and placed it on the floor beside the table.

“*Dave*, is that you I see *hiding* in the corner?” came the voice of doom from the bar area.

I looked at Sofia.

“What did I tell you?” I said, shaking my head.

"What a *coincidence*," Betty shouted.

We both looked over to see her waving at us.

"Hi, Betty," shouted Sofia.

I waved and gave a half smile.

"*I've just texted Doris* to ask if she fancies joining us," she shouted.

I looked at Sofia and shook my head again.

"Are you aware of any other dark, secluded bars on the island?" I asked.

"There are a few caves we could try?" she said.

She did her best not to laugh.

"How fast can you drink that drink?" I asked.

"*Very*," she said, laughing.

"Can you run fast?" I asked.

"*Very*," she said.

I looked over at Betty.

"*Betty*, we have booked a table at another restaurant, so we aren't staying long," I shouted.

"What a coincidence, we haven't eaten yet either. Should we join you?" she shouted.

Sofia looked at me, "Dave – what are we going to do?"

"*Relax*, I'll sort it," I said, squeezing her hand with reassurance.

"*Betty*, I'm really sorry, but when I said restaurant, I actually meant it was a table booked for just two, sorry," I explained.

"Oh well, that's a shame. Never mind, maybe next time, eh."

"Of course, Betty," I said.

I looked at Sofia.

"See, I told you, we can now chill at least, finish our cocktails and then get the hell out of here," I said.

"There are no *restaurants* around here, Dave. We will have to grab a taxi into town," she said.

"We could just slip into the bar next door. What are the chances of them following us?" I asked.

She looked over at Betty and her husband, who were engrossed in conversation, then looked back at me.

"Let's get out of here while they're not looking," she suggested.

She quickly finished the last of her drink and put a piece of mint in her mouth to chew.

I picked up one of the lanterns, opened the little glass door and blew out the candle inside. I then left money to cover the drinks on the table.

"That should assist with our escape," I whispered in her ear.

We quietly moved away from the table and slipped into the bar next door. This bar looked like a "locals" bar; there were no "tourist types" here. It was busy and short of options to hide.

We found a couple of stools at the bar and sat down.

"Another cocktail?" I asked.

"Why not," she agreed, grabbing the drinks menu.

*"You two didn't get far,"* came a shout from behind.

"Permission to swear," I said, looking at Sofia.

"Permission granted," she said, doing her best not to laugh.

"For fucks sake," I whispered.

Suddenly, Betty's face appeared between us.

"Is it one more for the road before you go to the restaurant?" she asked.

Betty was loving this.

"Have I introduced you to my husband, *Brian*?" she asked.

"I don't believe we've had the pleasure," I said, turning my stool to face him.

Brian looked a similar age to Betty, equally short and stocky, and sporting a thick black beard. He was short and tanned. He wore a pink Lyle & Scott polo shirt and tan chinos. He looked like he was about to go for a round of golf.

"You *must* be Dave," he asked, his hand reaching out to shake mine.

He then looked at Sofia – "and this must be your wife?" he asked.

Sofia laughed. Betty laughed even louder. It was exaggerated and a tad animated.

"Oh *Brian*, they are just dating, darling," she said.

"Oh, I see – one of them *holiday* romances, is it?" he asked.

"I think Dave would like it to be a bit more than a holiday romance," came the unmistakable voice of – *Doris from behind.*

"*Doris*, what are you doing here? I left you with a magazine and Greek TV?" I said.

"My fault, Dave, I invited her," Betty said, almost apologetic.

"Well, listen guys, without sounding rude, what chance is there of any romance when we keep getting ambushed by you lot?" I said.

"Let's all calm down. No harm done. I can see Dave has a very valid point. We won't be cramping your style any *longer*," said Brian.

"*Brian*, are you a diplomat?" I asked.

"No," he said.

"You should be," I claimed.

"Dave, may I have a word in your ear?" he asked.

"Sure," I leaned forward so he could say his piece.

“You’re a *very lucky* man,” he whispered.

“What, having a friend like Doris?” I asked.

He laughed.

“I think you know what I mean,” he said.

His face creased with a big smile.

“Lucky?” I said.

“Brian, seriously, if I bought a graveyard, people would stop dying,” I said.

He laughed, then looked at Doris and Betty.

“Right, you two, come on, we can go and have a drink somewhere else,” he said.

He grabbed them both by the arm and escorted them to the exit.

“See you two love birds later, Dave,” shouted Betty.

I looked at Sofia and smiled.

“He’d make a good doorman, too,” I said.

She laughed, but I could also see the relief on her face. I sat back on my stool and grabbed my cocktail.

“It’s exhausting,” she said, sipping her drink.

“Do you fancy going for a walk on the beach after these?” I asked.

She smiled and nodded.

“You’re quite the romantic, aren’t you?” she asked.

“I do try,” I said, taking a big gulp from my glass.

*If she sees me polishing mine off quickly, she'll get the hint.*

We finished our drinks and made our way to the beachfront. It was a warm evening, with just a gentle breeze. The sea could be heard crashing on the rocks a short distance away. It was a sound I could never get tired of.

We walked hand in hand.

*This doesn't feel like a holiday romance. It feels real.*

"You *okay,* Dave?"

"Don't know if it was that cocktail or something I'd eaten earlier, but my stomach feels a bit iffy," I said, reaching to undo a button on my shorts.

"Iffy, what does that mean?" I asked.

"Oh, sorry, it's an English expression for when you feel bloated," I explained.

"Agh, okay, I see."

It got worse by the second. Suddenly, discomfort turned to cramps. I had to stop and crouch to my knees in pain.

"Dave, do you need a bathroom?" she asked.

My stomach rumbled again, and I creased.

"Can you walk?" she said, her face etched with fear.

She helped me back to my feet, but no sooner had I stood up that I felt my bottom muscles give way, and what could only be described as a sudden wet sensation filled my boxers.

This was quite possibly the worst moment of my life. It was worse than failing my driving test for the third time, which was a low point.

*Oh fuck, oh fuck of all fucks – I have shit myself.*

I began to walk like John Wayne.

"Dave, you're all hot and sweaty. Let's get you to a *bathroom*," she insisted, her arm around my waist.

"Listen – I have a bit of a problem down below," I explained.

"Yes, I know," she said.

"No, stop, listen – I really don't know how to say this. I'm so embarrassed," I said.

The deposit in my pants went from warm to cold rather quickly. The acidity made my bum cheeks tender, and just walking a few steps made for a painful experience.

"I have had a serious accident down below," I explained.

"Oh my god, what is that smell?" she asked.

"It must be something I had eaten earlier."

"Oh, my God," she said, her hand over her mouth.

"Not even God can help me now," I said.

"Oh Dave - listen, don't panic, you poor thing, let's grab a taxi back to yours," she suggested.

I reached into my pocket to grab my key.

"Oh *shit*," I said.

Sofia looked horrified, “What *again*?” she asked.

“No, I mean, I’ve *forgotten* my key,” I pulled my hand out of my pocket, empty.

She was thinking.

“Right, well, you need to clean yourself up, Dave. You’ll have to come back to my house.”

“Sofia, I can’t face your dad like this. Is there any chance you can sneak me into the house without being seen?”

I was frantic.

“Listen, we’ll work something out. Let’s grab a taxi,” she said.

We got back onto the main road and flagged a taxi down.

“Wait, what if the driver complains about the smell?” I asked.

“Don’t worry, I’ll just make sure you sit in the back with the window down, and I will sit in the front and keep him talking.”

We managed to return to her house without any additional drama, but I was in a bad way.

Twice in one evening, I found myself outside the metal gates to her father’s empire. We asked the taxi driver to wait a short distance away before discussing our strategy for getting in and out of the house unnoticed.

The house was in darkness.

"It's only 9:40, a little early for them to be in bed, isn't it?" I asked.

Sofia looked at me as if to suggest that was normal.

"They do sometimes have an early night, which is good news for us because it means we can creep in and out without being seen."

"I admire your confidence."

"I have a key for the side gate, just follow me," she said.

We crept across the lawns and over to another gate leading us into the rear of the courtyard.

"I would normally go in the front way, but I think getting in via the kitchen is the best idea," she proposed.

"Listen, I may have to throw away my old boxer shorts. I'm really sorry, Sofia. I'm so embarrassed."

*"Dave*, don't panic. You can borrow a pair of my fathers."

There was no way of knowing if she was taking the piss or being deadly serious.

"I *know*, but I will need to throw these ones away," I said.

"Just take them off in the bathroom and hand them to me. I will get rid of them."

"I can't let you handle them. You'll be traumatised for life," I said.

"Just give me a plastic bag, and I will seal them, and we can take them with us when we leave. It'll be easier to dispose of them in town," I said.

"Okay, good thinking. I will grab a plastic bag from the kitchen," she said.

The door to the kitchen creaked ever so slightly as we made our way into the room.

"Right, you go to the bathroom. I will be there in a moment. Just let me find a plastic bag," she said.

"Where's the bathroom?" I asked.

"Third door on the left, but don't put on any lights; just feel your way in the dark," she suggested.

*Easier said than done.*

I walked slowly and felt the first door and then the second, all without sound. Luckily, the floor is stone and not wood; otherwise, the creaks would have been a big giveaway.

I could hear Sofia still rummaging for a bag, with the sound of drawers being opened and closed.

*Bloody hell,* my heart was racing.

"Have you found one?"

She shuffled across to me and handed me a bag.

"Be as quick as you can, Dave. I need to use the bathroom too."

"This might take a while," I said.

“Ok, don’t worry, I will use the one upstairs,” she said.

“Wait, where shall I meet you?” I asked.

“Meet me in the kitchen in five,” she said.

Then she was gone. I found the door handle of the third room on the left and pushed the handle. It was locked.

*How can it be locked? There’s nobody in it.*

I twisted the handle, hoping it might just be stiff, but nothing.

*Oh shit, what now.*

I had no choice. I had to get this kit off. I will just have to use the kitchen sink.

I walked back into the kitchen. Finding the sink in the dark wasn’t too hard, as the moonlight shone through the window, helping to illuminate the fixtures and fittings.

I took my shorts off, removed my boxers and put them in the sink. It was worse than I’d thought. The shit had soaked through my cotton boxers and into my shorts.

*Fuck this is terrible.*

I looked around for some napkins or a kitchen roll, but there weren’t any I could see.

I found a tea towel draped over the back of a chair.

*Fuck I will just have to use that.*

I wiped between my butt cheeks and rinsed the towel under the hot water tap. I then did it again, two or three times; I needed to be sure I got rid of the last bits. I then inspected my shorts. There was nothing else for it, and I had to rinse them. I kept the shitty boxers on the table.

*I will bag them up in a moment.*

I rinsed my shorts and gave them a squeeze. I could suddenly hear footsteps.

*Great, she was on her way back. We'll be out of here in a flash.*

I laughed and continued to squeeze the last bit of muddy water from my shorts. The water was brown, like gravy. It filled the sink and then washed away down the pug hole. I was struggling not to laugh.

The footsteps got nearer, and then they stopped near the door.

"I'm nearly done here, Sofia, but I'm naked. Just give me a moment to put these shorts back on," I whispered.

"Are you there?" I asked, expecting her to appear in the room at any moment.

Suddenly, the kitchen light went on, and the whole room lit up.

I turned to face Sofia – *oh, bollocks* – it wasn't her.

*Oh fuck.*

Standing before me was Stavros.

I squinted as my eyes adjusted to the light. I was naked from the waist down. Shit-stained underwear on the table and a half-cleaned pair of wet shorts in my hands.

# Chapter 20

It was somewhat of a delayed reaction, but I quickly placed my shit-stained shorts over my manhood and stood, frozen, nailed to the spot, my heart thumping in my chest.

He just stood there, across the other side of the kitchen table, looking me up and down, not a word spoken, his face expressionless, no emotion.

"Listen, I know it looks bad. I can explain everything," I said.

He said nothing; just stared at me.

"I was just about to bag them up and take them into town to dispose of them in a bin."

I pulled the plastic bag from my shorts' pocket and carefully kept one hand to hold my shorts in place. All the while, my hands were shaking, and I was terrified my shorts would drop to the floor and reveal my privates again.

He just charged towards me, grabbed me by my shirt collar, lifted me off my feet, and swung me like a rag doll to the other side of the room.

I was pressed against the wall, my feet were off the floor, my shorts had dropped, and my manhood was once more exposed.

"I don't know what kind of *pervert* you are, but I don't want to see you anywhere *near* my daughter or my property again – *do you hear me*?"

Lights went on elsewhere in the house, and I could hear footsteps getting closer.

Suddenly, Sofia appeared at the doorway. She ranted at him in Greek, and he let me drop to the floor in a crumbled mess.

He stood facing her, his hand on his hips.

"Dave has eaten something that has made him sick, father. We came back to the house to clean him up," she pleaded.

She looked at me, puzzled.

"I *thought* you were using the downstairs bathroom?"

"It was *locked*," I claimed.

"It's just a bit stiff," she said.

*It's very floppy from where I'm sitting.*

"I thought it was locked."

Barbara then appeared at the door.

"No, it's not locked, luv. It's just a bit stiff. You have to give it a shove with your foot," she said.

Barbara looked as though she had just walked into a completely normal situation. I grabbed the shorts off the floor and covered my privates again.

Babs still hadn't asked why I was sitting on the floor. She looked around the room, then noticed the shit-stained underpants on the table. It looked like a mass of white cotton, interjected with large wet splashes of brown.

"*Oh, Stavros*, why would you use a *tea towel* to wipe up gravy? Have I taught you nothing?" she asked.

She reached out, grabbed them, walked over to the washing machine, opened the door, and slung them in. She then looked at me, sitting on the floor.

*She really needs to wash her hands.*

"What *are you* doing down there, Dave?" she asked, and suddenly the penny dropped.

"I have had an accident, Barbara," I said before being interrupted.

"Listen, we were in town, Dave felt unwell, and he then had stomach cramps. He had no key to get into his villa, so we had to come back here so he could clean up," Sofia said.

*She's conveyed the message rather well*, I thought.

"Oh, you *poor* luv, but why are you on the floor," she asked again.

"Because your husband put me here," I said.

There was no other way of saying it.

"I can see you have your shorts, but what have you done with your underwear?" she asked.

She started to look around for them. I looked at Sofia and back at Babs.

"I appear to have lost them," I said.

"This guy is an *idiot.* Every night, there's *something new*, something else," he shouted.

He left the kitchen without saying another word and slammed the door behind him.

"Well, you can't put them back on Dave. They'll be wet and horrible," Babs said, all matter of fact.

"Well, I can't exactly borrow one of Sofia's dresses either. Can you not just hand me a bathroom towel and put these shorts in the dryer?" I suggested.

"Good idea, Dave, let me grab one for you," said Sofia as she went to the bathroom.

Sofia handed me a towel. I wrapped it around my waist and got to my feet. Babs grabbed my shorts off me, put them in the washing machine, added some powder, and put them on a cycle.

"Put them on a fast cycle, Babs, just so we can get them dried quickly," I insisted.

"You're teaching a granny to suck eggs, luv," she said, laughing.

She stood watching the drum fill with water.

"I can then throw them in the tumble dryer and have you *two* on your way out in no time," she said, still staring at the contents in the machine.

"Oh, *bugger,* I've just remembered Sofia - the taxi man will still be waiting?" I said.

"Don't panic. You sit and have a drink. I'll go and check. If he's still there, if he is, I'll tell him to wait for another half hour."

"It will cost a lot," I said.

"Yeah, it will, but my father can *pay* him," she said.

She walked out the door and made her way to the gate. I looked at Babs, who had just taken a bottle of beer out of the fridge for me.

"He won't like that," I claimed, watching Sofia walk through the main gate.

She twisted the lid off the bottle and handed it to me.

"Won't like what?" she asked.

"Paying for the taxi to wait."

I took a swig of the ice-cold Mythos. It had never tasted so good.

"No, he won't. But then he should learn to treat people with a bit more respect," she said.

"I can't blame him. He sees me as a tourist opportunist, out to take advantage of his daughter."

"Dave, it's only how Stavros and I met, same difference," she claimed.

"I *know*, but he seems to be finding me in rather compromising circumstances all the time. It's like we're being set up," I said.

"You certainly know how to make an entrance, luv. I'll give you that."

Sofia walked back into the kitchen and closed the door behind her.

"He's still there; he'll wait, and my father has just paid him double, which should cover us to get back into town," she said.

"That was very good of him, Sofia. I wouldn't have minded paying," I said.

"It's the least he can do, Dave, after traumatising you," said Babs.

I wasn't about to argue.

"Right, come and grab a drink," Babs instructed, twisting the lid off another beer bottle.

Sofia sat down next to her, facing me. She smiled.

"How was your father about the whole thing, finding me semi-naked by the sink?" I asked.

She shook her head.

"Did he pass any comment?" I asked.

Sofia smiled, "I'm not sure you'll be exchanging Christmas cards this year, but give him time," she said, laughing.

"I think we, me and your father, have got our wires crossed," I said.

"Why do you say that?" Babs asked.

"Because I've already bought him a Christmas card," I said.

They both laughed.

"Let me check on that washing," Babs added.

"Is it nearly finished?" Sofia asked.

"That's strange," Babs said, now crouched on her knees so she could take a closer look.

"What is?" Sofia asked.

"There should be a pair of shorts and a tea towel," Babs said.

"I have a bit of a confession, Babs. I'm really sorry, but the tea towel you picked up was, in fact, my soiled underpants. I tried to stop you, but it all happened so quickly, and before I could do anything, you'd put them in the machine," I said.

Sofia looked at me and put her hand over her face to defuse her laughter.

"Dave, that's *so gross*," she said, creasing with laughter.

Babs looked horrified.

"Compromising circumstances, eh Dave?" Babs said, her face etched with horror.

"I hope you washed your hands," I asked.

"Yeah, I did, thank God."

Babs whipped them out of the washer and inspected them.

"They look alright to me, guys. Right, let me get them blasted in the dryer," she said.

She then opened a drawer, pulled out a small packet, and placed it on the table before me.

"Imodium Dave, just take two to be safe, eh," she said.

Sofia laughed again.

"It's normal to be a little nervous on a date, Dave, but you don't need to *shit* yourself," whispered Babs in my ear.

They both laughed again at my expense.

"Well, I'm so glad I have kept you ladies amused for the last hour."

"Babs, while they are drying, why not give Stavros a shout and see if I can break the ice with him?" I requested.

"Wave the white flag?" she asked.

"Yeah, I will go and find him," Sofia said.

She left the table and disappeared.

Moments later, Stavros appeared at the door, being practically pushed by his daughter. He exchanged words with her in Greek and judging by his frown, they weren't words of approval.

She then spoke to him in English.

"Father, sit at the table," Sofia had total control; this was a first.

Sofia remained standing by the table while the rest of us remained seated. Stavros couldn't sit silently for long and began moaning at her in Greek as if to say he had better things to do with his time. He was all agitated; he just didn't want to comply.

"Both Dave and I have been on a couple of dates, and we like each other, and that is it. We don't need my father doing his best to make Dave uncomfortable because it's no different from when he met you, Barbara," she said.

Babs nodded.

"Listen, you're not *kids*, you're grown-ups, and I think it's about time a certain person, no names mentioned, should start to let you make your own decisions."

Sofia smiled.

"Dave is a warm, kind, funny and charming guy, and I enjoy his company," she added.

"I'd take just one of those attributes, Sofia, but thank you," I said.

"The taxi is *waiting*," said Stavros.

He rose from his seat, pushed his chair under the table and made his way out of the kitchen, again, slamming the door behind him.

Babs looked at us both and smiled.

"*Ignore him*. I will deal with him later," she said.

I looked at Babs; she was half the size of Stavros, but I wouldn't want to go toe to toe with either of them. They both had a fire in their bellies.

"Come on you two, *get a move on* before it's too late to go out," she said.

"Here, don't forget these," she said, handing me the box of Imodium.

## Chapter 21

We walked hand in hand through the main square.

I glanced at my watch. It was 10:20 p.m., and the bars and restaurants were still bustling.

"Fancy a drink in Zico's?" Sofia asked.

"I could murder a cold beer right now," I said.

We sat people-watching, drinking, laughing, and finally having some quality time together. It was the most normal evening of my entire holiday, and I didn't want it to end.

"It isn't completely *impossible* to have a night out without drama," I said.

She smiled.

*Bloody hell, I love that smile.*

"You do realise we haven't even had our first kiss?" I asked.

"Are you feeling brave, Dave?" she asked with a glint in her eye.

"Blimey, those cocktails are going down well," I said.

"They are so amazing. You should have one next," she suggested.

She took a sip through her straw and fixed her gaze on me.

"Close your eyes," she said.

"What?" I asked.

She laughed.

"Just do it," she insisted.

I closed my eyes and waited.

"Don't open them unless I tell you to, agreed?"

"Agreed."

I then felt her warm lips press on mine. It probably only lasted seconds, but every second counted. She then moved away.

"Can I open my eyes now?" I asked.

"You can."

*"Did you like it*?" she asked.

*She is a total tease, but I love it.*

"Hmmm, I'm *not so sure.* Maybe we should try that again, the best of three?" I asked.

She smirked.

"The best of three?" she asked.

"Just to be sure," I insisted.

"You will have to earn them," she said, laughing.

"So, was that kiss worth the wait?" she asked.

"I have a terrible memory. I can't even recall if it was worth the wait or not, so there is only one solution: you'll have to kiss me again."

"*Nice try, Dave!*"

She laughed. She was enjoying the tease.

"I need to nip to the ladies - back in a moment," she said, leaving the table.

"Yeah, no worries, don't be too long. I might forget what you look like."

She looked back at me and laughed.

I took another swig of my beer, sat back and watched people going about their business. The Imodium had done the trick. My bottom felt like it had been zipped up, and I had my swagger again.

Suddenly, a waiter approached me with another beer and another cocktail.

"Did you read my mind?" I asked him.

"Sorry, sir?" he said.

"I was about to order the same again."

"No sir, the two gentlemen sitting at the bar bought them for you," he smiled and walked away.

I looked over at the bar area but couldn't see anyone, so I got up and walked around the other side of the bar. I couldn't see anyone at first, until then, in the far corner of the bar, I saw two shapes sitting on stools, engrossed in conversation.

One fat, one thin – *what are those two arseholes up to now?*

I casually walked up to them and tapped them on their shoulders.

"Gentleman, how generous of you to buy us some drinks, or should I be thanking Stavros, your *boss*?"

"Look at it as an apology, funny guy, for our recent misunderstanding," said the skinny guy.

I nodded.

"You're all heart," I said.

The fat guy laughed.

"No hard feelings, eh? Enjoy your drinks," he said with a disingenuous smile.

"You're too kind," I added.

I didn't have time to hang about - I made my way back before Sofia returned. I sat back down and waited.

"Oh, you got the drinks in," she asked.

"Not quite. It appears a couple of locals did."

"Locals?" she asked, her face puzzled.

"Was I gone that long? Did you feel the need to make new friends, Dave?"

I laughed.

"I personally went over and thanked them," I added.

"Really?" she asked.

*"No,* who would I *know* in Naxos? They probably just sent the drinks to the wrong table?" I claimed, shrugging my shoulders.

"Wait here, I will go and have a look. I might recognise them," she said.

"Wait, Sofia. There's no need. It's no big deal; they probably mistook us for someone else, so come, sit, enjoy your drink."

*"Wait,* I will be back in a moment," she insisted.

She was gone no more than a few moments before she returned.

"Did you recognise anyone?" I asked.

*"Of course*, they work for my father."

"Oh yeah, I thought I recognised the skinny guy from earlier," I said.

"Sofia, I need to speak to you about something that happened yesterday."

Her normal warm glow switched to a more pensive expression.

"Sounds serious," she said.

"I don't know how to tell you this, but please, no harm was done. I'm here with you, and that's all that counts," I said.

"Dave – tell me what happened."

"The two guys at the bar bundled me into a van outside the shop near our villa and took me to meet another man at some warehouse. I was told I would be taken back to our villa, and they would help me pack my things and then put me and Doris on a plane back to the UK," I said.

"This is a joke, right?" she asked.

I shook my head.

She looked gobsmacked.

"Are you serious?" she asked.

"I had a sackcloth over my head at first, but as they took me back to the villa, they removed it so I could see their faces."

*"Oh my God, Dave,"* she said, her hands over her face.

"*That's* how I recognised them," I added.

"I wanted to tell you earlier, but I didn't think you'd believe me," I claimed.

"Did they *hurt* you?" she asked.

"No, at no point did I come to any harm, but it's not something I'd recommend."

"I need to confront my father," she said, all flustered, "I need to do it now, Dave."

*"Listen,* he was just looking after your best interests. He clearly doesn't want you hanging around with a tourist," I said.

Though, why I was defending her father's behaviour was beyond me, and I should really be using this as an opportunity to get my revenge.

She looked at me apologetically and yet seemed pretty relaxed, all things considered.

"He's an idiot. He won't let me find my own way in life, and he wants to control everything," she shouted.

"Is he really that bad?"

"Nobody is good enough for my father, whoever they are, Dave."

"Listen, why don't we spend tomorrow doing our own thing? I can hang out with Doris before she suggests I'm ignoring her, and maybe you can get to the bottom of your father's issue with me?"

She looked disappointed, which was the reaction I wanted. I wanted her to look like she cared, and she clearly did.

She grabbed my hands in hers and smiled. It was a gentle smile, and the warm breeze teased her hair.

*Shit, she is so dam fit. I am, no question, punching well above my weight.*

"So, you're happy with my suggestion?" I asked.

"Okay, let's do our own thing tomorrow. Like you said, it will give me time to sort my father out."

"Listen, at no point was I harmed yesterday, Sofia. I just think your father wants me out of the way for whatever reason."

She looked at me and smiled.

"Let me deal with my father. You just spend some time chilling by the pool with Doris."

"Anyway, finish your drink, and I'll sort a taxi," I said.

"We can text chat later if you like, and I'll see you in a couple of days," I said.

I waved my arm to grab the attention of a taxi.

"Sounds like a plan," she said,

She smiled at me with those pearly whites and ever-so-kissable lips. To me, she was like the perfect kebab. I didn't want the odd bite or the odd nibble; I just wanted to get stuck in.

"Are you sharing this taxi, Dave?"

"Do you know what? I really f*ancy* a kebab," I said.

She laughed.

"I can wait. It's not a problem."

"No, you get back. I will walk back; it'll only take me half an hour."

She looked at me, all concerned.

"Dave, are you sure you're ok?"

"Not yet, I'm not, but when I'll be tucking into some grub in about five minutes, I'll be just fine."

"Ok, no accepting lifts from any strangers then," she said.

"I won't."

She leaned in and kissed me on my lips. It was soft and warm and bloody amazing. Her tongue met with mine, and it gently danced in my mouth. It was only brief but utterly sensational.

She stepped back and smiled.

"Wow – I wasn't expecting that."

She laughed.

"Well, do you *think* you'll remember that one?" she asked.

"I think you need to get in that taxi before I get even more excitable."

She laughed again and climbed into the front seat of the taxi. Before it pulled away, she wound the window and popped her head out.

"See you soon, Dave, and don't *worry*, things will work out *just* fine."

I smiled.

"See you soon," I shouted.

# Chapter 22

The villa was in darkness; Doris must be in bed. I looked at my watch; it was just after 1:30 a.m. I walked into the kitchen, grabbed a beer from the fridge, unlocked the door leading to the balcony, and made my way outside.

I twisted the top off the bottle, took a big gulp and leaned on the railings. I'll just have this one and then go to bed. I just stood there and admired the moonlit view.

Moments later, I could hear the faint sound of conversation getting closer from down below. Then, a couple of staggering silhouettes came into view.

The chat got louder; it was the unmistakable sound of two old ladies.

"Doris - is that you?"

"Who's that?" she shouted back.

"A burglar, who knows you by name, who do you think it is?"

They both stood below the balcony, looking up at me, arms around each other, swaying like a pair of drunks on a boat.

"Why's Betty with you? Has she forgotten she has a husband?"

"He's still at the bar," Betty shouted.

"Betty just wanted to make sure I got home safe," she shouted, followed by a hic-up.

"No taxis?" I asked.

"Yeah, we did, but the taxi driver got a bit offended," said Betty.

"How?" I asked.

"When Doris *vomited* on the back seat."

"Did he charge you?"

"30 euros," said Betty.

"How far did he take you before Doris vomited?" I asked.

"About a hundred yards," shouted Doris.

"Bloody hell, right, well, get your backsides up here, then."

They staggered in the door, hands and arms flapping about on the door frame for support.

"Right, you two, just sit down on that sofa and don't move," I instructed.

"Oh, my head's spinning, Dave," shouted Doris.

"Don't be sick on that sofa, Doris. We don't need another bill," I said.

I put two empty glasses on the coffee table and poured them a glass of water from a jug.

Betty leaned forward, grabbed a glass and took a big swig while Doris leaned back her head to face the ceiling, her eyes closed.

I sat in a chair opposite them, leaning forward to keep an eye on Doris.

"Doris, how's the head?" I asked.

She opened her eyes, faced forward and smiled. I looked at Betty.

"What is she looking so *happy* about?" I asked.

"*Doris* has a date," Betty announced.

"Really, with whom - you?" I asked.

Doris took a swig from her glass of water and began to chuckle.

"He's a lovely man called *Steve*," she said.

"Careful, Doris. I know you have a weak bladder, and I wouldn't want you going for a pee before I hear the full story," I insisted.

"Did you meet him in the bar then, or what?" I asked.

Betty laughed, "No, she met him on Tinder."

I topped her glass up and sat back.

"Tinder, she doesn't even have a *smartphone,* and Tinder *isn't* for *grannies*."

Doris looked at me, her face creased like a well-used tea bag.

"Don't be so ageless," she said, pointing a bony finger at me.

"You mean ageist, Doris?" I said.

Betty looked at me and smiled.

"I have a smartphone, Dave," said Betty.

She shuffled about in her handbag to reveal her mobile.

"You do surprise me," I said.

"I joined on her behalf, took a few photos, uploaded them, and then *bingo!* What do you know, a lovely-looking chap called Steve popped up," said Betty.

Doris smiled, "He's ever so handsome and looks about my age, though I didn't ask. He sent me a mojo," she said.

"A what?" I asked.

"A mojo," Betty added, fiddling with her phone and then passing it to me.

"What are you two on?"

I swiped the screen, and there he was – Steve.

"He's sent an emoji, ladies, not a mojo."

"Oh yeah, one of them," said Betty.

"It's like hanging out with the Chuckle Brothers in drag with you two."

"Who *are* they?" Doris asked.

"Doesn't matter. It would hurt my head explaining."

I flicked through his pictures and looked up.

"Well, if this is him, he looks too normal for you, Doris."

"How old would you say he is then, Dave?" asked Doris.

"Probably early 70s, I'd say, so younger than you for sure."

"You cheeky bugger, how do you know how old I am," Doris asked, her face creased again.

She finished the last of her water and slammed the empty glass on the table.

"Dave, you should never ask a lady her age," said Betty, all matter of fact.

I looked at Doris.

"So what exactly have you *arranged* with this Steve bloke?" I asked, reverting to my protective self.

"Well, we just exchanged a few words. Betty did the typing, and we just agreed to meet tomorrow night at a bar in the square."

"Bit random, even for you," I said, doing my best to contain my amusement.

"You may laugh, but who knows *what* may come of it," said Doris.

"Bit *late* for a holiday romance. We go back in 5 or 6 days."

"Never *too* late, Dave. I might *not* come back at all."

"Like Shirley Valentine?" I asked.

"Who's she?" asked Doris.

I shook my head.

"Yeah, I'll stay *here,* Dave, and rent my house back home."

"You have two cats to feed, and *I'm not* having them. I've got my own."

"I'll *fly* them out here," she added.

I looked at Betty.

"Have *you* put these daft ideas in her head?"

They both laughed.

"*'Steve and Doris'* has a nice ring to it, don't you think?"

Doris looked at me for approval.

"Let me have another look at his photos," I insisted.

I reached out to grasp the phone. I swiped away two or three times on his profile.

"No body shots then, just his face, says nothing about his age either, and there's no way of knowing how old these pictures are. He could be ten years older in the flesh," I said.

"Why do I need to see his body, Dave – you young people are obsessed with sex."

She wasn't amused.

"Well, from experience, when someone only shows face shots, it means they're fat," I insisted.

"How rude, Dave," said Betty.

"I don't expect him to have a six-pack, but … "

Doris interrupted me before I could finish.

"*Dave,* thin or fat, doesn't matter to me. As long as he isn't a short arse, I'll be happy," said Doris.

"Yeah, exactly, Doris my lovely, just ignore him. Dave is clearly *very shallow*," said Betty.

She looked at me, her face creased with a disapproving frown.

"I'm right you mean, he's clearly hiding something."

I took another look at his profile.

"Says nothing about his height here," I said.

I looked at them both and shook my head.

"Give me strength."

I put my empty beer bottle in the kitchen and rinsed the dirty cups we'd accumulated over the past few days.

"Eh, don't go – you haven't told us about *your* night out with Sofia," said Doris, all inquisitive.

"Nothing much to tell, ladies."

"Really?" asked Betty.

"It was low-key. Nothing much happened."

"No drama then, Dave?" asked Betty.

"I'm done with drama. I need a rest," I added.

"What's the plan for tomorrow then, Dave?" asked Doris.

"Well, I'm free tomorrow evening, so I might just hang out with you and Steve."

"Why aren't you seeing Stella?" asked Betty.

"Who's Stella?" I asked.

"Dave, don't tell me you're two-timing Sofia with Stella?" asked Doris.

Betty laughed.

"Sorry, my mistake. I meant Sofia."

"She's got a family thing to attend, so I said I'd hang out with a couple of grannies instead."

"You *bloody won't*. I haven't met Steve yet, and I don't want you scaring him off," shouted Doris.

Betty laughed with her all too familiar deep rumble that made Barry White sound like a choir boy.

"Right, as much as this conversation is stimulating, ladies, I'm now heading for bed."

Doris turned to face me.

"Betty is crashing over here tonight, if that's alright?"

"Is *Brian* alright with that, or is he expecting you back?" I asked.

Betty looked-up.

"I've just texted him, and he's fine."

"I bet he is. He will get some peace after all."

"*Sorry, Dave*, what did you say?" Betty asked.

"I said I bet he'll miss you."

She smiled.

"Of course, he will."

"*Goodnight, ladies.*"

# Chapter 23

Doris wasn't due to meet her date for at least half an hour, so I decided to head to the bar early and grab my vantage point.

It was early evening, and the bar was beginning to get busy. The place had a nice vibe complimented by melodic ambient beats with some floaty female vocals; it was a good choice, and a nice combination.

*Well, if her date suggested this bar, he at least has good taste.*

I pulled up a stool by the bar and waited to grab the waitress's attention. I watched as she mixed cocktails for a couple of tourists. She was tall and slim, with big blonde surf chick hair, and she rocked a pair of hot pants, a baggy top and flip-flops. She was easy on the eye. I very much liked the recruitment policy at this bar.

She glanced over and smiled.

“I’ll be with you in a tick, mate,” she said.

I smiled, “No rush.”

I looked at the bar menu to kill time.

“What can I get you?” she asked.

She had a beaming smile and big blue eyes. She was even better up close.

“You’re a long way from home, aren’t you?” I asked.

“I am,” she smiled, “So are you,” she said.

“I am.”

“South Africa?” I asked.

“Yes, JB,” she said.

“I take it you’re from England?” she asked.

“I am.”

“London?”

*Bloody hell, do I sound like a Southerner?*

“Wigan.”

“Wigan, isn’t that the home of Wigan Rugby?” she asked.

I nodded.

“And Pies,” I added.

“But little else, if I’m honest.”

“Are you hanging around for long?” I asked.

“Well, long enough to *serve* you a drink, at least.”

“Not much demand for bar staff in South Africa, then?” I asked.

“Well, there’s less chance of me getting mugged, shot or eaten by a Lion in Naxos, so I might hang around for a while longer…What can I get you?”

I looked at the beer menu and flicked through the pages.

“So you like your *beers,* do you?” she asked.

“I do”.

“Are you a blonde or brune?”

I looked up, “Are we talking about beer or something else?”

She laughed.

“I think you’re probably a blonde kind of guy.”

“Well, if I wasn’t, I am now,” I said.

I couldn’t help being cheesy. It was second nature.

“Could I have a bottle of La’chouffe, please?”

“Good choice. You like Belgian beer then, do you?” she asked.

She flipped the lid off the beer bottle into the bin and grabbed a branded glass off the shelf. She then gently poured it, placed it on a mat and pushed it towards me.

“Thanks for the beer, by the way.”

“You’re welcome.”

“I’m Dave.”

She smiled.

"I'm Vanessa."

"That's a nice name."

*She didn't comment on mine. Why would she?*

"Are you waiting to meet someone?" she asked.

"I'm here not so much to *meet* someone, but I'm waiting for someone to arrive for a date, and I've been asked to keep an eye on them from a distance. It sounds weird, I guess because it is."

She looked intrigued.

"Tell me more."

"I'll let you serve those two gentlemen first."

She looked at me and laughed.

"What a tease," she said, "Back in a mo."

I looked around for anyone who might be sitting alone and who might remotely resemble the bloke in the pictures. There was plenty of time before Doris arrived, so I had enough time to spot him and watch where he sat.

She came back over and leaned on the bar.

"Sorry about that, so go on, tell me more about your friend and her date."

I kept it brief; I didn't want to freak her out completely.

"I'm here with an old lady called Doris; she's my neighbour back home. She won a holiday for two and had nobody to take, so she asked me and I said yes. Now, she has met a bloke online, and tonight is her first date."

"Wow, I wasn't expecting that," she said.

I took another swig of beer.

"So how are you going to know it's him? I mean, people often look very different from their photos."

"He will be wearing a name badge, so it should be pretty easy."

*"Really?"*

She laughed.

"No, but it would have helped," I said.

"I'm sure this Steve is a really nice guy. What could possibly go wrong?" she said while wiping the top of the bar and keeping herself busy.

"You don't *know,* Doris."

"Listen, if your friend needs help, you can step in and rescue her?"

"I'm not *David Hasselhoff."*

"Skinny legs and a pigeon chest is not my thing?" she said, laughing again.

"I didn't think my legs and chest looked that bad?"

"Not yours, his."

She smiled. She was cute, and it was a nice place to hang out at this moment. She then averted her gaze to someone approaching the bar to my left.

"Eyes to the left. Could this be your man?" she asked.

I glanced. Suddenly, a little man jumped on a stool beside me and leaned on the bar.

"Bottle of beer, please, darling," he said.

He had an unmistakable Essex accent.

"Coming up," she said, making another return to the fridge.

I had another look at the little man. He was a dwarf, I mean, a proper dwarf, with small legs, arms, body and a normal-sized head. He wasn't just a little man. I would say he was probably in his late 70s, but it was hard to tell. He was well dressed, wearing beige chinos, sockless slip-on brown leather shoes, a pink tucked-in shirt, and slicked-back grey hair. He had a swagger about him. He'd certainly made an effort.

He looked at me and smiled.

"There you are, sir."

She poured the beer into a glass, placed it on a mat, and pushed it towards him.

"*Thanks,* my sweet, and one for yourself, love."

He handed over a ten euro note and sat back on his stool. I looked at him again and smiled.

"Nice evening," I said.

I took another sip of my beer.

"Well, that all depends," he said.

"Depends?" I asked.

"Well, that depends on how well my date goes?"

He took another big gulp of his beer as though to calm his nerves.

"Oh, *you're* on a date, are you?"

"I must be mad," he said.

"I'm Dave, by the way."

I'm unsure why I needed to tell him, but I just did. He put his beer down and leaned over to shake my hand. His hand was small and clammy, with a loose grip.

*"I'm Steve."*

*Oh bugger.*

I looked at him more closely in the face. If it was the man in the pictures, then he's definitely ten years older. Now, one of two things could happen right now. I could text Doris to let her know her date is on the *short* side or not bother. I opted for the latter.

"What time are you meeting your date?"

He glanced at his watch, "We agreed at 8 p.m."

He took another swig of his beer, then removed a napkin from his inside pocket and wiped the sweat from his sunburnt face.

*"I hate dating.* They're like job interviews, don't you think?" he asked.

"I'd take a job interview over a date any day," I said.

He looked at me.

"Less pressure?"

"Exactly," I said.

"I wish I was more like Julio Iglesias. He's bedded 2000 women, you know," he said.

He finished his beer and looked to grab the barmaid's attention again.

"Granted, his CV *is* pretty impressive, though I'm sure his hit rate has tumbled recently," I said.

He looked at me and laughed.

"You single?"

"Almost always," I said.

"You gay?" he asked.

I laughed.

"Do I look gay?" I asked.

"No, but then lots of blokes don't *look* gay, but they are."

"Well, I'm *definitely* not gay. My track record just isn't that dazzling," I added.

"Why's that then?" he asked.

"I have a habit of picking unsuitable partners basically, a terrible sense of judgement, some would say."

He looked at me and smiled.

"That bad?" he asked.

"If I had the choice of a round wheel and a square one, I would pick the square one," I said.

He laughed.

"What's the problem with a round wheel?" he asked.

"Too easy, too normal. I like a bumpy ride," I said, taking another swig from my beer.

He looked at me and laughed.

"You want to try *Tinder,* mate? Never too old to meet the next victim," he added, chuckling to himself.

"To be honest, I'm actually having a bit of a holiday romance thing with a local girl, which is going alright."

"You're a *dark horse*," he said.

"More of a black sheep, mate," I said.

Steve got the attention of the barmaid.

"Excuse me, love, I've booked a table for two."

She grabbed a book from behind the bar and opened it.

"What name is it, please?"

"Steve Jackson - no relation to Michael, though he did borrow some of my moves."

She looked up.

"Never did like Michael Jackson," she said.

*I imagine his one-liners are a bit like a dishcloth; they've been used many times.*

She then continued to try and find his name.

"Yeah, must admit, you don't see much of him these days," he added.

He looked at me with a puzzled expression.

I wondered if that was genuine humour or if he hadn't read a paper for the past ten years.

"Found you – would you like me to show you to your table, or would you prefer to wait for your friend to join you at the bar?" she asked.

He paused for a moment, his face creased with indecision.

"Any chance we could sit there?" he asked.

He pointed to the nearest empty table with a reserved sign.

"You're in luck. That's exactly where I was going to put you."

She looked at me and smiled.

"Could I have another beer and one for my new friend, please?" he asked.

"Sure - I just need to grab some from the cellar. Back in a mo."

She made her way down some steps and out of sight. He then looked at me and smiled.

"She's a *right sort*. I think I'm in there."

"I agree, mate, so at least you have a plan B now, eh?"

"Do you think my date will want to eat?"

"Well, *probably,*" I said.

"I've got a bit of a dilemma then."

"Oh, like what?"

"Well, there's good news and bad news. Bad news, I left my reading glasses back in the UK. Good news, I have my prescription swim goggles with me."

"Why didn't you agree to meet her by the pool bar at your hotel?" I asked.

"There's no pool where I'm staying," he added.

*He thinks I'm serious.*

He then proceeded to reach inside his pocket and out popped his goggles.

*I can't wait for Doris to arrive.*

He put them on his head and positioned the lenses over his eyes. They were blue rubber Speedos with yellow tints. His eyes looked huge.

I laughed out loud.

*I am so looking forward to watching this date from a distance.*

I checked the battery level on my phone, just in case I decided to film it. He looked at me and laughed. I was praying he left them on until the barmaid returned.

"What do you think?" he asked.

"Nobody would even *know* they're goggles. I'd leave them on," I said, taking another swig of my beer.

*"Very funny."*

He removed them from his face and put them back in his inside pocket. I looked at my watch.

*Shit, Doris will be here any moment.*

The barmaid reappeared, placed one beer in front of Steve and one in front of me, and smiled. She really wanted to laugh; I could tell.

"What's with the red marks on the side of your face?" she asked.

He took a big swig of his beer but made no comment. She looked at me, puzzled.

"If I told you, you wouldn't believe me," I said.

"Right then, you two, I'd better get into position, ready to do battle - wish me luck."

"I'm sure you'll be fine!" she said,

She was clearly enjoying her job tonight.

He jumped off his stool and walked towards the table. She looked at me and then started to giggle.

"Maybe you should just text your friend to at least give her a heads-up that he's a bit smaller than she might expect?"

"Why would I do that?"

She laughed.

"Well, I think you *should* tell her."

I took my phone from my pocket, swiped the screen.

"Dam."

"What?"

"Out of battery."

"Liar."

She looked away for a moment, and I followed her gaze.

"Is that your friend?" she asked.

Doris was making her way across the road towards the bar.

"Yep."

She walked straight into the bar area and headed right towards where Steve was sitting. He had either texted her to advise her where he was sitting or she had a radar. I don't think it was the latter; she was hopeless with directions.

I watched with my heart in my mouth.

*Who will recognise who first?*

Steve recognised her almost immediately. He rose from his chair and stepped out in front of her, stopping her progress.

*Shit, she nearly walked over the top of him.*

"*Hello,* you must be *Doris*?"

She looked speechless.

"I'm *Steve*, pleased to meet you."

Doris glanced towards the bar area and spotted me, her face a picture of horror. She then looked back at Steve and smiled. It was a good recovery. At least she pretended she wanted to be there, so that was progress.

"Oh, you *must* be Steve?"

"Steve Jackson, no relation to Michael."

"You're a bit shorter than I *expected*."

I could hear every word; this was brilliant.

"Don't you *worry,* my love. I might be *small,* but I pack quite a punch."

*Shit, did he really just say that?*

Doris looked nervous; I was nervous. I looked at the barmaid, and even she looked nervous; heck, my beer looked nervous.

He looked over to grab the attention of the barmaid.

"Bottle of your finest fizz, please, my love," he shouted.

Doris looked at me and smiled. I'd never seen such a disingenuous expression on her face.

*Shit, this could be a long night for us all.*

## Chapter 24

"Dave, my darling, fancy seeing you here?" Doris shouted.

I pretended not to hear.

The barmaid leaned over and whispered, "I think your friend Doris is trying to get your attention."

She was doing her best not to laugh, as though she knew the next instalment of entertainment was about to unfold.

I pressed the lip of the beer bottle against my lips and swigged the cold contents.

"I'm pretending I can't hear her - it seems to be working just fine."

"*Dave* - are you ignoring me?" she shouted again.

The barmaid smiled.

"You need a refill?"

"More now than ever, I think," I said.

I pushed the empty bottle towards her. I then sheepishly turned around on my stool and looked over at Doris, waved and smiled.

"Aren't *you* joining us, *Dave*?" she asked.

She looked a little desperate, and I felt bad. Steve looked over at me and smiled, his teeth so white, they hurt my eyes. He had way too many teeth, almost more than his mouth actually needed.

"I'm just finishing my beer," I said, raising the bottle aloft in demonstration.

I took another quick look at Steve, and it made me wonder in that moment, *was his smile a bit fake? His eyes looked a bit disappointed behind that smile, either with the quality of his date or the fact I was about to cramp his style; only time would tell.*

I grabbed another beer and made my way over to their table.

"*Doris* – fancy seeing you here," I said.

I placed my bottle on the table and smiled.

"Pull up a chair then, Dave. You're making the place look untidy just standing there," said Doris.

I pulled out a chair and sat between them.

"*Well,* what a small world, eh Dave? Doris tells me you two are actually on holiday together," he asked.

He looked puzzled.

"Call it care in the community," I said.

"Doris has told me all about it. I think you're an upstanding gentleman for escorting this lovely lady on her holiday," he added.

*Maybe I had misjudged his fake smile; maybe he had good intentions after all?*

I looked at Doris and stood up from my chair.

"Where are *you* going?" she asked, bemused.

"I'll think I'll leave you two love birds alone; three's a crowd," I added.

"*Sit back down*; Steve is about to pop his cork," she said.

"I bet he is," I said.

He laughed, grabbed the bottle of champagne from the ice bucket and began to remove the foil. He twisted away at the metal casing to reveal the cork. He then began to remove the cork with his teeth.

Doris looked at me and smiled.

"I like a man in control," she said, her gaze fixed on Steve.

But he then began to struggle. I looked at Doris; she looked at me, and her face of concern matched mine. His face contorted, his eyes squinted, the lines on his face more and more pronounced, the blood vessels in and around his temple area packed tight against his skin.

*Take a deep breath, Dave, and leave him to it. He's got this.*

"I find hands are quite useful at this kind of thing *Steve*, just to make a suggestion," I said.

POP – Steve fell back off his chair as though the force had propelled his little body across the room. The bottle sat proudly on the table, the contents bellowing out. Doris leaned over and grabbed it with both hands, placing the bottle in her mouth, not one to waste the contents; she guzzled it back like a youth in a park who had just discovered cider for the first time.

I got up from my seat to find Steve flat on his back, with his chair lying on its side beside him.

*Shit,* he was choking on the cork, his hands grasping his neck, his face bright red, his eyes bulging with fear, his least breath edging ever closer.

"*Don't panic,* Doris; I'll *sort this*," I shouted.

I lifted Steve up off the floor and grappled him in a bear hug. His body was deceptively heavy for such a little man. I squeezed his chest three or four times until the cork popped out of his mouth, bounced on the table and rolled towards where Doris sat.

He coughed and spat, reaching for a napkin to wipe his face. The barmaid suddenly ran over.

*"Is everything okay? Are you hurt*?" she said.

"*Only my pride*," he whispered, as though he had no voice.

He limped back onto his chair, grabbed a glass of water and took a big gulp.

"I must *stop* doing these party tricks," he added.

He took another gulp.

"Are you sure you're ok?" asked the barmaid.

He looked up and nodded.

"If I can get you anything, just ask," she said before making her way back to the bar.

I glanced briefly around to see if we had any onlookers. If we had, they were doing a great job of pretending they hadn't noticed.

"Oh, Steve, couldn't you have done that somewhere else? You have spoiled my drink now. I'll need a new glass," said Doris.

"Eh, what's wrong with it?" I asked.

"Bits of cork floating in it," she said, swirling a bony finger around the inside of the glass in an attempt to fish them out.

"You were swigging from the bottle when I last saw you, Doris. Are you sure you need a glass? Why change the habit of a lifetime?" I asked.

I handed Steve my napkin to wipe his mouth.

"You alright, mate?" I asked.

He looked at me, his once-tanned complexion now a tad paler, his eyes a little bloodshot, and the veins in his neck still protruding with blotchy pink patches.

"I'm good, thanks, mate," he said.

He leaned forwards towards Doris and smiled.

"I wasn't *really* choking, darling. I was just pretending."

Grabbing his wallet off the table, he looked at me.

"I think I *need* a drink," he said.

"I *need* a holiday," I mumbled under my breath.

"Another glass of water might help?" I added.

"Not on my watch pal … *barmaid* … another bottle of Moet please, if you will, darling," he shouted.

He waved his crumpled napkin in the air like a flag to get her attention; his masculinity now seemingly restored.

"Have you two finished arsing around?" Doris asked.

She sipped the bubbles from her flute glass, most of which seemed to find her face instead of her mouth.

"Why are flute glasses so bloody *narrow*," she moaned.

"It keeps the contents nice and fizzy, Doris. If you used a wide glass, it would go flat faster," I said.

I was doing my bit to educate her.

"Can you two hurry up and look at what you want off the menu? I've already decided," she said, all frustrated.

"Oh *really*, did you find egg and chips on there then, Doris?" I asked.

"I'm *more* refined than you give me credit for, *Dave,*" she added.

Steve leaned over towards her again, caught her eye and smiled.

"Like an E-Type Jag, lovely lines, timeless design, as refined as it gets, darling," he said.

She laughed.

"You're quite the charmer for a dwarf, aren't you?" she asked.

*Shit, did she really just say that?!*

He looked pretty calm about it, but I could see he was gearing up for a punchy reply.

"I like to think of myself as a Mini Cooper, a small package with plenty of power."

She smiled. She was enjoying this, I think.

He fiddled again with his napkin, rolling it like a cigar on the table. Doris pushed the menu across to him and sat back in her chair.

"Wait one moment, please, madam, if you will."

Out popped the pair of prescription swimming goggles he showed me earlier.

*Oh shit, I'd almost forgotten about them.*

I looked at Doris and smiled. I was loving this.

He put them on and continued to look at the menu. I looked at Doris, and she looked at me, her face priceless.

"What on *Earth* are those things on your face?" she asked.

"Are you guys ready to order?" the barmaid stood before us with a notepad in her hand and a smile on her face.

He looked up at her, his eyes enlarged, almost fly-like through the thick lenses.

"I'll have a slice of you, please, if I may?" he joked.

He looked her up and down; I looked her up and down.

"Can you two put your tongs away, please?" Doris tutted.

She looked at the barmaid almost apologetically. The barmaid was enjoying it; that much I could tell. She had definitely touched up her lip gloss, too, and made her big blonde hair even bigger, more surf chick than before. The rips in her jeans subjected us to flashes of soft, tanned skin, making me forget what I was about to order.

"*You okay, Dave*?" she smiled, "Need a little more time?" she asked.

"Dave, what's wrong with you? *Sofia* wouldn't be very impressed with *your* flirting," Doris blurted, her bony finger pointing at me.

I looked at the barmaid.

"She's *just* a friend," I added.

She smiled.

"Who, Doris or Sofia?" she added, her smile switched to a frown.

Doris looked up at her and smiled.

"He's having a *holiday* romance with a local girl."

Doris couldn't help herself; the cat was out of the bag.

"Thank you for that, Doris," I added.

"I'll have the Greek Salad, please," Doris confirmed, "Oh, and a cheese and ham sandwich," she added.

"It's not even on the menu," I queried.

"Don't worry. I can rustle that up for you."

The barmaid then looked at me.

"What about you, sir?" she asked.

"I'll have the Calamari and a Greek salad, too, please."

I smiled at her, but she didn't respond. She then looked at Steve.

"I'll have the cheeseburger with fries, please, if I may, darling," he asked.

*What menu was he looking at? This isn't McDonald's.*

"We don't do burgers, sir, but I'll see what I can do," she said.

"You're *too* accommodating," I said.

I tried to make eye contact but failed.

"I would say *talented*, the ability to think outside the box, sir," she said, glancing at me.

"The ability to spot a couple of leeches that should know better," said Doris.

"Exactly, madam," she said.

She put her notebook and pen in her top pocket, glared at me, and then walked back to the bar.

"You've blown it there, pal," said Steve, all matter of fact.

"I should have let you choke on that cork," I said.

"*Eh,* I'm on your side, buddy. It was Doris dropping you in it," he added.

Doris swigged from her flute again. Some of it found her mouth, but most of it fizzed around her face, so I handed her a napkin.

"Doris, if you can't drink from a flute glass, should I get you a mug instead?" I asked.

"I thought you *really* liked Sofia," she said, her eyes all pensive.

"Listen, I had a few beers, I was a bit merry, and I was chatting to a barmaid, nothing more. I was hardly asking for her hand in marriage."

"You undressed her with *your* eyes," she added.

"*You did,*" said Steve, his cheesy smile returning.

"Oi, and you can pipe down. Dave's eyes only removed the barmaid's top; your eyes removed her entire outfit, and you're supposed to be on a date with me?"

"Agreed, but then why is Dave sitting here if this is supposed to be a date?" he asked.

"Agreed; why are you sitting at our table, Dave?" Doris asked.

"You invited me, remember?"

She squinted as though she was squeezing out every last drop of short-term memory.

"Well, I meant, you may join us for a drink, not completely gate-crash our date."

Steve looked at me and then looked at Doris and smiled.

"Well, at least let him have some food. He can then bugger off."

He looked at me and laughed.

"I'm glad you two find all this so amusing."

I took another swig from my beer bottle; it was now flat and warm.

"What did you do for a living before you retired, if you don't mind me asking, Steve?" I asked.

He paused for thought as though he needed to think of a more interesting job than the one he really had.

"I worked as a male model," he claimed.

"Really?" Doris asked, her face not convinced.

I was speechless.

"Yes, really, short people strut their stuff on catwalks, you know," he said.

"Children's clothes?" I asked.

*I knew it's not PC, but I really don't care now.*

"Hmm, no, it was actually modelling for a fancy dress online store," he said.

He looked rather proud of his revelation.

"What exactly did you *model*?" I asked.

"Pixie outfits, gnomes, that kind of thing."

He was deadly serious. Doris laughed.

"Hardly Armani, are you?"

She laughed again. He wasn't amused. He continued to molest the napkin with his fingers.

"Oh, looks like our food has arrived," said Doris,

She played around with her fingers in her mouth, possibly adjusting her teeth in anticipation; it was gross.

"Hi guys, here are your Greek Salads."

Steve moved the condiments to make space, and two large salads were placed in the middle of the table.

"One burger," she announced while placing it in front of Steve.

"One ham sandwich," she placed it in front of Doris.

"Last but not least, one calamari."

"Drum roll, please, everyone," I said.

I began to tap a beat with both hands on the table. I looked up at her, trying to make eye contact, but nothing. She then proceeded to place it on the table when suddenly, the plate upturned, and the contents landed on my lap.

"Oh, I'm *so* sorry, sir, how terribly clumsy of me."

I looked down at my lap. Most of it had now found its way past my lap and onto the floor by my feet.

I looked up. Doris and Steve were desperately trying not to laugh, but the barmaid was pensive and expressionless.

"These things happen; such a shame. I love calamari, not to worry, plenty more where that came from, eh," I said.

"Well, if you mean plenty more in the sea, then yes, if you mean, do *we* have any left, then I'm sorry, sir, that was the last of the calamari. Perhaps I could interest you in something else?" she said.

I let out a sigh.

"Do you know what? I will just stick with the salad, thank you and another beer if I may please?"

"I'm sorry, sir, we have run out of that particular brand of beer. May I interest you in an alternative?"

"You've run out of Mythos, the best-selling beer brand in Greece, but I saw a fridge full earlier?" I queried.

I looked at alternatives on the rear of the menu.

"Hmmm, I'll have a bottle of Alpha then, please."

"Of course," she said.

I looked at Doris, then at Steve and shrugged my shoulders.

"What was *that* about?" I asked.

"Dave, will you never learn? You had clearly been chatting her up earlier," she said.

"*She* told her you had a girlfriend, mate. Game over," he added.

Steve looked all smug, leaning back in his chair, his arms behind his head.

"I was merely being friendly; there was no intent. I'm the happiest man alive; I have Sophia, well, at least I think I do, so why would I have a *burger* when I have .. "

"*Steak* at home," said Steve.

He was doing his best to finish every sentence I started. The barmaid returned, bottle in one hand, a glass in the other. She tilted the glass and gently poured the contents until the glass was full. She then went to place the glass on the table and then…

"Shittttt .. now *come* on, that was deliberate," I shouted.

The glass dropped on my lap, beer everywhere.

"I'm so sorry, sir, I'm terribly clumsy, sir," she said.

She was doing her best to wipe away the excess beer from my trousers while using the world's smallest napkin.

"First the calamari, then a beer. Is there anything else you'd like to throw at me?"

Doris and Steve couldn't contain their amusement.

"I'm sure your *Boss* would think differently," I added.

I looked around to see if I could see anyone who might resemble a person of authority.

"He will sack you for this. Where is *he*?" I asked.

"Well, *she*…is not here tonight, sir," she added, her hands on her hips.

"Oh really, tomorrow night then," I suggested.

"I finish tonight, for good. I won't be working here again."

She was very smug. She looked at Doris and Steve.

"Enjoy your meals."

She then made her way back to the bar.

They both laughed loudly, loud enough for people to look over. Steve looked at me, and for a moment, his amusement stopped, and his face contorted as he leaned over to look at my wet lap.

"What are you going to do about that then pal? Looks like you've wet yourself!"

"I've done worse!" I added, "Fuk it," I said.

"That was your problem, Dave. You wanted to, but then she found out you had a girlfriend."

They both laughed.

"Doris, did you bring your hair dryer?" he asked

"Well, let me take a look in my handbag," she was loving this.

She pretended to rummage in her handbag.

"Well, I could have sworn I had put it in there before I came out."

"Do you know what? I think I will *leave* you two comedians to enjoy the rest of your evening."

I stood up, put several wet napkins on the table and placed a twenty euro note under a glass.

"That's a very generous tip, buddy. I didn't think you rated the service *that* highly," he gloated.

"Have a drink, on me."

"Oh, Dave, don't be like that," said Doris.

I pushed my chair back, bid them a good night, and left.

## Chapter 25

I left the bar and made my way to the main square. I stopped at one of those little street pop-up shops, the types that sell pretty much everything.

"Do you sell cigars?" I asked.

The little man grabbed several from the shelf behind him and placed them in front of me.

"All very good, sir, all special prices," he said.

"I will take those, please, buddy, and one of your lighters too, please."

I made my way towards an empty bench and sat down. I looked at my phone; there were no texts from Sofia, but it was early, and I suspect she had much talking to do with her father. I just sat back and watched people going about their business.

My pocket vibrated; I had a text.

*It's either Doris or Sofia.*

It was Sofia.

*"Hi Dave, just a quick hello to say I have spoken to my father and expressed just how unhappy I was that he didn't approve of me dating you. He has apologised, and I have asked him to apologise in person to you. So, I was thinking, would you like to come to our house for a meal, say tomorrow evening at 7 p.m.? If that suits you? xx."*

*Bloody hell, he's going to apologise in person, really?*

I text back straight away.

*"Hi Sofia, lovely to hear from you; glad things are better with your father. Yes, tomorrow's good for me. I will look forward to it, see you at 7 p.m. xx."*

Knowing I was seeing her again tomorrow helped me relax even more. I took another puff on my cigar and allowed the tobacco flavour to waft around the roof of my mouth.

My pocket started to vibrate.

*It must be Doris this time.*

It was.

*"Dave, why don't you come back? Steve and I are about to go for some drinks in the square, and we'd love you to join us."*

*"Have you finished eating already?"*

*"No, we're about to have a dessert, but then we'll go have a drink somewhere else."*

*"So what time, about 1/2hr?"*

*"Yes, that's fine."*

*"Steve has suggested you meet us in Zorb. It's in the main square."*

*"Ok, I'll see you shortly."*

I placed my mobile back in my pocket. I took another puff on my cigar and watched people go about their business.

Suddenly, in the distance, I spotted a couple of familiar-looking faces walking through the square.

It was fatty and his thin accomplice, Stavros's two most trusted heavies. I watched them walk into one of the bars and disappear out of view. I took one last drag on my cigar, dropped the butt on the floor, and crushed the embers with my shoe.

I then made my way to Zorb. It was a lovely little place, nestled in a low-key little back street, just off the main square. I could see it wasn't overly busy, which was a result.

I sat by the entrance at a cute little table and waited to get the waiter's attention.

I decided it would be a nice gesture for me to get a couple of bottles of Prosecco, not that Doris had earned it, but I was happy she was enjoying her date, and I wanted that happiness to continue.

"Hello, sir. How are you this evening?"

"Very well, mate. Could I possibly order two bottles of Prosecco and an ice bucket, please?"

"Of course, sir, for how many people?"

"There will be three of us."

"Very good, sir."

After all this effort, they had better bloody turn up or I'll be getting wasted on my own. Two bottles sat in an ice bucket at the corner of my table, waiting.

I looked at my watch. It had been half an hour since we agreed to meet.

*Where the bloody hell are they?*

Suddenly, in they walked, hand in hand.

*Bloody hell, they are getting on well.*

"*Dave!!*" shouted Steve, all exaggerated, like I was his long-lost cousin.

They both looked well on their way to being royally smashed.

*Perhaps my getting two bottles of Prosecco was a bit excessive?*

"*Come and join me*," I said with a big smile.

They both pulled up a chair and sat next to each other, facing me.

"*Dave*, are we sitting at the wrong table?" asked Doris.

She looked puzzled.

"No, why?"

"Is that Prosecco for us?" she asked.

"Doris, sometimes, I even surprise myself with my generosity."

"She said you were as tight as a cramp, Dave?"

"She gives me bloody cramps," I added.

He laughed.

"Don't believe everything you hear, mate," I said

"Ignore him, *Dave.* He's quite the *cheeky* chap this one."

"I had noticed."

I poured us all a drink and leaned back in my chair.

"So, how was the dessert?"

"We shared a cheesecake. We wanted to save some space for more drinks," said Doris.

"Good skills," I said, taking another big gulp from my flute.

*"Anyway*, enough small talk, Dave. Have you heard from Sofia?" she asked.

"She has invited me round her house tomorrow evening for a meal."

"Sounds very formal," said Steve.

"Yeah, I've not exactly hit it off with her old man, so I'm apprehensive, to say the least."

"Doris tells me you're really into this girl, which is great, but what will you do when you have to go home?" he asked.

I sighed, put my glass down, grabbed the Prosecco and topped our glasses up.

"I'm probably going to cry like a baby to be honest, mate."

"*Good answer*," he laughed.

"What about you, Steve? Will you cry like a baby when you say goodbye to Doris?"

He laughed again, looked at Doris and smiled.

"Could this Greek bird not move to England?" he asked.

"It's only been a few dates, pal. I don't think you need to buy a hat just yet."

"Yes, but what Steve is saying, Dave, is that you're pretty smitten already."

I nodded.

"How could it work? She works for the family business, so it wouldn't exactly be practical to move to the UK?" I said.

"Oh, I see, a bit more complicated," he said.

He looked at Doris as if to encourage her input.

"*Dave* doesn't do simple. He likes complicated," she said.

"Well, would you consider moving to Greece for a girl?" he asked.

"What job would I do, pick olives? Work in a bar? I'm not 21 anymore, mate."

"And you're butt ugly too, so chances won't be too plentiful, eh mate?" he asked and laughed.

"I don't want to think about it. I've been on a few dates, and I'm already talking about the rest of my life with this girl. Is this not crazy, even for me?"

"Do you want me to be honest, Dave?" asked Doris.

"No, preferably not, Doris."

"Well, you love a challenge, but you're right. Just enjoy the rest of the holiday and the time you spend together, and *see* what happens."

Steve looked at me and nodded his head.

"Pen pals?" he added.

"We're overthinking all this shit, guys," I said.

"Maybe," he said.

"Anyway, enough of this shit. Let's get *pissed*," Steve said, reaching for the bottle.

Suddenly, in walks the fat guy, and standing just by the door behind him was the thin guy, finishing his fag,

*Shit, these two knuckle scrapers are following me, I swear.*

The fat guy spotted me straight away. He nodded his head and smiled. I didn't mention anything to Doris as I didn't want to worry her.

"Are we low on fizz, Dave," she asked.

"You thirsty?" asked Steve.

"No, but it looks like the waiter is on his way over here with another bottle," she said.

I looked up.

"Hello, *another bottle of Prosecco, sir,*" the waiter announced.

"I didn't order another bottle," I said.

He glanced towards the bar.

"No sir, it is a gift from the gentleman at the bar," he said.

He placed the bottle in the ice bucket, smiled and walked away. Doris and Steve looked confused.

"*Dave*, aren't those the two blokes from the other day?" she asked.

She looked at them as they sat at the bar, swigging beers.

"It is. Maybe they aren't such arseholes after all," I said.

"How do you know them?" asked Steve.

"They work for Sofia's father. I've met them a couple of times, *lovely* blokes."

"So, have you two discussed *date* number two yet, assuming you're having another date?"

They both looked at each other and began to laugh.

"Well, if *Steve* plays his cards right, I could be persuaded," said Doris.

She looked happy and distracted, which was a good thing. It meant I would finally have some freedom over the next few days.

"I just need to nip to the gents, back in a mo," I said.

I made my way past the bar.

*"Thank you for the wine!"* I shouted.

I made my escape as I didn't have much appetite for small talk. Walking back to our table, I could see they had moved their chairs a notch closer. They looked like a cosy couple.

Steve is a dwarf, granted, but Doris is tiny too. I'd guess 4ft 10, not even 5ft, so the height difference, although obvious, wasn't obscene.

"*Dave,* look, your Greek friends have bought us some shots, perfect timing," said Steve.

I sat down, grabbed my Prosecco flute, and took a big swig. I looked over at the bar area where they were sitting.

The fat guy waved.

"*Doris, why are you waving back,"* I asked.

"I'm saying thank you. What's your problem?" she asked.

"You look a bit agitated, Dave. You alright?" asked Steve.

"I'm just a bit freaked out that these guys are buying us drinks, that's all."

They both looked puzzled.

“So I think we finish the last of this bottle, swig these shots, and then move on, unless you guys want to call it a night?” I asked.

“No way!!” shouted Doris.

“Calm yourself, super gran,” I said.

“We’re in no rush, buddy. Happy to move on, though,” said Steve.

We finished the Prosecco and grabbed the shots. I lifted the glass to my nose. It was not a smell I was familiar with, though whatever it was, it was strong.

“You oldies up for downing these in one?” I asked.

Without even waiting for the green light, Doris just downed hers, slammed the glass on the table, and belched. Steve and I looked at each other and followed suit, both slamming the glass on the table.

Steve also belched.

“You two are definitely a perfect match.”

“That was bloody *horrible*,” he said, his face creased.

“I rather liked it. I might have another,” Doris said, looking towards the bar.

“You bloody won’t. I don’t think Steve wants to be mopping up your vomit on a first date, Doris.”

Suddenly, the waiter appeared at our table. I cursed Doris; she had probably got his attention while Steve and I were necking our shots.

"I think we're okay for drinks. Thanks, mate," I said.

"Excuse me, your friends at the bar have arranged a taxi for you."

"Really?" I asked.

"Yes - to take you to a special VIP bar called Vespa."

"VIP bar, eh Dave? Well, whoever these two guys are, I think you've made quite an impression on them," said Steve.

His face was beaming with excitement. Doris looked bemused, probably because she was pissed and had no real facial expression of note when she was gassed.

"*Maybe, just maybe, Stavros has asked them to look after us, his way of an apology?" I asked.*

"Apology? For what exactly, Dave?" asked Steve.

"For being a complete dick," I said.

"Well, whatever he's said to his friends, I agree. Let's not miss an opportunity to milk his apology," he added.

He was loving this.

"Doris, getting past your bedtime, are you in?" I asked.

"*Hell yeah*!" she shouted.

"Bloody hell, where do you get your energy from?" I asked.

Steve laughed.

"You're high on life, aren't you, my lovely?" he said.

He stood up on his chair, put his little arms around her and gave her a big, wet kiss on the lips.

*Shit, I didn't see that coming.*

"*Oh Steve,* you're such a *nice man*, not many of them about anymore," she beamed.

"Do you two love birds need to get a room?"

"*Dave, it's not all about sex, you know*," she said.

"Is it not?" I asked.

We saw a car pull up outside the bar. I leaned forward to get a better view. It was a Merc, not too shabby. The driver looked over towards the bar and gestured to the waiter.

"May I escort you guys to your taxi?" the waiter asked.

I sat in the front, the other two in the rear. We hadn't been driving long when I started to feel very tired. I looked over my shoulder to check on those two, and they were both asleep, snoring their heads off.

*I knew it was a bit ambitious; expecting two 70-plus-year-olds to have the stamina to stay out this late, what was I thinking?*

I looked at my watch. We had been driving maybe just shy of half an hour.

"Are we nearly there yet?" I asked the driver.

He glanced at me and then re-focused his attention on the road.

"Not far now," he said.

Bloody hell, I was seriously struggling to keep my eyes open. I could feel my eyelids getting heavier by the second.

Before I knew it, I had dozed off.

## Chapter 26

I began to wake with the sensation of the warm sun beating down on my face.

I could feel my body rocking gently from side to side and the familiar sound of the sea.

Something was creaking; it sounded like timber. I was forcing myself to wake from what felt like a deep sleep. I was feeling very disorientated. I lifted my head up from what felt like a hard surface, and rubbed the back of my neck. It was stiff, so I gently rocked my head from side to side to flex it.

My eyes were now half open, but I was still squinting; the sun was so bright, and my head was throbbing.

*Where the fuck are we?*

I now sat upright, my eyes wide open, and I rubbed my head to try and relieve some of my discomfort.

Looking around me, it quickly became apparent that this was a wooden rowing boat. Doris and Steve lay together on a blanket next to me. They were asleep, no different to when I last saw them.

*Where are we?*

I did my best to adjust to the bright sunlight. I steadied myself, rose to my feet, and then sat back down as the boat rocked and I lost my balance. I crawled forward to the wooden seat before me and rose gently into a seated position.

I looked all around me frantically.

*Fuck, we are in the middle of the sea.*

I could see the very distant shape of Naxos.

*How the fuck did we get here?*

I checked myself out, making sure I wasn't injured. My clothes appeared intact, and my shoes were on my feet. I moved my fingers and toes.

*Fuck, my wallet, no panic, found it, nothing missing, shit, my mobile was gone, fuck. Why take my phone but not my wallet?*

I just sat for a moment and gathered my thoughts. I had a flashback of us drinking that last shot.

*Bastards, they spiked our drinks.*

I looked at my watch. It was obviously the following day.

*Fuck, did we spend a night out here on the sea?*

My heart was racing. It was 2:14 p.m. I looked around the boat to see if there were any ores, but nothing, *so no way of rowing then, fucking marvellous.*

There were, however, several bottles of water.

*Oh, so whoever put us here at least wanted us to last a day or two, then. How nice of them.*

From what I could see, the wooden boat looked pretty sound. It was a good size, both in length and width, and it had a good height to the sides, which at least gave me some confidence that it wasn't about to fall apart.

*Shit - we could be floating for days. I will miss my date tonight, and with no mobile and no way of contact, Sofia will think I have had a change of heart!*

*One thing I do know is that this was the work of Stavros, no question.*

I quietly checked Steve and Doris, who were, in fact, asleep and not *dead.*

I didn't want to wake them, as I needed time to think and establish some calm, and to recall what Bear Grylls had said in one of his DVDs that I had recently watched: *panic is your enemy, calm is your friend.* I'm not *entirely* sure he said that, so if he didn't, then I might just claim that myself.

I checked out the boat again and found three life vests in an old tin box under my seat.

*Brilliant, at least we won't drown. So, we have water and life vests; I just need to find a fridge.*

Suddenly, I could hear a groan; it came from Steve. I reached forward and tapped him on his leg.

"*Steve, Steve, wake up, mate, wake up*."

His groans got louder as he began to wake, his eyes squinting with the bright light.

"Wake up, mate, wake up."

His eyes opened fully, and his faculties returned instantly as though I had switched on a battery-operated toy.

*"Dave, what's happened? Where are we?"* he asked.

"Here, take a drink of water, mate. Just take your time."

He grabbed the bottle and took several gulps.

"I needed that; mouth feels like a flip-flop."

He slowly looked around, observing his new surroundings. He looked at me, and his face shrieked in horror.

"Unless I'm mistaken, Dave, are we at *fucking sea*?"

He looked around frantically.

"Steve, look at me. Remember the shots we had in the bar before we left in the taxi?"

"Yes, obviously."

"They were *spiked*. We all fell asleep in the taxi," I said.

"Makes no sense, Dave."

"We were then put on a boat and towed out to sea," I added.

"Any paddles?" he asked.

"Not a paddle or a pot to piss in," I said.

"We don't need a pot, Dave. We can piss over the side, surely?"

"It's a figure of speech, but yeah."

"*Oh fuck*, I can't swim," he shouted.

His face was terrified, and his eyes were panicked. He grabbed the side of the boat to steady himself.

"*Don't panic.* We have a life vest each; you're safe."

I handed him a life vest and told him to put it on.

"Surely someone will see us, Dave?"

"I'm not worried about the fishing boats; they would see us if they got close enough at least. In fact, that's our only hope of rescue, but it's the cruise ships and freight ships I'm worried about."

Steve looked puzzled.

"But won't they potentially rescue us, too?" he asked.

"They won't see a little wooden boat like this, Steve. They would smash us to bits."

"I love your honesty, Dave."

He turned to look at Doris. She was still snoring her head off.

"Should I wake her?" he asked.

"I wouldn't, not yet. Let's just sit here for a while and take stock of the shit we're in," I said.

"How much daylight hours do we have left?" Steve asked.

"Bloody hell, mate, you'll ask me to navigate by the stars next."

He laughed ever so briefly. This was no place for prolonged humour; it was very real.

"The sun will drop out of the sky by 8:30 pm-ish, so we have time. I don't think we need to panic just yet."

Steve nodded.

Suddenly, a waking groan came from Doris. She moved from lying on her side to lying on her back. Steve gave her a gentle nudge.

"My Darling, it's Steve. Can you hear me?"

I stepped a bit closer, doing my best not to rock the boat. Her eyes opened, and without even a squint, she gazed at the sky, looked at Steve, and looked at me, her face bewildered.

"Are we back at the villa?" she asked.

Steve looked at me.

"Dave, I'll let you explain."

"Doris, first of all, we are all alive, well, and perfectly safe."

"*Cut the bull!* How much *shit* are we in, scale of 1-10?" she asked,

"I think a 9," I said.

"Why not a 10?" she asked.

*"You know me, Doris*, ever the optimist."

"Correct me if I'm wrong, but why are we in a wooden boat?"

*"Doris,* listen, please put this life vest on. It will keep you safe, and I will *then* explain our dilemma," I said.

I handed her a life vest. She sat upright and looked around. She shrieked in horror, with Steve helping her to put her vest on.

"I don't need a *bloody* body warmer. I'm warm enough as it is," she insisted.

She pushed the vest back onto Steve's chest.

"Can you swim, Doris?" he asked her.

"Yes, of course I can. I used to swim for my school when I was a child."

"Can you swim about five miles?" I asked.

"Why do you ask such a daft question?" she asked.

"Take a look; that's how far we are from the land," I added.

She got up slowly, turned to face Naxos in the distance and sighed.

"Now, put your vest on and sit down," I instructed.

"Listen, the boat is solid. We have life vests and each other, and we are perfectly safe," I said.

She looked at me and shook her head.

I put my hand on her shoulder and gave it a reassuring squeeze.

"What the hell happened?" she asked.

"Our drinks were spiked, we fell asleep in the taxi, and it's highly likely Stavros is behind this; that said, we are in a boat, close to land, and we will be picked up by a fishing boat very soon," I said.

"Close to land, are you having a laugh? Close to land if you're a fish, maybe," she said.

"Is there a bathroom on this boat?" she asked.

"Hmm, no," said Steve.

"Do you need to go?" I asked.

"Well, yes, I need to wee. I always need to wee when I wake up," she said.

She looked around as if to search for a spot to do it.

"You have two options: over the side, while one of us holds your arms, and that won't be me, or just wee at the other end of the boat," I said.

"How does the first option work?" she asked.

"You sit on the edge, facing inwards, your bum over the side, you lift your skirt, and then you wee while *Steve* holds your arms," I said.

"What about my *dignity*?"

"Doris, look around; we're on a boat, There is no *dignity*. The ship called '*dignity*' has already sailed," I said.

"What if I need a *poo*?"

"Then it's an *undignified* poo," said Steve.

His face was struggling not to break into laughter.

"If you need a *poo, just do it,*" I added.

"Don't worry, darling, you're in safe hands with me," he said.

He gave her a big, exaggerated smile.

"It's your *hands* I'm worried about," she said.

She looked at me for reassurance.

"*Steve,* you have just nominated yourself as her carer."

"Eh, what?" he said.

"Welcome to my world," I added.

"What if we aren't picked up by a fishing boat before dark?" he asked.

"Then we huddle together for warmth and wait for the sunrise," I said.

"Is there anything out here that could attack us, Dave?" asked Doris.

"Not unless you fall in the water," I said.

"He's pulling your leg, Doris; ignore him," he said.

"Can you two not get out and push it?" asked Doris.

I looked at Steve.

"If the water was only a few feet deep, trust me, we would," I said.

"*Well, how bloody deep is it*?" she queried.

"It's not a *duck* pond, Doris. Trust me, it's *deep*," I said.

"Dave, have you got your phone?" she asked.

"No, they stole it, so I assume they have stolen yours too? I would also check for your wallet or purse," I said.

They both rummaged.

"Bastards, I liked that wallet, Italian, lovely leather, looks like my phone's missing too, what about you, darling?" asked Steve.

"They've taken everything, evil *scumbags*! What are we going to do?" she said, her face looked fragile, beaten, and lost.

"Don't worry, darling, you have me and Dave by your side."

She looked at Steve and then looked at me.

"Yes, that's exactly why I'm worried."

*"Here*, have some water. There's enough for a couple of days at least - but no sign of them leaving us any food," I said.

Steve grabbed a few ripples of fat on his belly and wobbled it.

"A bit of hunger won't do me any harm," he said.

"I know Sofia's father is doing his best to *sabotage* you dating his daughter, but don't you think this is a *little* extreme?" he asked.

"Well, yeah, but clearly, he's got it in for me. I thought maybe he hates the English, but then he married an *English* woman, so I think he just *hates me*."

They both laughed.

"Let's focus on us, the here and now," I said.

"Yes, like helping me have a pee," Doris said.

"Oh, *sorry* darling, I got distracted."

She reached out for Steve to assist.

"I'll look away," I said.

*What's that rolled up under that seat? It was some plastic sheet that could potentially keep us dry, at least, should it rain.*

*There are a couple of rolls of thin rope, too, so maybe we could fashion and secure a bit of shelter.*

Other than that, there was nothing we could use. It's a bit cruel of them not to leave a fridge. A few beers would do very nicely right now.

Doris had done her business, and sitting back down again, she huddled with Steve.

"Listen up, guys, this plastic sheet is the same length as the boat, at least."

They both looked blank.

"I still have my key to the villa, so I can make some holes along the sheet length and use this string to fasten it to the seat edges."

Their faces were still blank.

"We can sit under it for some shade."

"Won't we cook?" he asked.

"It's not transparent, so it won't be like a greenhouse, but it'll do. It's better than sitting in the sun and cooking like a lobster, mate."

They both nodded.

"Agreed?" I asked.

"Need a hand, mate?" Steve asked.

*"No, I'll sort it. You two just sit and chill."*

"We could make a sail with it instead," he suggested.

"No mast mate and no way of steering, as we don't have a rudder."

"Bloody hell, this is *proper* survival," he added.

"Of course it is. I don't do things by halves, Steve."

He slumped back into his seat and removed the sweat off his forehead using his shirt.

"I *now* need a *number two!*" shouted Doris.

"You can *hold* it in, surely?" I asked.

"I was just asking," she said.

I shook my head.

I fashioned a shelter from the plastic sheet and ensured it was secure enough not to blow away. It at least gave some protection, and there was just enough room to squeeze all three of us under it at a push.

"You're very proud of it, aren't you, Dave?" asked Doris.

"It's not exactly the Hilton, but it'll do," I said.

"Smashing job that, mate," said Steve,

I grabbed a bottle of water and passed it around.

"Just take a *few* gulps. We have to manage on what little we have," I said.

Doris, took a few gulps and passed it to Steve. She looked at me, her face etched with discomfort.

"You need that *poo,* don't you?" I asked.

"Oh, Dave, don't be so *vulgar!"*

"I'm just asking," I said.

She nodded.

"So that's a yes, then?" asked Steve,

"Steve will help you do your business over the side of the boat. With some luck, it might kill a few fish, and we'll have something to eat."

"Oh, Dave, I never thought of that. Do we have anything to cook them on?" she asked.

"I have some matches and firewood, Doris, so yeah, we'll light a fire," I added.

"What a good idea, Dave. I'll leave you to it," she added.

I looked at Steve, smiled and shook my head. He was equally amused.

"You see, Steve, I told you Dave wasn't as *daft* as he looked."

I looked away and waited for the unmistakable sound of a poo hitting the water. I counted three gentle plops as they splashed into the Med. In that moment of grossness, I imagined a couple of curious fish, maybe approaching the poo for a nibble. I retched with the thought.

"You can *turn around* now, Dave. She's all done," said Steve.

His face contorted with disgust.

"You ok, Doris?" I asked.

*"I am*, but not so sure about my dignity."

"So what now, Dave?" he asked.

His face was worried, his shoulders dropped, and his spirit was broken.

"Well, I don't wish to alarm you, Steve, but I now need a poo myself. Would you mind assisting me?"

His face was seriously grossed out - he slumped back in his seat and let out a big sigh.

"I'm *joking,* mate, trust me. I'll wait a week for a poo if I have to."

"What are we going to do, Dave? Any chance we can somehow propel this thing towards land?" he asked.

"I'll start the engine," I said.

"After all this time, we've had an engine?" shouted Doris.

"Calm down. We have shelter, and *someone* will find us."

I slumped back in my seat and looked out to sea, watching the islands in the distance.

"Listen, guys, we may have to accept that unless we get freakishly lucky, we aren't going to be picked up today. It'll be dusk in a few hours, and our only hope is that a squid boat sees us this evening," I said.

"*Squid boat,* what's that, Dave? A boat shaped like a squid?" Doris asked.

"That's right, so keep an eye out, eh," I said.

Steve looked at me and smiled.

"How can you be so laid back, Dave? I don't want to cause panic, but safe to say we're in the shit, aren't we?" he asked.

"Listen, a positive mental attitude, that's all we need," I said.

"Dave, you're a *good* swimmer. Why don't you go get help, and we'll wait here for you," said Doris.

She was serious.

"What a *great* idea. Why didn't I think of that earlier?"

"How long will it take you, Dave?" she asked.

"If the sea stays calm like this, I reckon 4 to 6 hours," I said.

"Really, and you can swim for that long, Dave?" she asked.

"Of course, did I not tell you about the time I swam across the Atlantic to America?"

"*Really?*" she asked.

"No, Doris, I didn't, and no, I can swim maybe 3-4 miles, but not 10-15 miles, which is likely how far land is from here."

"*We're fucked then*," she said.

"What about you, Steve? Are you a good swimmer?" she asked.

Again, she looked very serious.

*Has she really just asked a dwarf how far he can swim?*

He didn't look amused, as though he thought the question was a blatant piss take, but I knew it wasn't; I *knew* Doris.

"I think Steve is probably about my level, 3 or 4 miles."

I didn't want his morale to take another beating.

"*Yeah*, I would agree with Dave on that," he said.

"So what are we going to do?" he asked.

"Sit and wait; it's all we can do. We have enough water, so we won't go thirsty until tomorrow, at least," I said.

The sun beat down, even with the breeze. I knew it was time to get those two underneath the plastic cover and to fashion some head protection as best as I could, even if it meant taking my chinos off and using them. I'd rather burn my legs than my head, and I'd at least reduce the risk of sunstroke.

"Right, you two, it's time to get under cover. I know it means lying down, but at least you're out of the sun."

"I want to top up my tan, Dave," said Doris, bemused by my suggestion.

"Not an option, darling, just get underneath," said Steve.

He hadn't been assertive for a while, so his cooperation was very welcome.

They both shuffled under the cover. Steve made Doris as comfortable as he could. Taking his shirt off to reveal his vest, he made a pillow out of it for her.

"Dave, seriously, mate, what are our chances?" he asked.

I looked at him. I was no less scared than he was, but I couldn't show it; I had to remain calm.

"We're close enough to land for us to be within range of small fishing boats, sailing boats, that kind of thing, so we just need to sit tight, mate."

"But you're exposed to the sun," he said, all concerned.

"Don't worry about me."

I removed my trousers and quickly fashioned a hat, using the trouser legs to make a knot.

"What do you think?" I asked.

"*Bin Laden!*" Steve shouted.

"Ironic, his ashes were scattered at sea, weren't they?" I queried.

*"Yeah*, that's right. I hope this isn't fate, eh Dave?" he added.

"*You two quit your talking*. I'm trying to *rest* here," said Doris.

I looked at my watch; it was now 4:23 p.m. The sun was beginning to drop in the sky, which could be a welcome relief, but there was no way of knowing how cold it might be tonight.

"Are there any blankets or pillows about, Dave?" asked Doris.

Her head turned slightly so her voice could be heard more clearly.

"Hmm, wait, what do we have here? Yes, we have a quilt each, a couple of pillows, some spare socks, hats, and a fridge full of food," I said.

I shook my head.

"*No need to be sarcastic,*" she shouted.

Looking out to sea in all directions, I stopped for a moment and fixed my gaze on what looked like a boat, probably a mile or more away; hard to tell, I was no navigator.

It was too far away for them to notice us, so there was little point in me telling the others.

*What will Sofia think when I don't turn up for the family meal? She will just think I have bottled it, probably think I couldn't face her father again. Surely she would text or ring when I don't show and maybe figure something wasn't right when I don't respond?*

My mind was wandering, and in that moment, I was more bothered about missing my date than *our* survival. I needed to get a grip on reality.

"One thing is certain, guys. We'll see one hell of a sunset out here," I said.

I was trying to lighten the mood.

"Are you still here, Dave? I thought you'd started swimming to shore," asked Doris.

*At least she hasn't lost her sense of humour.*

"I did consider it, but the thought of bumping into your floating poo helped to change my mind."

"My poos don't float," she added.

"*How do you know*? Have you looked recently?" I asked.

Steve was clearly amused by the direction the conversation was taking.

"No, but *I just know*. They're pretty large, I think."

"Judging by the sound they made splashing into the sea earlier, I can believe it," I said.

"Have you two finished? I'm like the elephant in the room," Steve said, laughing.

"You're a small bloody elephant, luv," laughed Doris.

He didn't look amused.

"I thought you didn't have an issue with my size?" asked Steve.

"Are we talking about your height or your…" Doris was interrupted by me.

"*Shoe size, Doris*," I said.

We all laughed.

My objective was to talk shit for long enough so that these two would fall asleep. I could then quietly contemplate the night ahead.

I watched the sun slowly climb out of the sky and reach for the water below. It was majestic, and even in this time of crisis, I was in a calm place.

I glanced towards the other two; they slept like babies. My eyelids felt heavy, but I had to try and stay awake, at least for now. I grabbed a bottle of water and took another gulp.

Like a deflated balloon of warmth, the glow rippled across the distant sea, and the sun began to smudge in the water.

On the positive, the breeze was gentle and still warm. I took my makeshift trouser hat off my head and put them back on my legs. My hair felt sticky, caked to my head, like it had been glued; it felt greasy and horrible.

I decided that once darkness was upon us, there would be little point in me sitting here. I would huddle next to the other two and try and get some sleep.

I could see squid boats in the distance. They always fish at dusk as their lanterns are used to attract the squid to their fishing lines. I just hoped that one of them might come this far out, close enough to see the silhouette of our boat against the moonlit sky.

"*Are we there yet,* Dave?" Doris grunted, half-asleep.

"*Go back to sleep.* I will let you know when we arrive."

I leaned back on the boat's side and watched darkness slowly gobble us up. All I could see now were the lanterns on the three small fishing boats in the distance, each probably a mile apart.

I couldn't sit here any longer, wishing the boats would get closer when it was hopeless in reality. My thoughts now turned to the prospect of a larger ship that might spot us tomorrow.

I nestled undercover, lying on the hard, creaking floor beside Steve. I was careful not to wake him. There was no point in me trying to sleep; it was early evening, and although I was exhausted, my mind was busy.

The boat rocked gently; it was like being in a large crib without the comfort of blankets, but the rocking motion was very calming, very soothing and before I knew it, I had nodded off to sleep.

I don't know how long it had been since I nodded off, but I woke suddenly.

*Shit, has our boat hit something?*

I could hear voices shouting. I slowly moved my creaking limbs from under the cover and sat upright towards the bright light being shone on my face.

Voices were shouting in Greek.

Clambering to my unsteady feet, I grabbed the side for stability and did my best to stand upright to make myself appear larger. I squinted my eyes towards the bright lights.

*Is it real? Am I dreaming?*

"*Help us, please*," I shouted.

"*Help us, please, help us*," I shouted.

Steve and Doris were now awake. I could hear their groans and chatter between them from beneath the cover. Like two frightened children, they huddled together and watched.

The torchlight shone away from my face to reveal the silhouette of a fishing boat and what looked like two men standing on deck, looking down at us.

*"You English?"* a voice shouted.

*"Yes*," I shouted.

"*What happened*? W*hy are you here? Has your motor broken?*" one of them shouted.

"*No*, we have no motor. We don't know how we got here," I shouted.

I looked at the other two, still huddled under the plastic sheet. They looked back at me, their eyes like saucers.

"What are you two waiting for?" I shouted.

The other guy threw a rope into our boat. I grabbed it with both hands and started to pull our boat towards theirs until they came together with a bump, side by side.

"Oh my God, we have been *rescued,*" shouted Steve.

He looked at me and smiled, his pearl-white teeth almost as bright as the torch lights from the other boat.

"How did they spot us?" shouted Steve.

"They saw your teeth mate. They couldn't miss us," I replied.

I had to shout to be heard over the noise from the diesel engine on the other boat. It burbled and groaned like a sleeping giant; it was a serious bit of kit.

"Are you two staying here then?" I asked.

They both clambered to their feet and steadied themselves. I put my hand around Doris' shoulders.

"You ok?" I asked.

"*Just get me home, Dave*, that's all ask. I need my bloody bed," she added.

“*Don’t move. Let us throw you a ladder*,” came a voice from the other boat.

I looked at my watch. It was 8:14 p.m.

Doris was now shivering. It was a bloody good job we were rescued tonight. I’m not sure her bones would have lasted the night.

The rope ladder dropped into our boat from above, and I quickly grabbed it and made it secure.

“Ok, one at a time, please, take your time, *do not rush*,” came a voice from the boat.

I looked at Doris, then at Steve.

“Steve, we’d better let Doris go first. I will help her.”

He nodded in agreement.

“What about me?” he asked.

“What about you? You can go after Doris,” I said.

“Yeah, Dave, I’m not being funny, pal, but in case you hadn’t noticed, I’m really rather short, and I don’t think this ladder is made for a dwarf?” he said.

I looked at him and pondered.

“Should I ask if they have a children’s ladder?” I asked.

He had a look of fear on his face.

‘Well, I can’t *stick* you on my back, mate.”

“*Can you not try?*”

“I will make sure you get up that ladder in one piece - *trust me*.”

"*Stop arguing, you two,* and help me get up this *bloody* ladder. I'm *gasping* for a cup of tea."

"Hurry, we have no time to wait. The sea is getting choppy," came another voice from the boat.

I looked up at him. I could now make out his features more clearly. He was short, fat, with curly wavy hair and had a beard. He was smoking a cigar, the smell briefly wafting past my nose before being gobbled up by the breeze.

"I could murder a cigar, Steve."

He looked at me and smiled.

"Yes, me too, mate."

Doris didn't hang about. She climbed the ladder like a woman possessed. She made it to the top of the ladder and was grabbed and lifted onto the deck by two blokes. One of them put a jacket over her shoulders and hurried her inside.

I looked at Steve, and he looked at me.

"Come on, mate. How hard can it be? An *old lady* practically ran up it," I said.

*"Hurry*, what's taking you so long? C*ome on*," came another shout from the boat.

He scampered up the ladder like a rat up a pipe, and I quickly followed.

Stood before us were three men with bewildered expressions, like they had seen a couple of ghosts.

The short, chubby one was clearly the captain of this modest-sized vessel. He stood with his hands on his hips like he meant business.

"You're *very lucky,* my friends. We don't normally fish this far out, so it's a *miracle* we spotted you," he said.

"We'd have been ok. The boat was safe enough," said Steve.

The captain shook his head and laughed.

"Not a chance. A big swell is coming, and that little boat would have been swallowed up!"

Steve looked horrified.

"You've saved our lives. Thank you so much," I added.

I nudged Steve.

"Don't mention this to Doris. She will freak," I said.

"Come - follow me. Your lady friend is in the cabin below; it's *warmer* down there."

"*Thank you so much,*" I said.

"You can explain to me what happened when we are all together, yes?" he said.

He guided us to the rear of the boat, walking past baskets of fish and whatever else they'd caught. The smell was amazing.

*I love fresh fish.*

We followed the man down some narrow steps and into a small cabin area. It had a small table and a L-shaped wooden bench seat, with a scattering of well-used cushions, a small sink, a mess area and a porthole window which had seen better days; it was loose and rattled in the wind.

Doris sat, holding a paper cup with what looked like a cup of black coffee.

"*They had no tea,*" she moaned, taking a sip from her cup.

"You *nearly* had *no life*. Consider the coffee a respectable substitute, Doris," I said.

*"Sit down, please,"* the man said.

Steve squeezed up close to Doris and put his arm around her. One of the other men handed out bottles of water while we waited for the captain to speak.

He stood before us. He wore sky-blue shorts and a yellow T-shirt. With that colour combination, it looked like he could play for Brazil.

"So, tell me again, *how the hell* did you find yourselves out there, in a small boat, with no engine, no sail, nothing?" he asked.

His face creased with confusion. I looked at Steve.

"I'll let *you* explain this one, Dave."

"We went out for a meal in a restaurant last night. We were befriended by two guys at a bar, who we knew, well, sort of knew; they both worked for a guy called Stavros. He owns the vineyard on the other side of town."

"Go on, I'm listening," he said.

"They bought us some drinks, then they organised a taxi to take us to another bar, and then we fell asleep, and when we woke, we were in a boat, floating on the sea."

He placed his hands on his hips and shook his head in disbelief.

"So you *think* these guys spiked your drinks, loaded you into a small boat and pushed you out to sea?" he asked.

His face was still puzzled.

"You heard the man," said Doris in my defence.

"*Doris,* let me do the talking."

"Do you know this Stavros guy I'm talking about? He's married to an English lady, and they have a daughter?" '

"*Yes,* Sofia, yes, I know them."

*"Dave's* been *trying to shag* her," said Steve.

"Steve, *please*, let me speak," I said.

I gave him the eyes.

"*Well, have you*?" asked the captain.

"No, I've not been *shagging* her. I've merely *kissed* her probably twice," I said.

He said nothing; just looked at me blankly.

"Agh, so you *think* he arranged for you to be kidnapped and put in a boat?"

I shrugged. He nodded his head.

"I know Stavros. He wouldn't have tried to kill you, scare you, yes, but to put you in a boat, no way. You could have *died* out here, all of you," he said.

He looked at the other two.

"Not his style. Had you *shagged* his daughter, then maybe, but even then, unlikely, so this is not the work of Stavros."

"He was due to have dinner at his house this evening," said Doris.

He looked at me.

"Is that correct?" he asked.

"His wife invited me round, but Stavros wasn't keen, but I wanted to see Sofia, so I agreed."

"Then you need to go to the police because this is someone else's work," he added.

I suddenly had a lightbulb moment.

"Listen, can I use your phone?" I asked.

"You want to call *him?* I don't have his number."

"Do you have a smartphone?" Steve asked.

He grabbed his phone from his back pocket and handed it to me.

"Try Google, Dave," shouted Steve.

*What would I do without him?*

I frantically typed in GOOGLE in the search engine.

*Oh fuck, what a dumb ass. We're too far from land, no reception.*

"It's no good, mate. We will have to wait until we get closer to land," I said.

I passed the phone back to him.

"Okay, you guys stay here. We are on our way into the port. It should take about half an hour," he said.

"Listen, thank you, you've saved our lives," I said.

He looked at me and smiled.

"I will take you to the police station when we dock."

"Thank you very much for everything," Steve said.

He reached over to offer a handshake, which was ignored. The captain made his way back up on deck.

"*What was his problem? I offered my hand to shake, and he ignored me.*"

Steve wasn't amused. He slammed his bottle of water on the table in disgust.

"He probably didn't even notice your outstretched arm," said Doris.

She found it amusing.

"Maybe he just doesn't like dwarfs," he added.

"Maybe you're right, mate."

I took a swig from my bottle of water and smiled.

"Fishermen are afraid of little people, you know. They give them the creeps," I said.

"*Little people*, you mean dwarfs," he said.

"Steve, listen, I'm just pulling your leg; chill, we're safe, that's what's important," I added.

"He's only got short legs, Dave. Don't go pulling them too hard; you might hurt him," said Doris.

She laughed.

"Alright, you two, enough," he finished his water and squeezed the plastic bottle as if to release some frustration.

The boat rocked from side to side, the diesel engine rattled like an old tank, and my head began to hurt.

Moments later, another man popped down into the cabin with some chocolate bars and a plate of mixed cold meats, sliced bread and some cheeses for us to share

"Thank you so much, you're very kind," I said.

He looked, smiled, nodded his head and went back up on deck.

"I'm bloody starving," Steve said, his eyes like saucers.

He made a grab for the plates.

"*Leave some for us,* you bugger," said Doris.

She slapped his hand, forcing him to drop one of his cheese slices. We all grabbed our share and scoffed away.

"Do you think they'd make me some cheese on toast, Dave, if you ask?" Doris asked, all serious.

"Yeah, sure. Would you like a Greek salad with that? Maybe a gin and tonic as well?" I asked.

She looked at me, chewing away, her face pensive.

"Well, you can only *ask,* Dave," she added.

"It's a fishing boat, not a floating restaurant, Doris," Steve said, rolling his eyes.

We scoffed the grub like we hadn't eaten in days; there wasn't a crumb left.

Voices were heard from above, and the engine sounded like it was slowing down. We were probably getting close to port.

I glanced at the other two. *Bloody hell*, they had slumped back in their seats and fallen asleep.

Steve used his arms as a cushion, and he snored like a moped with his face down. Doris had her head leaned back, mouth open with her false teeth; it looked like they had dislodged slightly, and it wasn't pretty.

I spotted a packet of cigars nestled between a couple of books on a shelf above Steve's head. *What an opportunity*. I reached across and grabbed them but lost my footing and pulled the books down on Steve's head.

*"Eh, bloody hell, Dave,* what's happening," he shouted.

He rubbed his head with his hands.

"Mate, I'm sorry, but if it's any consolation, I have two cigars in my hand, and *one* of them has your name on it."

He rubbed his head as if I'd dropped a fridge on it.

"Can we smoke in here?" he asked.

“No, but come on, let’s go and have smoke on deck,” I said.

“What about Doris?” he asked.

“She doesn’t like cigars,” I added.

“No, I meant, are we leaving her here?”

“She won’t even know we’re missing Steve.”

“*Oh, will I not?*” said Doris.

She sat upright, eyes wide open. Her face creased like an old pound note.

## Chapter 27

"*Put them cigars away.* You'll blow the whole boat up," she insisted.

"They're cigars, not sticks of dynamite, Doris," I said.

"Never mind, you can save them until we land," she instructed.

Steve sat back down.

"You staying here then?" I asked.

He glanced at Doris.

"I need to play my cards right, Dave."

"Is Doris the Joker then?" I asked.

"No way, she's an Ace."

She didn't look amused.

The engine note had dropped another few notches, so I decided to venture up top for a better look.

The lights from the port lighted up the sea ahead; we had made it. The crew went about their business and prepared to dock.

I ran back downstairs to tell those two.

“Right, you two, shape up, we’re about to arrive at Naxos.”

It was 9:20 p.m., and all I could think about was how soon we could get to the police station.

“I don’t fancy partying much. I just need my bed,” said Doris.

“Bloody hell, Doris, there wouldn’t be many club 18-30s that would be out partying after what we’ve just experienced,” I said.

Steve laughed.

“Well, I wasn’t about to suggest we go clubbing. I’ll sort you two out with a taxi and go to the police station to report the crime.”

More shouts from above, then footsteps and the skipper walked into the cabin.

“Ok, we are about to dock. I will take you to the police station straight away,” he said.

“I was going to suggest I put these two in a taxi, and I’ll go to the station with just you?”

He looked at them both.

“No, they will need to see all three of you, I’m pretty sure of that; you will have to give a statement,” he said.

"*Bloody hell, Dave*, I *need* my bed," shouted Doris, her face was all agitated.

"The man's right, we're in this together," I said.

"Right, well, let's just get this done and dusted, and we can all be in bed by ten," said Steve.

When provoked, he was a good diplomate but looked no less agitated than Doris.

"Ok, follow me, please," the skipper said.

We made our way up the stairs, walked along the short deck plank onto the port side, and followed the skipper towards his jeep.

I jumped in the front passenger seat while the other two sprawled in the back. His jeep looked like it had seen better days; the paint had once been yellow, but it was now more white, complimented by rust patches and doors that creaked when opened. I felt their pain. I wanted to comfort them with a dollop of grease.

He took several attempts to fire up the engine, which knocked and clattered like copper pans in a busy kitchen.

"*Just had this old thing serviced,*" he shouted.

*It sounds like it was last serviced when it left the factory.*

The gearbox was equally agricultural, with every gear grinding as he forced the spindly gear stick into whichever slot would accept it.

"*You alright in the back?*" I asked, leaning my head to look.

*"I think I preferred it on the boat,"* shouted Doris.

"*Which one*?" I asked.

"The wooden thing we were rescued from," she shouted.

We juddered and rattled up the hill past the main square, and then stopped at what looked like the world's smallest police station. It was a door, in a wall with a window. It was hardly Scotland Yard HQ.

He looked at me and smiled. His face was weathered and creased.

"My name is *Frank*," he said.

*"Oh shit,* sorry, how rude of us, I'm *Dave*, this is *Doris* and her friend *Steve*."

*"No problem*, I just thought we had better formally introduce ourselves before we go in the station," he said.

"*Agreed*," I said.

*"Ok, time to make a statement, people. We need to do this as quickly as possible, as I need to get back to help my men unload the fish."*

"Absolutely," I said.

We got out of the van and followed him into the station. It was a small room with just a couple of desks. Each desk had what looked like a 1990s computer and some plastic trays stacked with bits of tatty paperwork.

There was only one policeman. He was short, fat, had curly black hair and a tanned, wrinkled face. He wore a white shirt that looked like it had once fit him. He was in his early 60's, I'd have guessed.

He sat at his desk, reading a newspaper and slurping from a coffee-stained mug that looked like it had never been washed. Looking up, he greeted Frank in his native tongue.

"*Please, grab a chair and sit down here,*" the policeman said.

He took one last drag on his cigarette and stumped it out in an old glass ashtray filled with butt ends; it was pretty gross.

They both exchanged words in Greek while we sat, blank-faced, waiting for the outcome.

The room was muggy despite a large floor-standing fan in the corner. The fan had once been white plastic but was now a faded yellow.

I wiped the sweat away from my forehead using my shirt sleeve. I needed a wash; we all needed a wash. Now was not the time to befriend a mirror; I would probably crack it.

Frank talked, and the policeman listened, nodded his head and occasionally glanced at me and the others.

I tapped Frank on his shoulder - he stopped and turned to face me.

"*Sorry* to interrupt, but would it be possible to make a call to *Sofia*? I mentioned it earlier?"

He nodded, "Yes, of course."

Frank reverted back to speaking English.

"Would it be possible to use your phone? He needs to call *Stavobabsa Vineyard*," he asked.

The man nodded.

"Sure, no problem," he said."

"I don't have the number. Would it be possible to look it up on Google?" I asked.

"It's ok, I *know* Stavros, I have *his* number on file," he added.

He pulled out a dusty old notepad from his draw and began flicking through the pages. He grabbed the phone and dialled the number.

The phone at the other end was answered almost immediately, as though someone was sitting next to it, waiting for it to ring.

He paused his call and looked at me.

"I am speaking to *Stavros*. I have explained what has happened and why you haven't been able to have dinner with them. I'm not so sure he believes what you have said is true?"

"Okay, please ask him if I can speak to Sofia."

He continued with the conversation for a few moments and then paused again. He looked at me, and his face was apologetic.

"She isn't *there*."

"Not there?" I asked.

"He said she was *very* upset that you hadn't shown so she had assumed you had changed your mind."

"What do you mean *she's not there*? Where is she then?" I asked.

"He said she has gone out with a friend," he added.

"May I speak with Stavros?" I asked.

"He said he doesn't want to speak with you."

"Well, can you ask him where she has gone so I can try to find her?"

My heart was racing. Steve put his hand on my leg and gave it a nudge.

"Calm down, Dave. She has gone out with a friend. It's a big misunderstanding, that's all, mate," said Steve.

"Ok, I will ask."

He paused and looked at me again; his face appeared awkward.

"He said she has gone out with a *male* friend."

"I don't believe him," I said.

They continued their call for a few more moments, and then he finished, putting the phone back on the cradle with a thud.

He leaned back in his chair, putting both hands behind his neck.

"He's not convinced with your story. He thinks there's something *very* fishy about it," he said.

*"Fishy,* yeah, we've just been on a *fishing* boat," shouted Doris.

"What *male* friend?" I said.

I looked at Steve like he would know.

*"Dave*, let's just make our statement and get out of here and get some rest. You can contact Sofia again in the morning."

Doris butted in, "Steve is *right* - Just go round her house in the morning, Dave."

"Yeah, it's alright for you two; I'll be wide awake wondering who she's with."

"Just chill, it'll be fine. You're flapping like a fish," said Steve.

I wanted to punch him in the face at that moment; me, the least aggressive person on the planet.

My head was in bits.

*I can't wait that long; I need to find her. I will get these two back home, and then I will go back into town and look around all the bars. I have to find her.*

I felt my hair with my hands; it was dry like twigs. I needed a shower and a change of clothes; I couldn't go out like this.

Frank looked at me and smiled.

"Can you explain to the office what happened on the night leading upto when you woke in the boat?" Frank asked.

"Sure," I said, readying myself in my seat.

I leaned forward and began to recall the previous night's events. The officer typed away on his computer, occasionally nodding as his fat fingers smashed away at the keys.

"Ok, the officer now has all the information he needs, and I have included details of the wooden boat and the serial number so he can cross-check to see if any small boats have been reported lost or stolen," he said.

"What about our statement?" asked Steve

Frank looked at him and then at me.

"You don't need to make an individual statement, just a summary of what happened."

"What now?" I asked.

"I have to get back to help my men prep the boat for tomorrow. I can't help you any more; I'm sorry," he said.

"Hey, no, listen, you have been amazing. You saved our lives," I said.

The police officer leaned forward on his desk.

"I have all the information I need from Frank. There is not a lot to go on, I'm afraid, no names, no faces, no leads. It may or may not come to anything," he said

He looked defeated already.

Frank rose from his chair, looked at me and smiled.

"Listen, get home, get some rest, there's nothing we can do in this moment," he said.

He spoke briefly in Greek with the officer and left.

"So that's it?" I asked, looking back at the officer.

He lit another cigarette, took a drag and leaned back in his seat. The chair creaked under his weight.

"I'll make some calls. Leave it with me for a few days."

"We go back to the UK in a few days," said Doris, shaking her head.

I rose from my chair.

"Come on, you two, let's get back to the villa," I said.

I looked back at the officer and shrugged my shoulders.

"You have my number. Call me if you hear anything," I said.

"*Wait*, I will take you back to your villa," he said, grabbing a bunch of keys off his desk.

"Really? That's very kind of you," I said.

"Could you stop by a kebab house, please? I'm starving?" asked Doris.

Steve didn't say a word; his face said enough.

"I'll make you a cheese toastie when we get in," I said.

# Chapter 28

I closed the door behind me with a thud.

"We're back; we made it, Doris. What a *day,* eh?"

*"Bloody understatement,"* she said.

With a big sigh, Doris slumped onto the sofa and removed her shoes.

*"Do you think he will call?"* she asked.

"I'm not saying he's not a nice bloke, but I've met his type, and they're all the same; nothing will come of it," I said.

"*Bloody hell, Dave*. I thought you said you liked him?"

"He looks fat and lazy to me," I said.

*"Go on, say it,"* she shouted.

"*What's your beef?* I thought you'd think the same, Doris?"

"Go on, say it," she repeated.

"Say what?"

"That he's also a *dwarf,*" she said.

She looked outraged.

*"Bloody hell, Doris*, I was talking about the police officer, not *Steve,*" I laughed.

She laughed.

*"Well*, do you think he will call me or what?"

I nodded.

"Of course he will, why wouldn't he? He's obviously an adrenaline junkie," I added.

"Don't *they* jump out of planes and stuff?" she asked.

"They do, but hanging out with you is the alternative fix."

She shook her head.

"Right, enough small talk. Go get a drink while I take a shower," I said.

"What are you up to?" she asked.

"I need to get back into town."

*"Town* - what for?"

*"Sofia*, remember?"

*"Dave,* sleep on it. Just go around her house tomorrow morning."

"Negative. I need to find her, and I need to find her tonight."

"Well, let me phone a taxi for you then," she said.

"Good thinking, I haven't the energy to walk."

"Not just a pretty face, eh, Dave?" she added.

"Who, Sofia?" I asked.

"Do you want me to *help* you or not?"

I made my way into the bathroom and closed the door. Peeling back the plastic shower curtain, I switched the shower on and sat on the loo seat to gather my thoughts.

I was suddenly hit by the realisation that I hadn't seen my reflection for 24 hours.

Looking in the mirror might be a rather scary prospect, but then, Doris and Steve looked ok, a bit red, but hardly lobsters.

I stepped in front of the mirror on the wall. *Shit,* I was red, tanned and blotchy all at the same time, but then I had been more exposed than the other two, so it was never going to look pretty. I looked like a tramp. I needed Aloe Vera and copious amounts.

*"Taxi said half an hour, Dave*, so don't hang about," she shouted through the door.

*I have half an hour to give myself a facelift, no pressure.*

I looked at my watch: 10:52 p.m.

*Best case, I find her; worst case, she's not even there. I really need this to be the best case.*

My legs felt hollow, and my tank was running on empty. I didn't even have the energy to make a huge effort.

*Shorts, hoody, trainers - that will do.*

"*Did you hear me, Dave*? It'll be here in half an hour?" she shouted.

*"I heard you*, do me a favour. I need to borrow some of your Aloe Vera, if I may?"

*"What did you say?*" she asked.

"*Aloe Vera*," I shouted.

"My *friend* Vera, what about her?" she asked.

"*Doesn't matter*," I shouted.

"*What about her*?" she shouted.

*Oh God! Give me strength.*

I took a quick shower and then made my way into my bedroom, grabbed fresh underwear, some shorts and a hoody. I towel-dried my hair and applied hair product to shape it into my normal bed-head look. I wasn't about to win a contract with Armani, but I'll do.

I found my Converse and put them on.

*Right, where's my aftershave? Found it.*

It was Dunhill Racing, and I *knew* Sofia liked it, so I splashed it on. I stepped out into the living area, where Doris was still slumped on the sofa.

*"Will I do Doris?"*

"*Bloody hell, Dave.* You look like you're off to meet your mates down the pub?"

"Listen, this isn't *a date*. It's a one-man search party."

"*You asked for my opinion, Dave.*"

"The shabby *look* is on trend, trust me."

"I have a pocket torch in my handbag if that'll help?"

"Are we expecting a power cut in town?" I asked, "I think I'll manage, Doris, but thanks all the same."

"I've just heard the taxi horn beep; you'd better go."

I grabbed my key and wallet off the coffee table and made my way to the door.

I turned to face her before I left.

"*Get to bed.* I don't want to find you still up when I get back."

*"I will,* I'm going, just stay safe, eh Dave? No more drama!"

"I'll be careful, don't worry, see you later."

The taxi dropped me off in the main square. It was packed, even more than normal. I watched the taxi drive away, and for a moment, I just stood there, devoid of ideas like a cork on the ocean; I felt pretty lost.

The bars were bustling with people, was it ever not, but that made it all the more difficult for me to focus.

I found myself walking at a pace that most fell walkers would struggle to keep up with. I was frantic, walking in and out of bars, trying to find her *or them.*

Sweat was pouring from my forehead, and my hoodie stuck to my back. My palms were sweaty, my throat was dry, and I needed to sit, take stock, and chill the fuck out for a moment.

I sat on the only empty bench in Naxos. It was as though I had reserved it for myself.

The world around me was now in slow motion. I could see kids playing in the square while parents sat close by, engrossed in adult conversation.

The smells of seafood restaurants all around me aroused my senses. It was food porn, and under normal circumstances, I would indulge, but not now; all I could think of was finding Sofia.

I reached inside my pocket, *shit, my phone, my phone's gone,* but then I realised, it had been gone ever since we had been abducted. My head wasn't thinking straight, and I couldn't fight fatigue for much longer; I was like an empty vessel.

I leaned forward, placing my head in my hands and closed my eyes.

Suddenly, I felt the seat next to me compress with the weight of someone who had just sat down. I continued to hold my head in my hands.

Whoever sat next to me was smoking a cigar. It smelt great, and it made me want one more than ever. I leaned back in my seat, glanced at the man and said hello.

He looked like a local, a bloke in his 70s maybe, hard to tell. He smiled and nodded his head.

"Are you *English*?" he asked.

"Depends who's asking?" I said.

He took a drag on his thin cigar and exhaled a plume of smoke into the night sky.

"*That smells good,*" I said.

I smiled at him, and he smiled back.

"*Would you like one*?" he asked.

He looked like he would be disappointed if I said yes, but I was about to *disappoint* him.

"I would *love* a cigar," I smiled, but he didn't.

Reaching inside his jacket pocket, he pulled out a thin cigar and handed it to me.

"You need a light?" he asked.

"Please."

He handed me a near-empty plastic lighter. I placed the cigar in my mouth, lit it, and handed it back to him.

I leaned back and exhaled. *Damn, I needed this.*

I looked at him. He faced forward, not saying a word. He just sat there, enjoying his cigar.

My head wasn't in a place for small talk; silence suited me just fine.

"*You need to stay away from the girl,*" he said.

I looked at him. I knew what he'd just said but needed to hear it again.

"Sorry, did you say something?" I asked.

"You have no business here. You need to go home, forget about the girl."

"Excuse me, have we met before?"

He looked at me and smiled.

"Sometimes in life, we find a fire and play with it."

"We do?" I asked.

"What happens when we play with fire?" he asked.

I smiled, taking a drag on my cigar. I didn't comment.

"We get burned," he said.

"Do you work for the local fire service?" I asked.

He laughed.

*"No,* I am looking out for you, *David*. I want what is *best* for you."

"How'd you know my name? Was it a good guess?" I asked.

He smiled.

"Who tipped you off I was *here*, the taxi driver?" I asked.

His face was blank.

“Listen, forget about the girl,” he said.

“*What girl*?”

“You *leave* in a few days. Why don’t you spend some quality time with your friends?” he asked.

I turned to face him.

*“I’m sorry*, I don’t have any friends. Have you mistaken me for someone more popular?” I asked.

I could see he was rattled. He took another drag on his cigar and looked at me. His face creased with a smile.

“Like I said, if you play with fire, you get burned, David.”

“Not me. I like fire. It keeps me warm,” I said.

“Who sent you, *Stavros?”* I asked, “Please thank him for our lovely boat trip. It was a wonderful surprise,” I added.

He looked at me and smiled. He then rose from his seat, tossed his cigar butt on the floor and walked away. I just watched him disappear into the crowd.

I got up, dropped my cigar butt to the floor and put out the ember with my trainer. I walked into the nearest bar that had an outdoor terrace and sat on an empty sofa.

“*Hello, what can I get you?”* said the waiter.

*Bloody hell, that was quick.*

“Hmm, a large cold beer, please, mate.”

"We do three sizes, Sir."

"Yeah, I'll take a large, please."

"No, we do three large sizes, sir. We do a large standard, a large grande and a super large."

*Bloody hell, I just want a beer.*

"Hmm, I'll take just a normal large, please."

"Very good, sir."

"What type of glass would you like, sir?"

*What?*

"Hmm, just a normal glass, please, that's fine."

"We do three different types of glasses, sir."

*Good job, I'm not dying of thirst.*

"Whatever you recommend."

"We do a flute, a straight and a barrel glass, sir."

"Hmmm, a straight one is fine."

"Very good, sir."

"How cold would you like it, sir?"

*OMG, this can't be happening.*

"Cold, please, cold is just fine."

"We do three different temperatures, sir."

"What are they?" I asked.

"Cold, ice and super chilled, sir."

"Hmm, super chilled sounds good."

"Very good choice, sir."

I smiled; *finally, I might get my beer.*

"Would you like ice, crushed ice or snow, sir?"

*I'm about to lose my shit.*

"Hmm, just ice, please."

An hour later.

"How many cubes, sir?"

*I want to bash my head on the table.*

"Just one, please."

"Very good, sir. How would you like the shape of the ice cube?"

*Someone help me.*

"Hmm, let me think. You have *three* options?"

"Correct, sir."

"What are they?"

"Standard, tubular and bomb, sir."

"Hmm, okay, just *standard,* please."

*Bloody hell, I won't be coming here again.*

"Alpha or Mythos?" he asked.

"Alpha, please, mate, thank you."

"Very good, sir, back in a moment."

I sat back and looked around. The entire bar was pretty much lit by lanterns on tables, so all I could see were the silhouettes of groups of people and couples. It was a nice place to be. I felt safe, at least.

"*One Alpha, sir,*" said the waiter.

He placed the beer on the table with such a nervous force that the contents splashed in all directions.

"Thank you."

He had all the grace of an elephant.

"Sorry, sir," he said, his face all apologetic.

"It's *only* a drop, mate, don't worry."

It was a *big drop*, but I didn't want to embarrass him further.

He put the bill ticket in a little glass and placed it on the table with a small bowl of nuts.

"Cheers pal," I said.

The beer was ice-cold and was absolutely well-earned after that ordering episode. I leaned back in my seat and reflected on the conversation with the old man.

It was *clear* that Stavros and his heavies were conspiring to keep us apart. They were upping their game.

I bet that old man has just made a phone call to whoever Sofia is with and told him he needs to get them out of town before I potentially find them.

I was done, exhausted, and out of ideas. It was an effort just to pick up my glass.

"*Would you like another beer, sir?*" the waiter asked.

*Can I trust him?*

"*No, I'm fine, thank you. I need my bed, I think.*"

"Very good, sir."

I finished my beer, stuffed some euros under the bottle and left.

*So what now? I will go around Sofia's house in the morning.*

I needed my bed, and tomorrow was another day. I felt uneasy about getting a taxi, especially after encountering the old guy, so I walked back to the villa instead.

I was so deadbeat that I think I walked back to the villa in a trance. I quietly opened the front door to be greeted by darkness.

*Good, this means Doris is in bed.*

How late was it? I glanced at my watch.

*Bloody hell, 2:07 a.m.? How long had I been in town achieving absolutely nothing?*

The door to my bedroom creaked. It probably always had, but it wasn't helping me slip into my room undetected. Doris was a light sleeper; a flea scratching its leg would be enough to wake her.

I opted to leave the lights out, and there was no way I had the energy to brush my teeth.

I quickly got undressed down to my boxers and slipped under the thin cotton sheet, but as I lay down, I felt a presence. Was my mind playing tricks on me? Do I put the light on? No, I just lay there in silence, frozen.

I moved my head slowly to take a look.

*Shit, there's someone lying next to me.*

My mind was racing, and my heart was thumping in my chest.

*Shit, no way, could it be Sofia, had she come around earlier? Had Doris suggested she could stay over, told her I had gone into town to look for her? But surely she would have just slept on the sofa? Maybe not?*

*It must be her. She must have fallen asleep waiting for me!*

I kept looking, my eyes now fully adjusted to the darkness. Oh my lord, I could now make out the slender shape next to me.

*It must be Sofia, no question. What do I do? Maybe give her a nudge, or do I gently spoon her? Girls love a good spoon.*

Of course, I spooned her. It was bliss. If only I had the energy to stay awake longer, to maximise the moment, but I was shattered and drifted off to sleep in a matter of seconds.

I was woken suddenly, with the sensation of a pillow being repeatedly bashed over my head.

*"Dave, Dave, Dave, come quickly, I've been assaulted, Dave. Where are you?"*

I quickly rolled onto my back and reached out to stop the pillow, grabbing it with both hands like a goalkeeper saving a goal destined for the top corner.

"*Doris,* it's *me*, it's *me*. What are *you* doing in my bed?" I shouted.

My hand flapped about on the wall behind me until I found the light switch.

*"Dave*, *why* are you in my bed?" she shouted.

*"I'm in my bed, you crazy woman."*

"Take a look around, Dave. Are you into cross-dressing or ladies' make-up, flowery dressing gowns?'

"What?" I shouted.

"Take a look around you. It's my room," she shouted.

*Shit,* she was right, all her stuff was in it.

*Shit, I am in her bed.*

She stood there, expressionless.

*"I thought you didn't like older women?"* she asked.

*"Shit,"* I shouted.

*"Sorry!"*

I leapt out of bed.

*"You're a bit young for me, Dave."*

I just stood there.

"*I'm gutted.*"

"*Don't be Dave*, let's just keep it as *friends,* eh?"

I looked at her and smiled.

"*Clearly*, I got the wrong room. I*t was dark*, and I thought I was in *my* bed and *you* were *Sofia."*

*"Bloody hell, Dave, how much have you had to drink?"*

*"Half a beer."*

"Only half?"

"The other half missed the glass."

"Eh?"

"*A clumsy waiter," I said.*

"No *luck* then?" she asked.

"What, getting the other half in my glass?"

*"No,* you know what I mean, Dave."

"No luck, Doris."

"Clearly," she added.

"Just go *around* her house tomorrow. You should have listened to *good advice.*"

*"I know*, anyway. I'm sorry I woke you," I said.

I picked my watch up off the bedside table and returned to my room.

I lay on my bed. It was hopeless; I knew I wouldn't sleep, so I got up, got a glass of water and sat outside on the balcony in darkness.

It was nearly 4 a.m., and the sun was already beginning to flirt with the horizon in the distance.

I lit a cigar, leaned back in my chair and reflected on the day ahead.

## Chapter 29

It was 7:43 a.m., and I was ready for the mission ahead. I even packed some lunch in my backpack for extra supplies; I wasn't taking any chances. There was every chance this could be a long day, so I had to be prepared.

I tapped on Doris's bedroom door.

*"Are you awake?"* I asked.

"*No, I'm not,"* she shouted.

"Good, I'm off out."

"Good luck, Dave. I think you might need it."

*"Thanks*, I'll see you later."

I made my way into town along the back roads. They were a series of elevated paths adjacent to the main road. The views were magnificent.

The walk to Sofia's house would take me about an hour.

Today was our last day, as tomorrow we would be flying home. With that thought in mind, I felt I had nothing to lose. This wasn't just a holiday romance, or was it?

*Then why the hell am I going to such extreme lengths to win the heart of a girl I may never see again?*

I sat on a large, flat, smooth stone under an olive tree and looked out over the harbour in the distance. I took a swig from my bottle of water, which helped quench the heat from an already unrelenting sun.

Suddenly, I heard the sound of a bell behind me. I quickly looked around to see what it was. A goat stood before me, bobbing its head up and down.

I rubbed its nose and had a feel of its floppy ears.

"Do you fancy a biscuit pal?"

I grabbed some biscuits from my tub and handed him a digestive. It grabbed and devoured it.

*"Fancy another?"*

I gave it another two or three, and it gladly chomped away. It then lost interest and made its way along the path to join another couple of goats.

I got to my feet and carried on walking. Eventually, I arrived at the gate to the house. It was a little after 9 a.m.

There, standing before me, was the commanding presence of the large gate. I pondered my next move.

I could hardly scale the wall, do a Rambo, throw grenades, and smoke bombs.

Unfortunately, I didn't have such weapons at my disposal. I had some cherry tomatoes, a couple of oranges, what was left of a pack of biscuits and half a bottle of water; this wasn't going to beat Stavros into a surrender.

*Let's just keep this simple.*

I pressed the button on the intercom and waited.

"Kalimera," the voice was Stavros, no mistake.

"Kalimera, could I please speak with Sofia *please*?"

"Who is this?" he asked.

"It's a friend. I was just passing and thought I would stop by and say hello."

There was a pause.

"So you think I'm *stupid*?" He asked.

I looked up; there was a small camera on a tripod on the other side of the wall.

"*Listen,* Sofia isn't here."

"Did you tell her what had happened, why I couldn't make your meal and that I had no phone?"

"She has gone out with a friend for the day and won't be back until late."

"Ok, may I speak with *Barbara*?"

"No, she isn't here."

"Is her friend a *girl*friend?"

"No, it's a *male* friend."

“Her ex, from years ago?” I asked.

I didn’t want to hear the answer, so I'm not sure why I asked.

*“Maybe,”* he said.

He was enjoying this.

“Okay, I will come back later.”

“No, *listen to me*. She will not be here. She has gone away for a few days.”

“You told me she was back later?”

*“I forgot to mention it.”*

“*You’re full of shit, Stavros.”*

I couldn’t keep my cool any longer.

He laughed. It was a deep rumble and crackled through the intercom.

“If you come here later, you are wasting your time. She won’t be here.”

“That’s ok. I will ring the house and speak to her over the phone.”

He paused.

“You’re wasting your time. I have put the landline on divert to my mobile until you have left the island, gone home, gone for good.”

I was fuming. I wanted to scream, but I gathered my shit and remained calm.

“I have just one more thing to say, if I may?” I asked.

"*Sure?*" he said.

*"You're a fucking arsehole,"* I said.

I then walked away. My mission had failed. I felt battle-weary and broken; I was spent.

I shook my head.

*"Bastard."*

I was playing with fire.

*If someone was so determined to keep me away from his daughter that he had me kidnapped, roughed up, then kidnapped me again and put me on a boat, what would he do next? Shallow grave?*

*Was he the Godfather of Naxos? Maybe?*

He had a tank, and I had a water pistol. There was no contest. It was time to retreat to my bunker for good. I flung my rucksack over my shoulder and made my way back.

I saw Doris sitting at a table by the pool as I approached the villa. She was flicking through some trashy magazines again, and looked like she was either having a glass of water or it was gin time already.

*"Oh, hello you, well, how did it go?"*

"Terrible. I spoke to Stavros through the telecom thingy at the gate, but he's blocking me. There's no way I will get a chance to see her before we fly back tomorrow."

She took her sunglasses off, put her magazine down and looked at me. Her face was pensive.

*"Go back and keep going back, and if she's still not there, then ring the house, do something, Dave. Don't let that arsehole beat you. He's fed her a load of shit, and she thinks you're now not interested. She probably thinks that no contact from you was your way of saying, 'Hey, I can't cope with your father, so I'm off.'"*

"I really appreciate your passion, Doris, I really do, but who is to say when they stole my mobile that they didn't unlock it and send Sofia a text, probably saying just that, that I can't get involved or whatever."

"Yeah, you're right. I'd hazard a guess that is exactly what happened. She probably replied. She was probably very upset, who knows, but it would have also given her total closure."

I grabbed a chair and sat next to her.

"You have very little time, Dave. We fly tomorrow morning."

"It's hopeless," I said.

"Didn't she give you her business card?" she asked.

"She did, but that's vanished too. They probably found it in my pocket when they drugged us."

She shook her head.

"Okay, wait until we're home and write her a letter."

"Not a bad idea, but who's to say he won't intercept it," I said.

She nodded her head.

“Anyway, as soon as he sees mail from the UK, he’ll know it’s me and burn it.”

“At the end of the day, Dave, you have to think logically. Even if you managed to speak to her eventually, and she believed your explanation, what then? What can possibly come from this?”

“I know.”

“She lives and works for her family business, end of story. She can’t just up-sticks and move to the UK.”

“I know, you’re right, Doris.”

“Would you be prepared to jack your job in and move here?” she asked.

“Obviously not, no. What would I do for work if I did?” I said.

“Well, the jobs are seasonal, and I can’t see you picking grapes on their vineyard.”

“Picking grapes won’t pay the bills, eh, Doris.”

“My advice, let it go. Write a letter by all means, try at least, maybe address it to Barbara with a cover note to explain the letter is for Sofia?”

I looked at her and smiled.

“Stavros wouldn’t open mail addressed to his wife, surely?” I asked.

“No, she would bust his balls for that,” she said.

"*Bloody hell, Doris,* you're pretty smart for an old bird, aren't you?"

*"Wisdom only comes with age,"* she said.

"Yeah, I will do that because, at the very least, it would be nice to stay in touch, maybe even come back next year. Who knows?" I said.

"Nothing is guaranteed, Dave, but it's worth a shout."

"What are you drinking there, gin?"

She looked at the glass and laughed.

"It's not even midday, Dave. Give me some credit."

I grabbed the glass and pressed it to my nose.

"*There's gin in this,*" I laughed.

We both laughed.

This was probably the first time I seriously considered Doris a friend. She wasn't just a neighbour; she was more than that. Her status was cemented into something more than just a hello over the garden wall.

"How did you leave it with Steve then? Obviously, we all had our mobiles stolen, so it's not like you can text him?"

*"Yeah,* he's coming over later. He didn't say what time. 'Afternoon,' he said."

"*Oh good*, so when does he fly back?"

"In a few days, I think we'll stay in touch. I did say I would write to him."

"Doris, you can *call* each other. This isn't medieval times anymore."

She smiled.

*"So,* what are your plans for your last day?" she asked.

"I will be reading my book by the pool and finishing the last of the beers in the fridge, I think."

She looked surprised.

"No last-ditch attempt to contact Sofia?"

"Like you said, it's best to get home and write her a letter; nothing more can be done here."

She nodded her head with approval.

"How does it feel?" she asked.

"Feel?" I asked.

"To *listen* to good sense," she added.

*"Feels horrible."*

She laughed.

"Right, enough of this small talk," I said.

I grabbed my book, sunglasses and a bottle of beer from the fridge and made my way to the pool.

"Got everything?" she asked.

"Yeah, why?"

"Towel?" she asked.

"Where would I be without you, Doris?"

She finished her drink and made her way back inside.

Just as I began to settle by the pool, I saw Steve walking up the path.

"Bloody hell, you're keen," I shouted.

He did a quick detour and made his way over to me.

"Keen?" he asked.

"She said you'll be here in the afternoon."

"Did she?"

"Doesn't matter. I'm sure she'll be pleased to see you mate."

"Any luck with Sofia?"

"Nothing, I will let Doris fill you in."

"Right, I'd better go in then," he said.

He wore the tightest pair of white shorts I've ever seen on a human and a pink Lacoste Polo. That, too, was so tight, it looked like it had been sprayed on.

"She's in the shower, mate. Sit and chill for a bit. She's not expecting you for ages."

He warmed to my suggestion immediately by pulling up a chair.

"So - are you two going out for the day?" I asked.

He scratched his head as though to look for ideas.

"A walk on the beach, I believe, mate. Maybe grab a bite to eat somewhere. What about you?" he asked.

"I'm keeping a low profile, last day, plane to catch tomorrow morning. I don't want to miss it."

He looked puzzled.

“I could get kidnapped again.”

He shook his head.

“You’re forgetting that it is Stavros behind all this. He wants you off the island, so he’ll probably personally escort you to the plane himself.”

I smiled and nodded.

“Of course, he would, so I’m pretty safe then, eh.”

“Well, you are if you *stay here* and keep out of bother.”

“I’m going nowhere today, mate. I have a fridge with a load of beers to finish and several cigars, so I’ll get quietly sozzled.”

“Sounds perfect, pal. I might join you later.”

“You bloody won’t; not enough beer for two,” I added.

“Right, well, I better go in and say hello,” he said.

But as he rose from his chair, I heard the unmistakable sound of trousers splitting. He looked down and looked up at me with horror.

*“Shit,* what’s happened?” I asked as though I didn’t know.

He had a feel about with his hands and shrieked with horror.

“Turnaround, let’s see,” I asked.

He turned and revealed a giant split that pretty much ran the entire length of his backside.

"Bloody hell Steve, I did wonder about how tight they looked when you walked across to me. I did kind of fear the worst."

"*Shit, Dave*, what am I going to do now?"

"Well, looks like you're off for lunch in your boxer shorts. I hope they're clean?" I asked.

I was seriously struggling not to laugh.

"*Very funny,*" he said.

"Well, we won't have time to sew you back up, mate, so you'll have to borrow a pair of my shorts."

"They'll be massive on me."

I laughed.

"Well, yeah, but I'll give you a belt, so at least they won't fall down."

He looked horrified.

"Listen, calm down, don't panic. I'll go fetch a pair."

"What colour options do you have?" he asked seriously.

*"Steve* - this isn't a personal shopper experience, mate. Whatever I *grab* is what you're having."

I sheepishly walked back into the villa.

*"Is that you, Dave?"* she shouted.

*She can hear a mouse fart.*

"Only me, Doris."

"Any sign of Steve?"

"I'm not about to send a search party out. You said he didn't give you an exact time."

She ignored me and carried on singing in the shower. I grabbed a pair of shorts and a spare belt and made my way back outside.

"These ok for you?" I asked.

He looked horrified.

"Dave, they will clash with my pink polo."

"They're the only colour I have, mate."

"What, all of your shorts are blue?"

I nodded.

"Yeah, pretty much."

He shook his head.

"Should I ask Doris If you can borrow one of her dresses?"

"*Point taken*," he said, leaning forward to grab the shorts.

I leaned back in my chair, struggling not to laugh. He began to remove the torn shorts with his face contorting and the vanes in his neck bulging.

*Jeez, he will need a glass of water after this.*

"*Hurry up,* you're too slow, Steve. Time is of the essence."

He finally surgically removed his shorts, slipped the replacements and fastened the belt.

He looked at me, then shook his head in despair.

"To be honest, mate, they just look like a pair of surfer dude shorts on you. Baggy? Well, yes. Too long? Yes. A bit odd? Yes…but in a cool kind of way."

He looked at them, then looked up and looked at them again.

"Mate, seriously, who looks *cool* in shorts anyway?" I asked.

"Tom Cruise?" he asked.

"Steve, he's about the same size as you, mate."

He looked up and smiled.

"Yes, but he's better looking," he added.

"I can't argue with that, mate, sorry."

He looked at me and laughed.

"You're not helping, Dave."

"Oh, so me literally saving your arse isn't helping?"

"So I don't look like a dick?" he asked.

"Mate, maybe we're more alike than you think?" I asked.

He looked puzzled.

"Similar size?" he asked.

"Like looking in the mirror, mate," I said.

"*Oh* – stand by your post. Doris is here," he spotted her unmistakable presence approaching.

"Act normal," I said.

"Hello, my lovely," he shouted.

She slowly made her way down the path towards us, careful not to trip in her gold heels.

"*Wow,* what a dress. You *look* stunning, darling," he said, all giddy.

She looked very 1980s: gold dress, with matching shoes and earrings.

"*Oh, Steve*, what on *Earth* are you wearing?"

"It's *fashion,* Doris. Get with the times, eh," I said in his defence.

He looked at me and nodded.

"That's right, hard to keep up, it changes by the day," he said.

She looked at me with a creased face.

"I wouldn't be getting any ideas from him. He's hopeless," she added.

Steve looked deflated.

"I can go back to my villa and change if you prefer?" he suggested.

"You look fine, mate. Just ignore her."

She pulled up a chair and sat next to us at the table.

"So, are you two going out for lunch then or what?" I asked.

"That's the plan, I think," she said, looking at Steve.

"You're welcome to join us, Dave," he suggested.

She looked at me and back at him.

"He bloody isn't. This is my last day, and I don't want any more drama," she said.

"I'm happy chilling by the pool. I had already suggested that was my plan."

She looked guilty as though leaving me here might cause offence.

"I didn't mean it like that, Dave."

"No, you're right. I think I need to lay low, lick my wounds."

"What about Sofia?" Steve asked.

"Yeah, what about Sofia?" said Doris, joining in.

I shrugged my shoulders.

"I'm sticking to the plan. I'll write her a letter when I get home."

They both nodded.

"Of course, yeah, good plan, clever, in fact," said Doris.

"Oh, you approve then?" he asked.

"It was her idea," I said.

Steve smiled.

"I admire your long game, Dave, I really do," he said.

"Like the courage of the first man to cross the ocean, you can't venture into the unknown until you have lost sight of the shore," I added.

He smiled again and pointed a finger at me.

"I *like* your style, Dave, big balls. I'm impressed, mate."

Doris looked bemused. She looked Steve up and down.

"Yes, well, I don't like *your* style much today. Come on, take me for lunch."

They both rose to their feet and pushed their chairs back under the table.

"You okay?" he asked.

"Yeah, of course, you two go and enjoy yourselves."

"We'll only be a few hours, Dave," Doris added.

"Go!" I said.

I was rather relieved watching them leave. I had craved a bit of me time all day. Sitting by the pool and reading was heavenly. It was just the tonic I needed to fix my head space.

After a few hours, I went inside and collapsed on the sofa. I glanced at my watch; it was just after 5 p.m.

I sat watching Greeks answer to First Dates when there was a knock on the door.

*Bloody hell* – I nearly jumped out of my skin. I spilt my beer all down the front of my hoodie and knocked the remote control onto the hard-tiled floor, breaking the back of it and sending the two little AA batteries rolling across the floor.

*Shit, could this be Sofia? It must be. Who else could it be? She has come to see me? She has managed to escape the grasp of her father.*

I ran towards the door, stopped, took a deep breath and opened it.

"Sorry, Dave, I forgot my key."

"*Doris!!*" I shouted.

She brushed past me, flicked her heels off and threw her bag on the sideboard. Steve followed her in and closed the door behind him.

"Nice lunch?" I asked

"Bloody marvellous," he said, all smiley and ever so slightly tipsy.

Doris flopped onto the sofa and put her feet up on the coffee table.

"So you still have a couple of days before you fly back, Steve. Any plans?" I asked.

He sat next to Doris, kissed her on the cheek, looked up at me, and smiled.

"I'll be drinking and smoking cigars but not much else, Dave."

"Very good, right, well, I'll leave you two love birds to it."

"What are you doing now, then?" she asked.

"*Packing*," I said.

"*Packing*, we have loads of time for packing, Dave. Come and have a drink," she insisted.

"We have to leave at 8:30. I'd rather just do it now."

She wasn't amused.

"8:30, Dave, exactly. We can chill by the pool and pack in the afternoon."

"8:30 in the morning, Doris. Do you ever listen?" I asked.

"Oh bloody hell, why didn't you tell me?" she asked.

"I did, several times."

Steve nodded his head and rose to his feet.

"Listen, Dave's right. I'll leave you two to get sorted and drop by early tomorrow before you leave."

Doris looked sheepish.

"You're welcome to *stay*, Steve, if you *like*?" she asked.

He looked surprised.

"Well, whatever you decide, no funny noises from your bedroom, please. I need a good kip."

She was impressed.

"Dave, don't be so vulgar," she said, shaking her head.

"What?" I added.

"We aren't all perverts like you," she said, pointing her bony finger at me.

I laughed and made my way to my room.

## Chapter 30

The alarm on my phone went off at 7 a.m. I was already awake. I had been since around 6.

I could hear the familiar sound of Doris making her first brew of the day and the distinct sound of the spoon tapping on the side of the cup.

“Make one for me, please, Doris, if you will,” I shouted.

*“Sorry, Dave. I just had the last bag.”*

“Great!” I shouted.

“I can fetch it from the bin if you like; try and squeeze another one out of it?”

“I think I’ll leave it. Thanks all the same.”

Steve was up. I could hear him chatting to Doris from the balcony. I grabbed my hoodie, put my watch on and went to join them.

“Morning, you two. Sleep well?”

Steve smiled. He leaned back in his chair and folded his arms.

*"I got off eventually."*

*Jeez, I hope there was no sexual innuendo in that comment.*

Doris took a drag on her first fag of the day, flicked some ash in her empty cup and smiled.

"It's been quite an adventure, eh, Dave," she said.

I shook my head, pulled up a chair and sat down.

"Not having a brew, Dave?" asked Steve.

I looked at Doris.

"Guess *not,* mate, no."

He took another slurp from his cup and put it down on the table.

"Nice *watch,* Dave," he said, looking towards my left wrist.

I looked at my wrist and smiled.

"Ahh yeah, cheers, mate."

"What brand?" he asked.

"Oris, it's a pro diver chrono."

He leaned forward to take a closer look.

"Expensive?" he asked

"I treated myself with a bonus."

"Nice thing that."

"You like watches?" I asked.

*"Oh please*, you two and your *boy's toys*," said Doris, her face creased like a paper bag.

"Right, well, I'd better leave you two to get sorted. Your taxi will be here in half an hour," he said, rising to his feet.

Doris smiled, rose to her feet and put her arms around him. It was heartfelt; there was love in the old girl yet. They hugged and squeezed for a few moments before releasing their grasp.

"You two will have me welling up."

They both smiled.

"I will call you when I'm back in Essex," he said.

"That'll be nice," she said.

He gave her another hug.

"I'll see you out, luv," she said.

"No, I don't like goodbyes. Finish your breakfast; I'll see myself out."

It was like a Mills and Boon novel.

He shook my hand and smiled.

"Don't give up on her mate."

I looked at Doris and smiled.

"*Not Doris*, I meant Sofia."

I nodded.

"Yeah, I know, I'm teasing."

“See you on the other side, eh, Steve,” I added.

“You shall.”

He smiled, blew a kiss at Doris and left.

Doris was okay until she could hear the door to the villa open and close. She then had a little weep, using a tissue from her handbag to wipe her tears.

“He’s had quite an impact on you, eh, Doris.”

She looked up and smiled.

“He’s such a nice little man,” she said.

“He is. I will vouch for that.”

I put my arm on her left shoulder and gave it a gentle squeeze.

“Come on, the taxi will be on its way.”

# Chapter 31

The airport was no less stuffy than it had been when we arrived. We walked through passport control and headed for customs.

"Traveling together?" asked the officer.

"Unfortunately," I said.

"Very good, sir. Can you both go to belt four, please."

I grabbed our hand luggage and placed them into the plastic trays provided.

"Take your watch off, Doris. It'll set the metal detector off."

She quickly removed it and placed it in the tray. I removed my belt.

"What are you doing?" she asked, all confused.

"I'm getting frisky; what does it look like I'm doing?"

She looked horrified.

"It's got a metal buckle."

"Agh, yeah, so it has."

I walked through the metal detector gate, smiled at the two friskers and made my way to the end of the belt.

My tray passed through without a hitch, and I gathered my bits. I looked up.

*Oh, bollocks,* her tray had been separated and was now parked up, waiting for an attendant to rummage through it.

"Dave, look, what's my case doing over there?"

"Have you got anything metallic in your carry-on?" I asked.

"No, just some kitchen knives."

"Doris, it's a carry-on. You can't put metal shit in your carry-on."

*It was my fault. I should have checked it.*

"What knives?"

"I took some from the villa."

"How many?"

"Oh, just a couple of bread knives."

"Are you short of bread knives at home?" I asked.

"No, not really."

I shook my head in disbelief.

The drama added another half an hour of aggro. I just wanted to get on the plane and have a drink.

"Can we look in duty-free now, Dave?"

"Remember, it's not free. It just means you don't pay tax on stuff."

"I know that."

"Well, you didn't last time. You walked around putting things in your handbag and nearly got arrested."

"It was a lot of fun, though, Dave."

I shook my head, put my arm on her shoulder and guided her through the terminal. It was just a relief to make it on the plane without any grief.

We sat in our seats and began to chill while other people went about their business.

"So happy I've got a window seat again," she said.

"Nothing but the best for you, Doris."

She peered out over the wing and looked back at me with an inquisitive look on her face.

"Do these windows open?"

"Only at 30,000 ft."

She looked bemused.

"Really?"

"Yep, well, you have to put in a request with the crew, and then they have to open it by remote control."

She nodded.

"Why would someone want to do that?"

"So you can take a walk on the wing and stretch your legs."

She looked out the window and looked back at me.

"You can't fit through that?"

"Oh, trust me, if it opened at 30,000 ft, you'd have no problem fitting through it, Doris."

She nodded.

"A fat person won't fit through that, Dave."

"No, but why would a fat person want to stretch their legs?" I asked.

She laughed.

"Fat people shouldn't be allowed on planes for two reasons: number one, they take up too much room, and number two, they eat all the food."

"Bloody hell, Doris, why don't you shout a bit louder?"

She looked apologetic, then looked behind her and looked back at me again.

"Shit, there's one behind us," she said, all sheepish.

"One of what?"

"You know, a fat person."

"Just keep your voice down."

"Well, I didn't know two fat people were sitting behind us," she shouted.

"Stop bloody shouting, what's wrong with you?"

"I want some Prosecco," she said.

"We have to wait until the plane takes off."

"Well, how long's that going to be?"

I grabbed the menu card and handed it to her.

"We should be in the air in about ten minutes."

She looked behind her again and leaned into my ear.

"Those two look like they like a sandwich, we had better order before them, Dave, or we're fucked."

"Just chill, there's a shit ton of food on a plane, stop flapping."

She leaned in again.

"Yeah, but they also look like they like a drink, too."

I shook my head and began to flick through the inflight magazine.

"Excuse me, luv," she shouted to get the attention of a crew member walking past.

"Hi, everything ok?" the attendant asked.

"No, we're a bit concerned that there's not enough food and drink to go around," she shouted.

The attendant smiled.

"Why would you think that?" she asked.

Doris pointed to the two people sitting behind us. I wanted the ground to swallow me up.

The attendant looked very uncomfortable.

"There will be plenty, madam, I can assure you."

She then made a quick exit.

"Just pipe down, Doris. Be quiet now, please, before you offend anyone else."

She shrugged her shoulders and continued to look out of the window.

We soon took to the air. I hated take off. I was always a nervous wreck until we got up to cruising height.

I leaned back in my seat and sighed.

"You ok, Dave?"

"Why?"

"That's a *big* sigh."

"Oh, yeah, no, I'm good. I just need to get home. The sooner I'm home, the sooner I can write a letter to Sofia."

"Agh, I see. Yeah, of course."

She smiled.

"Right, let's order some drinks, eh?" I suggested.

"We won't have to wait long, Doris."

"Why is that?" she asked.

"We're sitting near the rear exit, so we'll be on the early run for drinks and snacks," I added.

Doris turned around in her seat to get a better look.

“That fat couple will get served before us, knew it,” she grumbled.

“Doris, we are three seats from the back. I’d be very worried if they ran out of grub by the time the trolley got to us.”

She looked concerned. I gave her a look.

“What?” she said.

“Chill out.”

She slumped back in her seat like a petulant child. I whispered in her ear.

“Just wind your neck in and be patient.”

“I’m just saying,” she said.

She looked at her drinks menu card again.

*ADHD, she must have it.*

“What are you thinking?” I asked.

“Prosecco, there’s a deal: buy three for £10, that’s dirt cheap that.”

“They are only quarter-size bottles, don’t get too excited,” I added.

“Three each, then, Dave?”

“Go on then,” I agreed.

The hostess arrived at our seats.

“Hello, sir. Any drinks or snacks?”

“Six bottles of Prosecco, please, luv,” shouted Doris.

"Of course, any snacks to go with that?"

Doris looked at the menu again.

"Bacon roll for me and whatever he wants."

I looked up at the hostess and smiled.

"Make that *two,* please."

She handed the bottles over with plastic glasses and ice.

"Your bacon rolls will be with you shortly, sir."

"No problem, thanks."

"That'll be £27.00, cash or card, sir?"

"Card, please."

"Are the rolls ready yet?" shouted Doris.

"Give her a chance."

The hostess laughed.

*"It won't be long, madam."*

Doris began to remove the foil on one of the bottles.

"Would you like me to sort that?" I asked.

"Dave, I am more *capable* of popping a cork."

"That's what worries me, Doris."

*POP* - the cork hit the ceiling and disappeared somewhere behind us.

"Bloody hell, Doris."

*"Oi, what's your problem,"* came a voice from behind us.

We both quickly turned around.

*"Your cork has landed in my pot noodle!"*

"I'm *really* sorry. Can I buy you another one?" I suggested.

Doris was creasing with laughter.

*"You* - can get me another one," he said, referring to Doris.

"I'll take care of that, mate, just order another one, and I'll pay," I said.

His wife didn't speak. She was too busy stuffing her face with crisps while she read her book.

Doris looked over again.

"Good book?" she asked the lady.

The lady looked up.

"Yeah, it's alright," she mumbled.

Doris looked a bit closer.

"Bit ironic, don't you think?" Doris asked.

The lady looked up again.

"What is?" she asked.

"Well, there you are, stuffing your face while reading a book with the title '101 Ways to get thin'," Doris laughed.

The bloke was fuming; every vein in his neck began to bulge. I wanted the ground to swallow me up.

*"How bloody rude,"* said the lady, clearly disgruntled.

"No offence, luv," Doris added.

I smiled at them both apologetically.

*"Forgive* my friend. She meant no harm."

"Get me my pot noodle and shut it, the pair of you," he whispered.

"Of course, would you like a roll with that?" I asked.

"Yeah, and I'll have another bag of crisps for my wife."

Doris piped up again, turning to face the couple.

*"She* should be ordering a *salad*."

*"Doris*, sit back down, please."

We both sat back down again.

"Are you mad at me?" she asked.

"No, just mad at myself."

She looked confused.

"Yourself?" she queried.

"Yes, for agreeing to come on this crazy holiday in the first place."

"*Oh, Dave*, you don't mean that. We've had *quite* an adventure."

I shook my head and leaned back in my seat.

"That's it. Just relax, Dave."

"I'll try."

"I'll open *another* bottle."

"*No,* you bloody won't - give it here *now!!*"

# Chapter 32

The taxi dropped us at the end of Green Lane.

"Home sweet home, Dave."

"Yep, come on then, let's get indoors," I said.

I lived at No 4, Doris next door at No 2. We dragged our cases up our respective paths and stopped by our front doors. She put her key in the slot and opened her door.

*"Wait,"* I said.

She looked at me, puzzled.

*"What?"*

"Fancy a brew?" I asked.

"Are you not sick of the sight of me?" she asked.

"Yeah," I said.

She laughed.

"Well, considering I'm pretty sure I'm out of teabags, I'll take you up on that offer, Dave."

"Excellent, see you in five."

While we were away, I had entrusted my dad to look after my cat Mog by checking on her every day. I was still apprehensive, as that also included feeding her. My dad, at the tender age of 82, was getting forgetful.

"Mog, where are you?" I shouted.

There was no sound.

"Mog, come on, where are you?"

*Meeeeowwww.*

My furry black and white companion darted in and around my legs. I left my case for a moment in the middle of the living room and leaned down to pick her up.

"Kettle on, Dave," shouted Doris as she made her way up my path.

Mog wriggled from my arms, landed on the floor and darted behind the sofa. Doris closed the door behind her and made her way in.

"*Where's your cat?*"

Mog wasn't a fan of Doris. I couldn't, for the life of me, work out why.

"Oh, you know, she's always a bit nervous when she's been alone for a while."

Doris sat in the armchair by the door

"Tea, one sugar?"

"That will do nicely."

"Put your feet up. I'll be back in a mo."

I grabbed the kettle, filled it with water and switched it on.

*Bloody hell, I hope my dad's remembered to leave some milk.*

I opened the fridge, bingo, a bottle of milk lay in wait.

"Do you have any biscuits?" shouted Doris.

*"Don't push it,"* I shouted.

The biscuit tin wasn't in its usual place. It felt very light and I knew what the outcome would be on removing the lid.

"*Out of luck. I'm afraid we're out of biscuits."*

"You always have biscuits in," she shouted, with a disgruntled tone.

"Looks like my dad's demolished them."

Suddenly, there was a knock on the front door.

"You expecting anyone, Dave?"

"No."

"Should I see who it is?" she shouted.

"That's normally how it works," I shouted.

I poured the hot water into the cups and grabbed the sugar.

"Dave."

"Yeah?"

"You have a visitor."

"If it's my dad, just let him in."

"No, it's not your Dad. I think you need to come and see who it is."

I went to have a look.

*"Hi David..."*

# About The Author

David grew up in a sleepy West Lancashire village, not far from Wigan. He went to college, then university, and studied art and design with the intention of becoming a footwear designer. Unfortunately, this didn't happen, though he does have an impressive collection of shoes.

His alternative career choice was to work in the automotive industry, which he continues to enjoy till this day.

This book was written as a creative outlet during the lockdown. He wasn't sure if he had the talent to make this happen, until he started to share some chapters with his friends and work colleagues, who found his work very entertaining. Hence, he continued to write.

There will be a sequel to his first book, and he intends to write at least three in the Doris & Dave series, with his 2nd book well on the way.

"Dave & Doris will return soon! Their next adventure will be based in Barcelona, and I can't wait to share it with you!"

Printed in Great Britain
by Amazon

30515945R00240